T0356707

"Ariel's debut is a swoon-inducing second-chance romance featuring college sweethearts who never really got over each other. . . . At turns humorous and heart-wrenching, with a smoldering sensuality that underlies even the most fraught of the protagonists' encounters, this novel is highly recommended for all library collections."

—*Library Journal* (starred review)

"Fans of Hollywood romances and second-chance scenarios will enjoy Ariel's debut romance novel, a thoughtful story of love and self-discovery." —*Booklist*

"Ariel's sensitive debut explores the experiences of people of color in Hollywood. . . . Danny and Kaliya rediscover their old rhythms at a believable clip, making it easy to see why their relationship works, and Kaliya proves a wonderful heroine whose strength and passion in the face of adversity will have readers cheering. Ariel is an exciting new voice in romance." —*Publishers Weekly*

"The novel shines in its depiction of Danny's parents' story and in the scenes where the author weaves in Black joy and art. . . . The flashbacks to the romance between Kaliya and Danny during their college years in New York effectively evoke the thrill of first love. . . . Enjoyable." —*Kirkus Reviews*

ALSO BY MYAH ARIEL

When I Think of You

NO
ORDINARY
Love

MYAH ARIEL

BERKLEY ROMANCE
New York

BERKLEY ROMANCE
Published by Berkley
An imprint of Penguin Random House LLC
1745 Broadway, New York, NY 10019
penguinrandomhouse.com

Library of Congress Cataloging-in-Publication Data

Names: Ariel, Myah, author.
Title: No ordinary love / Myah Ariel.
Description: First edition. | New York: Berkley Romance, 2025.
Identifiers: LCCN 2024043330 (print) | LCCN 2024043331 (ebook) |
ISBN 9780593640616 (trade paperback) | ISBN 9780593640623 (ebook)
Subjects: LCGFT: Romance fiction. | Novels.
Classification: LCC PS3601.R536 N66 2025 (print) |
LCC PS3601.R536 (ebook) | DDC 813/.6—dc23/eng/20241001
LC record available at https://lccn.loc.gov/2024043330
LC ebook record available at https://lccn.loc.gov/2024043331

First Edition: April 2025

Printed in the United States of America
1st Printing

The authorized representative in the EU for product safety and compliance is
Penguin Random House Ireland, Morrison Chambers, 32 Nassau Street,
Dublin D02 YH68, Ireland, https://eu-contact.penguin.ie.

For the broken hearts in search of healing.

You have a right to require only love.

1

I don't necessarily want to be a "strong" person—I just keep going.

Tina Turner

SHOULDN'T HAVE WORN THE wig. It was bad enough Sheryl wasn't available to help me install it properly. Now it's sitting about an eighth of an inch too high on my hairline and digging into the base of my neck. But since it's my signature look—long, dark chocolate, with a body wave—I'm pretty sure that blue-pinstripe-suit-wearing dude positioned at my four o'clock near the turnstile just spotted me.

And, yep, now he's got his cell phone camera trained in my direction primed to snap a photo. I cock my head to the side and marvel at the boldness. Most people have the decency to at least *pretend* they're on FaceTime or using a selfie cam to check for a seed in their teeth. That he should be ashamed to openly invade my privacy is a notion entirely lost on this man, and I have to say . . . I'm impressed by the audacity.

Grunting, I angle my body slightly to reposition my purse strap on my shoulder while willing the elevator to put some pep in its descent from the thirtieth floor. Thankfully, this corporate lawyer type turned amateur paparazzo is waiting near the elevators for the odd floors, which means soon, I'll be free of him.

I could kick myself though. Because more than likely, by tonight his photos will have graced *The Shade Room* under a headline that reads something like *Ella Simone: Spotted! at Divorce Attorney's Office!* and my publicist, Lydia, will suffer a cardiac event. In her defense, my coming here alone *was* ill-advised. If she'd gotten her way, I'd have sent my manager, Angelo, who would have patched me in over Zoom. But if she'd *truly* gotten her way, there would be no reason for this visit at all. Because I'd be doing the "wise thing" for my career and staying attached to Elliot Majors.

But these days, I'm impervious to wise counsel. Ironic, given the reasons I've shown up here today.

"Excuse me, miss? I'm sorry but I'm *such* a huge fan." The words tumble down at me from about half a foot up and behind my left shoulder.

It looks like Blue Pinstripe Suit has gathered up the courage, or decency rather, to approach the subject of his impromptu photo essay. Behind my shades, I roll my eyes. *Damn this slow-ass elevator!* Suit Man probably just wants to confirm that I'm me before he shoots those grainy snaps off to the highest bidder. I turn and plaster on the trained smile I've adopted—it says I'm a nice person who's got both hot sauce *and* Mace in her bag.

Reluctantly, I extend my hand to shake his. "Hi, how are you?" I say politely, if a little restrained—a tactic meant to signal that this interaction will be brief.

He encases my hand with his damp palm, aggressively shaking it in return. "Wow. I can't believe it's you!" he exclaims, with beads of sweat dotting his brow. "Would you . . . would you mind?"

Assuming he's about to ask me to sign something, I reach in

my purse for a pen. But before I can object, he's angled himself next to me and raised his phone with the camera flipped to selfie mode. At the last second, I noticed it's toggled to *record*. Imaginary sirens blare in my ears.

I open my mouth to protest, but he steamrolls ahead. "Can you sing a little bit of that one song . . . what was it?" he muses. My face pricks with heat from mortification and then . . . he proceeds to perform a boisterous and breathtakingly pitchy rendition of "Bitch Better Have My Money."

He bobs and weaves, making little swiping motions with his hands and these . . . dance moves? are so aggressively unpredictable I have to take a step back to avoid being headbutted or sideswiped when he shouts the lyric "I call the shots, shots, shots! Like bra, bra, bra!"

I am simultaneously frozen, in shock, and utterly awed by what I am witnessing. Then I deflate. Not out of disappointment that I've apparently been mistaken for Rihanna, or that in this post–"listening and learning" and "doing better" America we find ourselves in, *some* people still fail at individuating Black folks with markedly distinct physical characteristics. But all that previous pent-up fear and anxiety whooshes out of me like a popped balloon. He hasn't the faintest idea of who I am. That means my secret's safe. For now, at least.

The performance, which lasted for probably fifteen seconds but felt like an hour, is over now, and he's gesturing toward me like it's my turn to do a little ditty for him. The nerve. I may be an entertainer, but I'm not here, at this moment, for his entertainment. And before he can tap the record button with his thumb, I reach up and block his camera lens with my hand.

"This has been fun and all but actually, I'd prefer it if you didn't," I say. Then I crane my neck and train a panicked *Help!*

glance at the well-dressed security guard who's been dutifully manning the turnstile.

Almost instantly, he clocks my distress and glides over to assist. "Excuse me, sir. But there's no filming allowed in the lobby."

Ding!

Like an answered prayer, the elevator opens depositing a handful of overly starched individuals with stern expressions on their faces. I step aside to let them exit, just as the security guard, whose name is Jamal according to his badge, gently nudges Rihanna's biggest fan farther away from me.

And before I step onto the waiting elevator, Jamal leans over and whispers in my ear. "Don't worry, Miss Simone. Promise I won't tell." He winks and I smile just as the doors close.

HER BODY LANGUAGE IS LIKE TEA LEAVES.

As if on cue, with the flip of each page, she raises an impeccably laminated eyebrow and releases a tiny, strangled sound of distaste from between her porcelain veneers.

It's hotter than I expected here on the thirty-seventh floor of 1901 Avenue of the Stars. But Janet Waterman is in her element, like they've programmed the thermostat with her DNA as the baseline. I'm seated in the main conference room of Waterman, Schuster & Milner trying not to sweat while the Ice Queen herself, as coined by the *Daily Mail*, appraises my fate. And by the looks of it, I'm fucked.

I've always wondered if that moniker had more to do with the chilly vibe she projects when strutting down Hill Street in red bottoms with cameras flashing and paps demanding statements on her high-profile clients, or with her reputation for protecting said clients' icy assets from being pillaged in the process of their acrimonious decouplings—now I'm thinking it's an even split.

I chart Janet Waterman's eyes as they descend past each cursed clause of the prenuptial agreement I entered into when I was just twenty years old. And even though hindsight has proven I was too young and too ignorant to comprehend the gravity of what I was signing away, perhaps more pathetic is the part where I was too in love and too drunk on the promise of a life with *the* Elliot Majors to care.

Finished reading now, she slides the crisp printout across the frosted glass conference table toward her paralegal and crosses two perfectly manicured hands. I notice a rose gold Patek Philippe encircling her left wrist, and I have to stifle a groan. Ten years ago, I'd have fainted in the mere presence of a forty-thousand-dollar watch. Now, I've got one to match sitting in a box somewhere in a penthouse I don't plan to return to.

Ironically, it was a gift from Elliot on our eighth wedding anniversary, which, with Janet's help, will have been our last.

"I'm sure you've anticipated what I'm about to say?" she asks, her voice clear and resonant as a bell. The kind of voice that cuts through the chatter of a crowded room. It sets me at ease in a way that's quite rare. Perhaps it comes with the territory of being a professional vocalist that I find myself instinctively appraising the timbre and tone of each new voice I encounter.

I shake my head, realizing my delay, and rush to answer her. "You're going to tell me I'm fucked?" I reply, startled by the thready, hollow sounds coming from my own throat.

"Ten minutes ago"—she shrugs—"before you walked in that door, I'd have said you were fucked." She leans back in her chair, using her forefingers to swipe narrow columns of pin-straight black hair behind each ear. "It's a shit situation . . . one of the most predatory I've seen. As it stands, you walk away from the marriage, you walk away from the music."

Instantly, a million tiny needles pierce through my flesh. She's done nothing but confirm what I already assumed. But somehow, quite foolishly, I thought retaining Janet might mean I'd secured some sort of fast pass toward a pain-free divorce. Never mind the fact that already, she had to petition a judge to compel Elliot's lawyers to provide me with the prenup documents since, after signing them ages ago, he never gave me a copy for my own records.

"But you knew this," she says. "When you decided to leave him. You knew what you could be leaving behind." Janet eyes me shrewdly. This look is far from the lusty, assessing one I'm used to enduring in boardrooms, not unlike this room, when I'm sitting across from suits that are more often than not filled out by much older, *male*-er forms. She's not even in a suit. She's wearing a sleeveless Alaïa shift that boasts a high neckline with tasteful cutouts—if there can be such a thing.

I nod, swallowing past a knot lodged in my throat. I've never felt more foolish than the day I fully reckoned with the rock-hard truth that marrying Elliot Majors might have possibly been the biggest mistake of my life. Now, I can only hope the Ice Queen might possess some alternative kind of magic. Because that's likely what it's going to take if I want to escape this marriage with my career intact—if I want to see a dime of revenue from the records Elliot produced for me, the songs that won us both Grammys and me millions of adoring fans.

Janet must sense my rising panic. "It's okay," she says. "When we say yes to marriage, divorce is the last thing on our minds. Especially at twenty."

Especially when the man you're saying yes to is the first man in your life whose love doesn't hurt . . . until it did.

"So, what are my options," I ask, squaring my shoulders and sniffling back the stinging threat of tears.

"Well, I like to start off by asking my clients to pick a 'D.' The answer will undoubtedly determine how we proceed," she says, smirking. "So, what's more important to you, handling the *dissolution* as quickly as possible? Or, are you more concerned about the *distribution* of your assets?" she asks. "Because if it's option A, we can wrap this up in California's standard six months. No fanfare or hand-wringing. We go by what you've already established to the letter. But as outlined in the prenup, everything reverts to Elliot."

At this, I flinch. But if she notices, she doesn't let on and continues. "It means you'd be free . . . in a sense. You'd retain your split on future earnings on all performances of the music produced by him. But he'd retain one hundred percent ownership of the masters. You'd be severing all ties and voiding your recording contract since you came in as his talent. In effect, you'd be starting fresh as an artist."

"That's not freedom," I say. "It's robbery."

"Okay." Now she leans forward, placing her elbows on the conference table and clasping her hands. "So let me ask you, then. What does freedom look like to you?"

I breathe in deeply and let it out slow and steady—summoning my vocal bravado. "Freedom looks like me walking away . . . with everything I have worked for."

"I was hoping you'd say that." She sits back and smiles. "*Distribution* it is."

And for the first time since I stepped off the elevator, I smile too. "So, what's that going to take?"

2

YOU MEAN TO TELL me that long-necked, narrow-assed pea-cock gets to flounce around Europe with Miss Thing, mean-while you have to sit back like Susie Homemaker just so you don't end up strung out on the streets?"

"Tuh! It's the gall for me."

"Honey, it's the gall. The gumption. The unmitigated audacity. Tell me where I can find some. 'Cause clearly I missed the flash sale."

"All right, all right. How about a round of the quiet game?" I not so calmly suggest before my irritation bubbles over. We are a third of the way into my three-hour glam routine, and for all intents and purposes, I am trapped in what I've come to call The Chair.

Typically, this is my sacred, safe space—the place where I center myself before a live performance or a major appearance. Where I get to savor the final moments of being just me, Elladee Robinson, before I'm transformed into the well-crafted popstar persona of *Ella Simone*.

But at some point, we all lost the plot. It probably happened around the time the *Waiting to Exhale* soundtrack found its way onto my Bluetooth speaker, which shifted the mood in my Sunset Tower suite accordingly. Now, Mary J. Blige is belting about how she's "not gon' cry," and my glam team is spiraling over my impending divorce from the most prolific hitmaker of the last twenty years.

At my passive-aggressive request for silence, three stares pin me in place as if to say, *Check us like that again, and we'll have you up on that Grammy stage looking a hot mess.*

But then Rodney, my stylist and oldest friend, pauses from dutifully steaming the chiffon skirt of my evening gown. His eyes soften as they meet mine in the vanity mirror, and he makes a sharp intake of breath, as if suddenly noticing the fine cracks in my otherwise buffed and primed exterior.

"Oh no! We've gone too far." His words are breathless and tinged with remorse, just above a whisper. Rodney's full lips droop into a pout as he turns to his cohorts. "Ladies," he snaps. "Maybe let's take it down a notch?"

"Miss me with the soft shit, Rodney!" Sheryl chirps as she swivels around to glare at him. Miraculously, she doesn't miss a beat as she deftly loops a long lock of my hair around her curl wand. "The one who needs to 'take it down a notch' is that triflin' ex of hers."

"Clock it!" Jamie chimes in, while gingerly applying moisturizer to my cheeks—the second step in her elaborate face-beat prep routine. "And you know what's *really* foul?" she asks. "The way everybody expects her to *keep it cute. Be the bigger person. Go high. Don't mess with the bag.* Trust and believe, I can see the logic in what that lawyer lady advised you to do." She pauses, sucking her lips until they smack. "But that doesn't mean I wouldn't like to bust a cap in a few asses right about now."

"Mm-hmm," Sheryl adds, pinning both me and Rodney with a pointed look. "Moral of the story, friends, is . . . we can keep it cute in public. But we sure as hell don't have to behind closed doors."

The two of them high-five as a long exhale whooshes out of me. With it, the tension in my shoulders begins to ease just slightly. As much as I've avoided exposing any raw feelings I have about the public disaster that has become my personal life to *anyone*—it's cathartic in a way to have my closest friends express theirs on my behalf. In a way they've become my anger translators, and right about now it's saving me from bursting at the seams.

These three have been my Day Ones since, well, the start of it all. Rodney and I go all the way back to my short-lived time spent studying songwriting at Boston's Berklee College of Music. Sheryl and Jamie were hired on by the label, but we instantly clicked.

So I know they mean well.

But while I am physically trapped by the ministrations currently happening to my head and face, I'm also now bound by Janet Waterman's rules. Ones I've been instructed to follow religiously— lest I run afoul of her million-dollar strategy and lose my shot at future earnings from a decade's worth of blood, sweat, tears, and life-altering music.

"Look, I get how fucked up this is, you guys, and I'm sorry for snapping. This week has just been . . . a lot," I admit. "Janet says, despite whatever Elliot throws my way in the press, while we prep for the divorce negotiations, I need to keep a squeaky-clean reputation in all of this. No juicy headlines. No bad PR. And no new relationships he can claim predated our separation."

"Okay. Now *that* brings me back to my original point about DJ Chlamydia and all that boppin' around town with Thing One . . . or is it Two?" Sheryl says, referring back to Miss Thing—which is her actual stage name.

"She's his artist," I reply, exasperated. "So he's got plausible deniability there."

Jamie scoffs while placing an aloe patch under my left eye. "Well . . . his tongue *was* just down her throat all over—"

"It's beside the point," I cut in sharply, and she rears back. "The prenup didn't stipulate cheating on *his* behalf . . . only mine." Something I only relearned yesterday, when Janet provided me with a copy of the very long document. Heaven knows, if it had, we could light a match to the entire document at this point.

"When they go low," Jamie mutters, shaking her head and sticking on the other eye patch, "apparently Elliot goes to hell."

I sigh again. As if sensing the need for a lighter mood, Rodney rubs my shoulder over my silk kimono. "It's okay, boo. One day at a time. We'll get you through tonight . . . lookin' flawless as usual. Then we'll plot from there," he says, before moving on to spot-checking the beading on the bodice of my gown.

Everyone falls silent as if in tacit agreement, just as Toni Braxton starts crooning about packing her tears away and letting go and letting it flow. I stare at my reflection in the vanity as the crew diligently gets back to work.

It's a total out-of-body experience, watching them mold me into a red-carpet-ready pop star in much the same way an artist sculpts an ornate bust out of marble—the common thread being that the end result is still a *product*. However beautiful it may be, she's not real.

Hoda Kotb once asked me what the most transformative step of my glam routine was, and without thinking twice, I answered that it was the hair. Whether I'm in color-treated fauxlocs, braids down my back, or have an install that's pressed straight, I haven't worn my own shoulder-length hair out and free for an appearance since signing with Onyx Records a decade ago.

Elliot, or "Majors" as everyone in the industry calls him, always loved having me dolled up with heavy makeup and hairpieces in public—preferring I reserve my "natural beauty" for him.

I already have to share so much of you with the world, he'd said. *Let me have this.*

At first, I thought it was sweet. I liked feeling like I was being kept safe by him. But later, after discovering that he was sharing *all* of himself with practically anybody willing, I started to find it intensely stifling and even perverse that he'd played on my emotions to assert control over my styling choices . . . and eventually *all* my choices. But by then, I had an image to uphold. One that was cosigned and underwritten by Onyx Records' top executives, the A and R department, and perhaps most importantly, millions of fans worldwide.

When I debuted, the robust R&B/hip-hop vibes that had dominated the charts during the nineties and early aughts had funneled down to a select few artists. The ones I'd grown up admiring and even imitating in my childhood bedroom—the Ashantis, Mýas, and Ameries of the world—were no longer releasing records at a steady clip. Streaming had flipped the entire industry on its head, and labels were reeling, scrambling to adapt new formulas for cultivating breakout talent. Gone were the days when you could get discovered busking on the street, at an auspicious open mic night, or from sending out demo tapes.

It was 2014, and I was a fresh dropout after my first semester at Berklee. It was a jaded adviser whom I'd apparently caught on a bad day who gave me a piece of advice that blew my mind—*Don't go into debt for a degree in something you already have what it takes to go out there and pursue.* I withdrew immediately, using the dregs of that month's student loan check to book a flight out to Los Angeles, where I'd spend the next six months crashing on

Rodney's cousin's couch. I knew absolutely no one, and even less about the recording industry. My only game plan was to audition for *The Voice.*

Televised singing competitions made for great ratings, but the same couldn't be said for promising music careers. Still, I subjected myself to the circus of it all, hoping I'd be the outlier to break the mold. Turns out, I wasn't.

But shortly after I was sent home on week three of the competition, a YouTube video of me singing Amy Winehouse's "Love Is a Losing Game" went viral. That's when the needle started to move in the right direction for me. Next thing I knew, Elliot Majors was in my DMs, asking to fly me out to New York for a month of recording sessions.

You're a star, he said on our first phone call. *Right now, I'm just the only one who knows it. Soon enough, everyone will.*

From there, it's all a chaotic blur. It took us two weeks to record my first single but only one to give in to the electric chemistry that pulsed between us. I'd never had a champion like Elliot—a man who makes you feel like the shiniest object in the room when his eyes are on you. And somehow, his belief in me rubbed off on everyone at the label, too, because my contract sailed through negotiations and I was a signed artist before I could legally drink alcohol.

At only thirty, he had that much pull within the industry already. Elliot was convinced I wasn't the next *fill in the blank,* but the first *Ella Simone,* a stage name he crafted by melding Ella Fitzgerald and Nina Simone—B*ecause you're an old soul, baby girl,* he'd said. *You stand apart.*

Standing apart would be easier said than done. Beyoncé had recently released her self-titled fifth studio album, and Rihanna's *Unapologetic* had come out two years prior. Needless to say, for a brand-new Black female artist like me, who straddled the lines of pop and R&B, there was little room for error in establishing and distinguishing myself.

I'm not exactly edgy, irreverent, or dripping in swag like Rih. And while I was blessed with enough of an innate sense of rhythm to find my way around a choreographed eight-count—I'd be delusional to put myself in the same category as Queen Bey when it comes to raw performance talent. But what I've always had in spades, since I was a little girl, was an ear for melodies and a way with words.

Rolling Stone said my first EP possessed a vibe that rang "fresh yet familiar, with sweet melodies and wrenching lyrics to remind listeners that R&B stands for rhythm and blues." Elliot read me the review from the opposite end of a bubble bath we'd shared in the presidential suite at the Four Seasons in Manhattan. That same day, he'd gotten the word *Songbird* tattooed on his wrist—his nickname for me and the title of my debut album. We were perfectly, incandescently happy. And later that night after we made love, we wrote the song that would win us our first Record of the Year Grammy.

The words. The melodies. The double and triple entendres that could turn a lyric about a summer breeze into a meditation on the lingering imprint of a stolen kiss—it all came easy to us. It was the rest that he'd eventually make so hard.

ELLA! ELLA! MISS SIMONE! OVER YOUR SHOULDER, ELLA!
   On your right!
   Over here, Ella!
   Give us a smile!
   Thank you! Can we get a smolder?!

Show us some leg!

Ella! Ella! Miss Simone! This way!

The heavy, steadying press of my bodyguard Sanders's hand at the small of my back and the firm grip my manager, Angelo, maintains on my left elbow anchor me as we burst through the Sunset Tower Hotel's double doors and into a sea of flashing lights. The Glam Squad brings up the rear as I'm ushered ahead on the stone walkway toward an idling black SUV.

We barrel through the chaos. A bevy of paparazzi surrounds our path, bolstered by a lively crowd of fans. I press forward as steadily as I can in six-inch platform heels, grateful as always not to be doing this alone. We reach the car, and before I'm hoisted up into my seat, I pause, giving Angelo's hand a firm squeeze and a questioning look, which he returns with a swift nod and wink. Nonverbal communication becomes essential when you're used to being observed in every public moment. I turn to my bodyguard and mumble quickly, "It's okay, Sandy, I can give 'em a few snaps."

I face the mob of flashes and deliver what they demand. Propping one foot up on a step to the SUV, I reveal a leg that's just been slathered in shimmering body butter. I then turn over my left shoulder and offer what I calculate to be a dazzling smile. The frantic shouts and frenzied camera clicks from seconds before erupt into the kind of deafening barrage that never fails to make my face and limbs go numb. Seconds later, when Sanders shuts me in the vehicle and all goes quiet—with Angelo having slipped around and into the seat next to me—I can finally breathe, even within the tight confines of my corset.

"So, the plan for the night," Angelo commences with business and absolutely no pleasantries. "You and Majors will do the carpet, take your seat for the opening number, then you'll go back for a quick change into the Balmain gown. Just like in rehearsal, at the mid-show mark, you're performing the 'Always Be My Baby' / 'Fantasy' medley with Ariana for the Mariah tribute. Then in the back quarter of the show, you're co-presenting R&B Song of the Year with Miles Westbrook . . ."

"I'm sorry, with who?" I ask.

"Miles Westbrook," Angelo repeats. Looking up from his phone, his eyes spear me like I've just asked him what day it is. "Starting pitcher for the LA Dodgers," he explains.

Suddenly jittery, I adjust in my seat and start to pick at my sparkly acrylics. "I know *of* him," I say, albeit a bit defensively. "But remind me why a baseball player is presenting at the Grammys? Did the Recording Academy strike some sort of deal with Major League Baseball?"

"Right on the money," Angelo confirms. "It's all part of a strategy to revitalize the telecast and draw in more ratings for the network. I'm told each award tonight is being presented by a recording artist and, I quote, 'someone of note from another field.'"

"Hmm," I murmur, not entirely sold on the gimmick. At the same time, it tracks. Given all any of us seem to be doing in this business these days is scheming for the *right* kinds of attention.

Angelo continues his briefing. "Anyway. Things you need to know about Miles . . . other than he's fine with a capital 'F'—"

"Also apparently a fuckboy with a capital 'F' . . . " I cut in. "But do go on."

Angelo, who has been with me for seven years, is entirely unfazed by my interruption.

"His rookie year with the LA Dodgers was 2014, and he's been with the team ever since. Four years ago, he became starting pitcher, leading the team to two World Series titles, which they failed to defend last year in a *devastating* loss," he says, and I note the deflation in Angelo's voice.

"Sounds like *you* took that personally," I add, hoping for a rise I know I won't get out of my unflappable manager.

"It was hard on the city," he says gravely, like the born and bred Angeleno he is. "Anyway. When this season's up he'll be a free agent. Word on the street is he's itching to jump ship to get as far away from LA as possible."

"Oh, that's right!" I remember aloud. "Wasn't there some sort of drama with an ex and a teammate?"

Angelo smirks, furiously tapping out a message on his phone. "So, she's not living under a rock after all."

"Sports, I could not care less about," I explain. "A real-life love triangle that ends in a brawl? Sign me up for season tickets." I say the words, but instantly, they sour in my mouth. If living in caustic limelight for this long has taught me anything, it's that nothing is as black-and-white as it seems in headlines or the salacious claims from the often questionable "sources" that accompany them. And if what I've heard of Westbrook's past year is even close to being accurate, he's been put through the ringer.

I do my best to avoid online gossip as much as possible. But given all my hours spent in The Chair with Rodney, Sheryl, and Jamie, inevitably I end up absorbing the latest scandals through osmosis. So I vaguely recall them talking about some big shot player's wife getting caught in an affair with a teammate of his.

"The aftermath was catastrophic for the guy," Angelo recalls somberly. "I mean, the *LA Times*, *SportsCenter*, and everybody else pinned the Dodgers World Series meltdown on that locker-room dustup between him and Morales right before the final."

I grimace. "In that case, who can blame him for all the swimsuit models and actresses that came after?" I say flatly, careful to curb the edge of bitterness, and maybe even a little bit of envy I feel. It's always pricked me how when men in the spotlight are jilted or betrayed, everybody seems to revel in their devil-may-care rebound eras, practically cheering them on to get over their exes by getting *under* any- and everybody they possibly can. But let a famous woman get a little too close to her trainer after her husband's been caught with his hand down the nanny's blouse, and suddenly she's "spiraling," written off as pathetic and sloppy. Worst of all, it's not even *just* her reputation that suffers. If she's not careful, her career will too. Not to mention her self-esteem.

Elliot and I haven't slept together in a year. We haven't lived under the same roof in months either. In that time, our marriage has been reduced to the tired cliché of a celebrity PR relationship. Which means I haven't been touched by a man in a way that wasn't intricately choreographed for a music video or live performance in more than three hundred sixty-five days. And if Janet Waterman has her way, this will remain the case for, at minimum, the next six months while she fights tooth and nail to nullify the restrictive clauses of our prenup and my recording contract.

Keep your side of Front Street clean. At least in the eyes of the tabloids, she said. And that should be easy enough for me, since I've perfected the act of keeping up appearances, even when my reality is a smoldering hot mess.

3

A S WE MAKE THE trek from WeHo to Downtown LA, a stifling sense of calm settles inside our black SUV. Tonight,
there are no nominations or make-or-break performances of
new singles to send me on a spiral of anxiety—only the pressure
of pretending like I'm having the time of my life while enacting
what are essentially the last rites of my marriage before a sea of
cameras.

Traffic on the 110 is stop and go, and apart from NPR chatter
droning low on the radio, everything's quiet. Sanders and my
driver Rohin are seated up front like clay statues, so stoically focused on the road ahead they might as well be set behind a parti-
tion. And with Angelo quietly returned to his emails, I'm left
alone to tussle with my thoughts.

If my manager can help it, he won't take calls for other clients
when he's out with me. It's this kind of deference that makes
me itch most when I'm all done up like this—even more than
the false lashes, boob tape, and shapewear. The way people

bend and contort themselves to please and placate me. Or maybe my discomfort comes from just how *used to it* I am at this point—how natural it feels to be accommodated without having to ask.

When Elliot and I first got together, I was mesmerized by the way he moved through the world, or better yet, how the world seemed to move *because* of him. How paths would automatically form when he walked into any room, how doors seamlessly opened, and how the people behind those doors made note of his presence. The man was mood music. He set the vibe for every space he occupied.

Someone with a firm grasp on pop culture or a true soundhead would likely recognize Elliot from all the cameos he's made in his artists' music videos, where he often plays it casually cool in the background, bobbing his head in designer shades while tucked behind the turntables and surrounded by writhing bodies. But pass him on the street, and the average person wouldn't know that the layered snare drum beat in eighty percent of today's hip-hop music was inspired by Elliot's work in the early aughts—back when he was discovering artists on MySpace. They also wouldn't know that if Prince were with us today, Elliot could hold his own onstage next to him with a rhythm guitar.

It all felt so foreign to me at first, being attached to a true musical genius. But soon, I got a contact high on the rarefied air he breathed, and before I could blink twice, his world became mine. This new land of celebrity was an adventure, and Elliot was my tour guide. As long as he was holding my hand, showing me the ropes, it was the time of my life. But somewhere along the way his grip loosened, and I learned how hard it is to keep hold of someone who's already decided to let you go.

"Change of plans," Angelo says, piercing through my cloud of thoughts. The unusual, frayed edge to his voice makes me sit up a little straighter. "Elliot's not doing the carpet," he says, aggressively rubbing his brow. "Coco just texted."

Elliot and I had agreed to do this one last red carpet together before allowing our teams to release a joint statement about our separation. This had been part of our plan to present an amicable and united front—show the world that conscious uncoupling isn't just for the Goop crowd. Selfishly, I hoped it could help curb the press and their rabid appetite for digging up dirt on us—despite Elliot's many not-so-private infidelities. Both our PR teams pushed for it too. And like a fool, I assumed we were set.

"Heeeey, C! I'm here with Ella." Angelo's already rung up Coco on speakerphone to get to the bottom of it. "So, listen, totally cool that Majors can't make the carpet. I'll just play seat filler until he gets here. Sound good?"

"Oh, darling. If it wasn't clear over text, he's not coming at all. Carpet or show," Elliot's manager says in her posh London accent. "It was a game-time decision or, of course, I'd have told you sooner."

I slump in my seat, releasing my head to let it thud against the smooth black leather.

These days, unless we're in the studio working on music, Elliot and I rarely speak to each other without an intermediary—usually the task falls to our management teams, who have drummed up a muted but still palpable distaste for each other. And exactly two days ago, Coco had confirmed that he'd be here. *With bells on!* she'd said with her typical faux sweetness, like a lie dipped in honey. And stupidly, I counted on it—even if I *was* a bit shocked that Elliot would agree to grace the Grammys with his presence after all the public swipes he's made toward the Recording Academy in recent years. But he'd given his word, and trusting it was another mistake on a long list of many for me.

But now, I have to wonder if his bait and switch is a form of punishment for me choosing to lawyer up. For me daring to scrutinize the prenup and then push back against it. A wad of anxiety starts to form in my chest. I'm suddenly scrambling for my phone. I don't have to swipe through the three-digit notifications of unread messages to know that none are from him or Coco. But I do so anyway, if for no other reason than to confirm my well-earned bias.

Suddenly feeling the kind of flustered anger that makes it hard to catch your breath, I turn to Angelo. "So, what do I say? When everyone wants to know where he is?"

"Let's think," he says, chewing on his lip. "Presumably, Elliot never got on the plane from London so . . . we'll just say he's at Abbey Road!" Angelo's brows shoot up like he's just conquered the daily Wordle. "Give 'em a line or two about his new artis—" He stops short as I tense at the mention of Miss Thing, the straw that broke my marriage's back.

A potent memory slams into me of the night I first met her at an album listening party thrown by the label. How I was eager to meet someone who reminded me so much of my younger self that I'd been casually scanning the room for a glimpse of her so I could introduce myself, maybe take her under my wing. How the moment we crossed paths, she couldn't seem to get away from me fast enough—how her eyes seemed to burn and retreat the instant they made contact with mine. It's only now, in retrospect, that it all makes sense.

"Oooor . . . we could come up with something else?" Angelo asks, snapping me back to the now.

"No. It's fine." I say the words the way I would if a manicurist had cut my cuticle to the quick and I was bleeding out on the table. I shrug away the sting. "I can plug their LP. With all the photos of them out now, I'm sure it'll track."

"You good?" he asks warily. "Because we can have Lydia issue a gag advisory to the red carpet press and squash all things Elliot."

"No. It's fine." I'm repeating myself now, like a glitching robot. Giving that sort of tip-off would be nothing short of a smoking gun. Surely Angelo knows that. So him even suggesting it likely means he's as thrown off by this curveball as I am.

"I can handle it," I add to assure him.

But when I glance over at my manager, it's obvious that he doesn't believe me either. Then I see the moment he backs down from his internal protest, when the tension releases from his shoulders and he sinks back against his headrest. I sink back, too, and try to ground myself with a few rounds of meditative breathing, shoring up my energy for the game I'm about to play.

"I'll let Lydia know we're doing the carpet solo," Angelo says, and the words sound like they were uttered from somewhere far away. Because I've already slipped back under the blanket of numbness that protects me from the sharp edges of all my swirling troubles. And after my final six-second exhale, I dive back into my clutch for my phone and tap out a text to my people. They may be close by, riding in the SUV that's trailing us. But I need them closer.

GROUP TEXT: The Glam Squad

ME: Elliot's not coming.

SHERYL: That negro better count his days . . .

SHERYL: Don't you go covering for him either!

JAMIE: What's she gonna do, tell Ryan Seacrest her man's across the pond swimming in a sea of 🐱

RODNEY: She can tell Ryan to have five seats in a basement is what she can do.

ME: I will tell anyone who asks they're working on the album.

SHERYL: You deserve the peace prize.

SHERYL: . . . and some premium side 🍆 tonight.

JAMIE: Yes hunty! Let's get you tossed around gf. Elliot can't have ALL the fun.

JAMIE: He deserves to have NONE.

RODNEY: I don't usually agree with you heffas but I can get on board here.

ME: Okay. This was a mistake. See you on the carpet.

SHERYL: She didn't say no to the side 🍆 so . . . that means there's a chance.

ME: There's absolutely zero chance.

JAMIE: Oh ye of little faith. Father God, forgive
her for her unbelief.

RODNEY: This just got real unholy up in here.

RODNEY: I'm not mad at it.

ME: Fools. I'm friends with fools.

ME: Lovable. Talented. But FOOLS all the same.

SHERYL: Iss ok boo. We got you. 😘 🥺 💦

JAMIE: 😋

RODNEY: 🙁

SOUTH FIGUEROA IS BACKED UP WITH A SNAKELIKE ROW OF
sleek black SUVs and Sprinter vans queued outside of Crypto
Arena. We sit for twenty minutes, slowly inching along, before it's
finally our turn to emerge and face the music.

Sanders hops out of the passenger seat to open my door and
help me step down on the pavement. This is far from my first ro-
deo, but still, it takes a beat for my eyes to adjust to the bright
white glare of the sun and the jarring mass of bustling activity
before us. Seconds later, the glam team materializes almost out
of thin air. Like the magical woodland creatures who get Cinder-

ella dressed for the ball, they waste no time flitting about, poking and prodding and tweaking me for my now solo walk down the red carpet. Within seconds, my gloss is reapplied, the flowing gossamer fabric of my skirt is smoothed out, and any flyaway strands on my wig are coaxed back into formation. Finally, with a subtle wink and purse of Rodney's lips, I have the stamp of approval to proceed.

He turns to my manager with a smirk. "The face card never declined on this one," he says.

Angelo winks at him before clasping my hand in his. "Ready to rock and roll?" he asks. I squeeze him back and take a deep fortifying breath, then nod and smile.

Next we're greeted by Lydia, my publicist from the label. She's dressed from head to toe in black business attire and wielding a clipboard in one hand and a walkie-talkie in the other. "Hi, Ella, you're right on time," she says while gesturing for us to follow as she leads us to the edge of the carpet—the mouth of the jungle.

There's an element of structured chaos to walking a red carpet on a night like this—when an entire industry descends on a single spot, and everyone's scrambling for attention. Rising stars are hoping to cement their status on an ever-shifting platform, while industry vets cling to their own ebbing relevance. On a night when we're supposed to be celebrating music, we end up focusing on everything but—the clothes, the plus-ones, the parties, the beef, the drama. The "content" over the art.

Elliot once explained to me how it takes a special kind of person to opt into this lifestyle. To willingly put the most vulnerable parts of themselves out in front of the world to embrace or reject. To stand in front of three hundred high-definition lenses, not to mention the millions of eyeballs at home, with flashbulbs all wielded by skilled photographers, eager to capture your every angle—each one expecting nothing less than perfection, but still hoping that they might get lucky enough to catch something even more valuable, like a moment of novelty—a sign of weakness or distress. It's the one reason I'm relieved Elliot's a no-show for to-night.

After nearly a decade of doing these "perp walks" together, I've grown increasingly weary of the act. It's one thing to find yourself on a "Red Carpet Mishaps" roundup because of smudged eyeliner or fabric that photographs a bit too sheer, offering everyone a peep show of your shapewear. That's par for the course.

But when you're a couple, the scrutiny is amplified tenfold. Any sign of tension between the two of you, whether it's an awkward head tilt and strained smile after a curt whisper or simply an extra half inch of distance between your angled bodies, and the next morning's headlines could read *Trouble in Paradise*, with a body language expert brought on to guesstimate how long you're going to make it based on whether or not your toes are pointed in or out.

So doing this alone makes things simple for me after all. I just have to (a) look the part and (b) not stick my foot in my mouth. Easy as pie.

Ella, straight ahead!

Over your shoulder, Ella!

Miss Simone! Can you give us a smile?

Three feet from the step and repeat, and I've already been spot-ted by the press pen. Some up-and-coming artist was just getting photographed voguing with their tongue out, but now they're not so gingerly being nudged aside by a carpet handler as another one ushers me to the very spot where they stood. I take my place in front of the flashing lights and instantly I'm *on*.

4

ADVANCE DOWN THE STEP and repeat like the well-seasoned pro that I am. After countless requests for smiles, pouts, hair flips, and a few jarringly abrasive demands for a twirl, it all starts to feel like some chaotic game of Simon Says, anyway. So, when Angelo whisks me off for a round of press, the relief I feel is a shock to the system.

"And now we have joining us, the *stun-ning* Ella Simone," Sherelle purrs. As I approach, she gracefully takes both of my hands to help me ascend the steps. Sherelle is dripping with diamonds in a floor-length sparkling green number that looks like something straight out of the Emerald City. It's doing amazing things for her legs and waist.

"Honey! You're just giving us *ev-er-y-thing* tonight!" she coos.

We beam at each other and air-kiss, careful to position ourselves so that the cameras capture our best angles. I try to center myself in the interaction and drown out the chorus of activity surrounding us. "But look at you! That waist is snatched," I croon, careful not to shout on instinct to counter the chaotic din of the carpet. Years ago, I learned the hard way that yelling into the mic on a red carpet makes you sound utterly ridiculous to anyone who's watching at home.

"Oh, stop it." Sherelle playfully swats at me with a gloved hand. "Now of course everyone's been *dying* to know where that handsome hubby of yours is tonight. Can you tell us if Majors will be joining you later?" she asks.

Somewhere a record scratches, sending a violent chill up my spine. Angelo and I rehearsed this in the car, sure. But after all the spins and twirls, somehow this feels like an ambush with knives. I figured if Sherelle was going to be the one interviewer to highlight the absence of my yet-to-be-announced ex, she'd at least *ease* us into it. Maybe, like the others, she'd ask me who I'm wearing or who lent me the million dollars' worth of diamonds that are digging into my neck and stretching out my earlobes. I school a sour expression before it has time to manifest on my face.

Where is Elliot, you ask? Probably with his head up a twenty-two-year-old's skirt, I think, but don't dare say. Instead, I shrug casually and glance to my left, where Angelo stands dutifully within earshot, ready to step in and rescue me if I start to bomb this interview.

If I gave Sherelle the whole truth, I'd tell her that as of this moment, Elliot Majors and Ella Simone are at war—two ex-lovers engaged in a battle to sever all ties. But on a less dramatic scale, he has been not-so-subtly blowing off this awards show ever since a very public falling-out with the Recording Academy over its refusal to televise the awards categories of his neo soul and alternative R&B artists—the ones the industry draws the bulk of its inspiration from but has no trouble relegating to the sidelines on its biggest night. So even though Elliot gave his word, via Coco, him showing up tonight would have been an aberration. But alas, I settle for the cover.

"He's at Abbey Road," I lie, with a smile.

"Oh! Londooon." Sherelle drags out the last syllable and waggles her eyebrows. "I assume he's working on something very special, then? I mean, to miss a big night like this?"

Absently, I finger the eight-carat ruby that sits above a white gold band, both weighing down my left ring finger. Per our prenup, he'll get it back when we formally divide our assets. Maybe that's when I'll feel the last string that binds our union snap.

Eager to satiate Sherelle's curiosity so I can be done, I return to my practiced script. "Elliot has signed an amazing new artist—"

"Mm-hmm, Miss Thing! Oh yes, honey, we've seen," Sherelle cuts in. I feel Angelo inch closer—a warning for Sherelle and her producer to stay in bounds here. Clearly everyone's seen the photos of Elliot's hot young protégé draped across his lap in the VIP section of Cirque le Soir in London.

"Yes, well they're working on a new album," I add with feigned enthusiasm. "I've heard some of the tracks they're recording, and it's truly phenomenal stuff."

In my periphery, I see Angelo, ever the enforcer, make a swiping motion across his neck with his right hand. His eyes are nearly popping from their sockets—all part of his nonverbal cue for Sherelle to cut the bullshit. She clocks it and visibly gulps before giving an almost imperceptible nod. Then, course correcting with a quickness, she says, "Well, I'm sure Majors is eager to get himself back across that pond with the way you're looking tonight! So tell us, who *are* you wearing?"

I thought she'd never ask.

AFTER BARRELING DOWN THE CRIMSON GAUNTLET, ANGELO and I follow hastily behind Lydia toward our assigned seats on the floor of the arena. We find them with only a few minutes to spare ahead of Thundercat's opening performance. Instead of hanging out backstage or in a greenroom, where he'd usually be, Angelo's next to me, filling in for Elliot. This way I don't have to sit next to a stranger all night or, worse, an exec from the label. Production has strategically placed me on the aisle for a comedic bit I'm supposed to do after the opener with our host for the night, Trevor Noah.

We've just been served our drinks, a flute of champagne for me and a tumbler of scotch for Angelo. I take a sip of the sparkly liquid and let my eyes flutter closed. When I open them, I sense an energy shift when a slight commotion breaks out around us. Turning, I find two seat fillers peering down the aisle with their jaws practically detached. I shrug it off—it's been a long time since a celebrity sighting has had that kind of effect on me. I'm about to turn back to the stage, when a tall, dark figure snags my attention from the direction they were gawking. I blink twice to try to reconcile this reality with the photos I've seen in the past. On the third blink, it's unmistakable.

Miles Westbrook has entered the building.

Under the dim blue-hued lighting of the arena, Miles's tall, athletic frame appears—dark, imposing, and devastatingly regal. Suddenly unsure of what to do with myself, and unwilling to be found staring, I hastily turn around. For what reason? I don't know. But that's when I notice a card with his name taped on the chair directly behind me. And next to his seat is a card that reads *Draya Nishelle*. I recognize it instantly and feel tiny pinpricks on the back of my neck.

Draya is a fitness model I once found Elliot getting a little too close for comfort with in the far corner of an album release party. He never supplied me with a straight answer as to whether or not things had started and ended there with her. But then, I *never* got straight answers from Elliot about all the countless scenarios that made me question my own sanity. It wasn't until I later caught him in the act that my reality became just that—real.

Feeling overheated, I swivel forward and take an oversized gulp from my champagne flute, nearly draining the glass. When I look up again, Miles and Draya are just a few feet away from us with her arm possessively interlocked with his. In a figure-hugging hot pink jumpsuit, she flicks her seventies Cher-like hair over a shoulder while smiling and blowing air kisses at attendees who are already seated. For Miles's part, he's sporting a warm, broad smile with a look of wonder in his eyes—almost like he's surprised by the warm reception. I have to admit it is a very welcoming embrace from a room that, for all the boisterous appearances on television, can be stilted and cold in person. But Miles is getting dapped up by everyone from Machine Gun Kelly to Ed Sheeran and Usher.

The chatter around us ratchets up several notches as more people start to take notice of his arrival. "Guess baseball really *is* America's favorite sport," I mumble, leaning close to Angelo's ear, mindful of the fact that in the arena, cameras are on us at all times, and any display of outsized emotion is likely to be captured and repurposed into a viral meme.

Angelo cranes his neck to peek for himself. "When baseball looks like *that* and has a nine-figure contract . . . what's not to love?"

At this I nearly spit up the bubbly. "I'm sorry, did you say *nine*?"

Angelo scoffs. "Spread out over ten years, but . . . yeah. The boy is paid."

Just as I begin to quietly contemplate my life choices, the house lights dim further and the couple of the hour nears us to brush past. But before they do, Miles looks down and our eyes lock. At this precise moment, something cold and hot slices through my entire body, and the promise I made myself not to stare at him is instantly forgotten. Our eye contact can't last more than two seconds, but the moment he turns away, I feel like I could fall. That's when Thundercat takes the stage and the crowd erupts with excitement.

Somehow, Angelo's procured a double shot for me, and I could kiss him with gratitude. Within seconds, I'm swept up in the groove of the song and have no choice but to get up and move my body to the hypnotic bass line. Three minutes later it's over, and Trevor Noah is standing in the aisle next to me with a spotlight trained on us. We didn't rehearse the bit in advance, but it's simple enough—we do an eight-count of a viral TikTok dance that's set to one of my singles, and the crowd awards us with polite laughter. He intros the show and we're off to the races.

Seconds later, Lydia scurries over to me and Angelo, our cue to get backstage for my wardrobe change.

THIS BALMAIN NUMBER COULD MAKE "BARELY THERE" LOOK matronly. It's basically one intricate circuit of multicolored silk straps that intersect in all directions to form a lattice pattern around my torso. The skirt tapers down in a tattered fringe effect that showcases the full length of my legs and only a portion of my ass. I loved it when I initially saw the sketch and tried it on during fittings, but now that I'm about to be onstage beneath all the lights, I'm wondering if maybe I'm doing just a little too much.

"Uh-uh," Rodney chirps as he notices me scrutinizing myself in the mirror. "Don't do that!"

"Don't do what?" I ask in mock confusion, already sure of what he's about to say.

"You know you look *damn* good. Don't come around here with that 'I shoulda went harder at the gym' look on your face. Nobody has time for that!" he scolds.

We watch the next segment of the show from backstage. It drags on in overlong speeches interspersed with a motley lineup of performances, some arguably more inspired than others. At the halfway mark, Lydia comes by the greenroom area to scoop me up so I can go join Ariana Grande for our duet honoring Mariah Carey, one of my all-around top-five favorite vocalists and probably my biggest lyrical inspiration.

The performance goes mostly as planned—save one iffy moment after the bridge of "Always Be My Baby" when our ad-libs begin to clash, so I back off the mic. But by the end we save it enough to garner a standing ovation. And by the looks of it, Mariah didn't hate it. If she had, that plus my divorce might be enough to put me off on an indefinite hiatus.

I spend another twenty minutes in the audience sipping a glass of wine with Angelo. By now the crowd is well lubricated and loosened up. Everyone's ready for the show to be over so they can head to the after-parties. But the biggest awards of the night are coming up, which means there's a healthy dose of anxiety in the air too. Without a new album released in time for this year's nominations cycle, the pressure's off me for the night—except for my R&B Song of the Year presentation with Miles. He and Draya weren't in their seats when I got back after my performance, and they haven't returned yet.

I find myself swatting away images of what they could be off doing together in secret corners of this arena. But before I lose that battle with my curiosity, I'm tapped on the shoulder once again.

I turn to find Lydia crouched down near my seat. "Miles Westbrook is asking for you backstage."

5

*Some of us need to be rescued, but
everyone wants to be seen.*

Mariah Carey

ILES WESTBROOK'S PRESENCE LOOMS large backstage.
Even with a frenzied sea of people separating us, I am keenly
aware of him standing in a dark corner chatting closely with a
member of his team. I can't remember ever feeling this affected by
a complete stranger before—wary yet intrigued at the same time.
Prior to tonight I *had* seen the man before . . . in photographs and
on TV.

Briefly, I revisit Sheryl's ridiculous contributions to the group
chat, along with Jamie and Rodney's relentless teasing. It's one
thing to make jokes with your friends about getting back in the
swing of things. But nothing could quite prepare me for the chem-
ical reactions Miles would draw out of me with just a glance.
That's all this is. The body's natural response when presented with
a desirable person, after its most basic wants have been neglected
for far too long.

In this case, the person stands a few inches taller than everyone else who is zipping between us and frantically occupied with
the business of putting on the show. And considering the fact that

almost half of us are tiptoeing around while propped up on what might as well be called stilts, that's saying a lot. The person has a bright white smile that stretches broadly over a strong chin, is framed by achingly full lips, and bracketed by dimples that curve deep within the rich brown complexion of his otherwise angular face.

"Ms. Simone, if you come with me now, I'll introduce you to Mr. Westbrook," a show producer says with a polite smile that knocks me out of my trance. I smile back and follow after her on stiff legs. Something elemental happens in the room as the distance closes between me and Miles. Like somehow, just by walking thirty feet, I've traversed a continent and entered a new climate. At about the halfway mark, Miles seems to take note of my approach. And when our eyes lock, for the second time tonight, I can only hold the contact for a moment before I glance away to break the tension.

In the final seconds before reaching him, I give myself the pep talk of the century. It consists of several *get it together*s, a few *girl, he is just a man*s, and a final resounding *Elladee Ashley Robinson, your grandmama taught you better than this*. So, by the time I am squarely in front of him, I've mustered the poise and control to act like the well-adjusted adult I am, but only in the most uncertain terms.

"Hi, Miles, it's nice to meet you," I say, extending my hand with a perfectly professional smile.

"Ella," he says my name and tapers off, like he meant to follow it up with something and never quite decided on what. But his eyes remain steady on mine. And there's an indecision there, like he's willing them to stay put rather than travel the length of me, like they *really* want to.

I can't shake the dangerous feeling that I want to be looked at by him. Like I want his eyes to drink me in, have their fill, and wordlessly affirm their delight. It's even more maddening that he won't give me the satisfaction of that coveted, languid perusal. Despite what the tabloids have said, Miles Westbrook has self-control, and *everything* in me wants to test it.

At some point in the past few seconds, we wound up alone. I have a faint memory of the producer telling us she'd be back with our sides. But I'm currently more preoccupied with the two loose buttons at the top of Miles's silk shirt, which reveal the divot at the base of his neck and just a hint of his strong chest.

My distraction is so utter and complete that I don't realize how long I've been staring as we've stood in total silence, until Miles clears his throat. "So, I'm a . . . fan," he says, piercing the awkward-ness. And surprisingly, his words are stilted, like now that we've been left alone for probably only a minute—at least I hope it's only been that long—he's nervous in my presence. "Of y-your music that is."

"Ah," I say, dubious of the claim. Most athletes I've come in contact with have Drake or Kendrick on their AirPods, not my subgenre of pop and R&B.

"You're about to quiz me, aren't you?" he asks, a sly grin creeping across his perfect face.

I fight the urge to fan myself as I feel sweat beading down my back. "I wouldn't dare," I lie.

"Oh, it's cool. My pop always said if you stay ready, you don't have to get ready," he counters, rolling his shoulders like he's preparing for a workout. He sports a panty-dropping grin that's as boyish as it's devilish.

"I'm waiting, then," I say, crossing my arms and cocking my head to the side. I'm aware of what the motion does to my chest in this dress, and I don't miss the moment his eyes swoop low and then return to my face—or the slight strain of his furrowed brow, like he's disappointed in himself for succumbing. I'm not.

He rolls his shoulders. "Okay, top-three Ella Simone tracks for me are . . . 'Cry Alone,' 'Thief of Hearts,' and the new one y-you just released. The Sade interpolation."

"'No Ordinary Love,'" I say, referring to the redux Elliot and I recorded a year ago and let linger to collect dust on a shelf until the label released it last week. Mostly, I'm stunned that Miles Westbrook just used the word *interpolation*. Not because I'd be so silly as to make the basic assumption that an athlete wouldn't have a vast vocabulary. It's just not a word you hear thrown around by people who aren't intimately involved in the process of producing music.

But before I can even respond, we're joined again by the producer, who's carrying a printout of our lines. She steps up to us gingerly, as if she's afraid to interrupt. "You don't have to memorize it," she says timidly. "There'll be a prompter. But just in case, sometimes people like to . . . well, you've both done this before. Anyhoo, holler if you need me. You're on in five!"

She hands us one printout to look at and scurries off to other duties. Now that we've got our assignment, we put the music talk on ice. Miles casually positions himself next to me and lowers the page so I can look on with him. Then we stand in silence. And I don't know about him, but I'm *looking* at the words on the page without really seeing what's there. Instead, I'm cataloging the subtle notes of his cologne, wondering exactly how tall he is, and fixating on how strongly defined his fingers are—curious all of a sudden to know if the hand holding the page is the one he pitches with.

Miles clears his throat. "Uh, so . . . it looks like they kept it pretty straightforward for us," he says, settling the mystery of whether or not he's as distracted by my presence as I am his.

I look up at him and notice his eyes are shifty and his jaw is tight. The swagger and ease from a moment ago has all but dissipated. "Wait, don't tell me you're . . . are you nervous about presenting?" I ask, careful not to sound like I'm teasing him.

He shrugs. Not dismissively, but more like an admission of defeat. "Public speaking. It's uh . . ." He pauses, eyes darting around as if checking for lurkers. "I stutter." He shrugs again, but this time with a small smile. And such an innocent gesture on this grown, gorgeous man is disarming.

"Oh. I see," I say, briefly at a loss for what to do or say to put him at ease. "Is there anything that helps when you get blocked? Anything *I* can do?" My best friend in middle school had a stutter, and eventually she discovered that clapping her hands or snapping her fingers whenever she got held up on a syllable or letter seemed to help get her over the hump. I can't assume the same trick works for everyone with the same speech impediment, but I figure it couldn't hurt to ask.

"Nah. It's okay," Miles says. "But most people don't even think to ask that, so I appreciate you."

I nod, probably a bit too aggressively, and my brain produces no additional thoughts. We stand in awkward silence for a few more seconds.

"I tap my thigh when I get stuck," Miles offers. "It doesn't always w-work, but it helps me often enough."

I'm about to say something totally inadequate for this vulnerable disclosure, like *thank you for sharing that with me* or *oh, that's nice to know*, when I'm saved by the bell.

"There you are!" shouts Rodney. Feeling uneasy and desperate for an escape, I turn and begin walking up to him and Angelo without realizing that one of the long tassels of my skirt is wedged underneath Miles's shoe.

I hear the pop of fabric before I feel the straps snap one by one.

"Oh dear," Angelo says without so much as an ounce of alarm.

Suddenly, the tight squeeze around my torso begins to give way. As if in slow motion, I feel the tug and slide of my dress as it begins to fall from my body. At the last moment, I grab hold of the cups at my chest to keep from fully exposing myself to four people, three of whom have already seen me in various states of undress, and one who seems to be doing everything in his power to avoid such a fate. Miles stands with his back turned to us, his nose practically pressed against the wall.

I turn and am instantly struck by the sheer panic on Lydia's, Angelo's, and Rodney's faces. We go on in two minutes, and with one wrong move, my dress might as well be a pile of tattered fabric. A single strand broke loose, and then another, then the whole garment unraveled.

"Okay, peeps, what's the plan," I say calmly, if only because I'm staving off true panic. "Clearly I can't go out there, you know, holding my dress up."

"I could hold it for you?" Miles offers very innocently while peeking over his shoulder. "This t-technically is my fault and I'm very sorry, and I—"

"Hush, man!" Rodney says, palming his cheek, seemingly drawing a complete blank.

"No, for real," Miles offers again, "I can just pinch the fabric at the back—"

"Hush!" they all shout at him in unison. At this, Miles seems to shrink a few inches and turns back to his corner.

"Okay, let's think," I say, cheerfully turning to Rodney. "Do you have time to run back to the dressing room for my red-carpet look?"

He turns to Lydia, who motions toward the countdown clock.

We've got one and a half minutes before the ad break is over. So the answer is a resounding *hell no*. Wordlessly, we all deflate.

Without an explanation, Miles starts unbuttoning his own shirt.

"What are you doing?" I ask. "Put your clothes back on! We have to go out there in . . ." I glance over at the clock. "A minute and fifteen seconds. We can't both be naked!"

He turns and winks at me. My stomach flips, and I have to fight to keep the muscles in my face from either scowling or smirking right back at him.

"And we won't be. You can wear this, and I'll just wear the jacket," he says, suddenly self-assured. That confidence melts when he's met by our silence. "It's Atelier Versace?" he offers, like a selling point. And I briefly wonder if he's a fashion guy or if his style team rehearsed that with him specifically for tonight. I have a feeling it's the latter, and I like it. Seconds later, he confirms it.

"That's what they told me at least?" Miles brandishes his shirt and then looks over at Rodney, who is suddenly casually smirking as if this wasn't a desperate wardrobe crisis of epic proportions a second ago.

"It's not a bad look," Rodney murmurs. "We can probably make it work." He turns it over in his hands, appraising it like we've got all the time in the world while I continue to marvel at his apparent lack of urgency. He points to Miles. "Okay. You, turn back around." Then to me: "You, step out of that and get over here."

With Miles safely facing the wall again, I do as Rodney says. He helps me into the shirt, and the moment I'm enveloped in the butteriness of the fabric, I'm hit with a wave of Miles's lush scent. The shirt isn't bad either. Admittedly, it's a great fashion piece. It hits me right at mid-thigh, and Rodney opts to keep it unbuttoned down to just above my navel. From somewhere in his magic fanny pack, he grabs a clamp that cinches it at the waist, which keeps it from looking like a full knapsack on me. I glance at the clock, and with forty seconds to spare, this is surely as good as it's going to get.

Angelo and Lydia have been securing the perimeter with wardrobe partitions to make sure no one else backstage witnessed this little snafu. But now they turn and admire Rodney's work.

"Okay, Miles. You can turn back around now," Rodney says.

As he slowly faces us, I can't help but feel like we're at a "first look" photo shoot on our wedding day or, worse, like I've just walked down a never-ending staircase as I'm presented to my homecoming date while he stands awkwardly in the foyer holding my wrist corsage between his sweaty palms.

"Well," I say impatiently. "How did we do?"

"You look . . . y-you, um." He coughs, to clear his throat. "You're beautiful."

My skin pricks with heat all over, and I wonder if I'm the only one who noticed that his eyes never once left my face. I also didn't miss that, as he spoke, he was tapping his thigh.

IF YOU DON'T KNOW WHERE TO TRAIN YOUR EYES ONSTAGE, it's easy to get blinded by the heavy orbs of light that are rigged up above the proscenium. And everything beyond the radiant halo is a sea of endless black. From stage left I can see DJ D-Nice spinning my biggest hit, "Make You Mine," for our "walk out" anthem. At the same time, I hear Miles and me announced as "Major League Baseball's former Man of the Year and two-time Grammy-winning pop and R&B princess." Convinced I look like the Tweedledum to Miles's Tweedledee in my Hail Mary ensemble, I take a deep breath and exhale the jitters. In ten minutes I fully intend to reunite with my glass—this time with something stronger than wine in it.

When we finally reach our mark near the mic, the clamor of applause and music in the arena begins to dissipate and our script appears on the prompter. I'm first up. I take another clarifying breath and launch into my opening line. "Tonight, Miles and I have the distinct honor of presenting the nominees for R&B Song of the Year."

Miles inhales shakily beside me before he goes for his part. "But before we do that, Ella and I have a few items to address." Despite the nerves I felt reverberating from him a moment ago, he manages to deliver the words with a cheeky flare.

"Mm-hmm. That's right," I declare, crossing my arms and turning toward my co-presenter. "I have it on good authority that the Dodgers locker room has a strict no R&B policy." I arch an eyebrow, cheating toward the audience and on cue, a series of *ooh*s and *aah*s ring out from the crowd. "Apparently, it's not the 'right vibe.'" I make exaggerated quotes with my hands, and this time we can hear boos.

"Hold up, hold up, hold up," Miles says, playing his part perfectly. "Let's not get confused. R&B music is timeless, don't get me wrong. Take tonight's nominees for example. I love me some Coco Jones. Some Giveon. Lucky Daye. But when the 'ship is on the line, it's all about setting the right mood for the task at hand. Now, I can think of a few *other* tasks that might call for some Marsha Ambrosius"—he nudges me playfully with an elbow—"*maybe* even some . . . E-ella Simone—"

"All right, all right," I cut in with a chuckle. "I think we get where you're going with this, buddy." I pat him gently on his muscled shoulder and almost lose my train of thought. I clear my throat. "So now that we've gotten that cleared up. Without further ado, the nominees for R&B Song of the Year are . . ."

The announcer takes over at this point, calling out the nominees while a live shot of each one in the audience flashes across the jumbo screens. When Elliot is announced as the final nominee for a record he wrote and produced featuring Muni Long, his glossy headshot fills the screens, as expected since he was a surprise no-show.

"I'll let you do the honors, my lady," Miles says in a low rumbling tone that makes something flip over in my stomach.

I shake off the feeling and look down at the card in my hand. "And the winner is—" The letters I see printed there on the stiff card stock take longer than they should to compute in my brain. Ever the professional, I press on to speak. But the syllables catch in my throat.

Then Miles gently places a hand at the small of my back as if to say, *Don't worry, I've got this*, before clearing his throat. "Elliot . . . M-majors!" Rescuing me, he says the name I know all too well.

Snapping out of my momentary trance, I look to the prompter, prepared to announce that we'll be accepting the award on my *husband's* behalf when the screen goes blank, refreshing in real time. When the words HOLD FOR WINNER flash on the prompter, my heartbeats kick into high gear. Next, I see Elliot's beaming, *live* smile flash on all the screens in the house.

He emerges from the dark arena, and all the blood drains from my face, slipping down my body and pooling at my feet—holding me in place. If I wanted to run, I'd be shit out of luck. Without a thought, my body begins to lean to the left until it meets flush with Miles's warm, rigid strength. The time lapse between Miles uttering Elliot's name and Elliot reaching the stage couldn't last more than ten seconds, but it feels like we've endured an endless summer when my estranged husband arrives.

He's in a head-to-toe black silk ensemble. Probably Gucci. Definitely not the look his stylist pulled to match my intended dress for the night. Guess that means we're both going rogue. He practically oozes up the stairs in deliberate, fluid motions—the man can't even walk like a regular human. The closer he gets, the wider the pit of dread inside me grows. Then, suddenly, he's receiving his Grammy trophy from Miles. Next, he's angled himself toward me with his arms outstretched to wrap me in an embrace.

Each movement rapidly blends into the next so fast I can hardly keep up, like a movie montage I'm watching on fast-forward. Elliot places one hand on my waist, and I inch closer to him, more out of practice than instinct. His broad, bright smile is for the cameras. But the intense look in his eyes, that's for me. He tilts his head down, as if angling in for a kiss. At the last second, I turn my head just enough for two things to occur: Elliot's kiss lands on the space between my ear and neck and then my eyes latch on to Miles's fiery gaze. The simultaneous jolt is sensory overload. I blink several times to snap out of what feels like a daze, stepping away from Elliot so he can give his speech.

Miles and I are still onstage, but with the spotlight on Elliot, we're now off-mic and bathed in shadow. "You okay?" he whispers. And the question alerts me to how heavy I've been breathing. When I don't answer immediately, the smooth warmth of his knuckles brushes against the back of my hand. I swallow thickly. "Yeah," I say. "I'm fine. I just . . . need some air."

He hasn't moved his hand, and now little electric firings are sparking at the point where we're just barely skin to skin. "Almost there," he says. And it's so tender it feels like an embrace, like our hands are entwined, fingers interlaced.

At some point, Elliot finishes his acceptance speech, and we're led backstage by a Grammy escort. The moment we're back in the wings, I lock eyes with Angelo and Rodney. In a split second I weigh my options for the night . . . stay and schmooze at the after-parties in Elliot's shadow, or get the hell out of Dodge. It's a no-brainer. I bolt.

Love is like a faucet. It turns off and on.

Billie Holiday

9 and a half years ago

ELLIOT HOLDS MY HAND as he leads me through the throbbing crush of pulsing bodies on the dance floor toward the back of a club where a reserved booth nestled between thick red curtains waits for us. Butterflies on acid flutter frantically in my stomach, making it hard to catch my breath as I struggle to adjust to the surrealness of the night.

We've just finished our third session at Wyclef Jean's Platinum Sound recording studio in Chelsea, and I think we nailed what Elliot's convinced will be my first single—once we have the label's buy-in. A grueling ten-hour day spent in the booth running every line over and over, grasping for that elusive perfection I can only seem to achieve when Elliot says so. Now, just after midnight, we're out to celebrate and unwind before doing it all over again tomorrow.

Just as we reach the table, Elliot gently tugs me forward, bringing our clasped hands to the small of my back. He draws me close at his side and leans into my neck. "Easy there, tiger," he purrs in my ear, bringing my hand up to his mouth to kiss, "your grip is like a vise. Why so nervous?"

"It's nothing," I say, my face flaming with embarrassment. I glance around us. "I just feel like . . . everyone's watching us."

He shrugs and quickly scans our surroundings too. But unlike me, jittery and shy, he's aloof and smug and sexy as hell. "And?" he says. "So what if they are?"

Maybe one day I'll get used to living in a fishbowl. I suppose I'll have to if I plan on being as successful with my music as I've always dreamed I'd be.

Elliot slips us into the booth, and seconds later, two servers materialize with supplicant smiles. He orders our drinks, whiskey for him, club soda and lime for me—because I'm old enough to do everything with him but drink. His long fingers massage the back of my neck as the sultry opening saxophone chords from "Is It a Crime" penetrate the space around us. In spite of myself, and my nerves, I instinctively begin to sway.

"Ah, so she likes Sade." Elliot sighs with a small smirk curving his mouth.

"Mm-hmm," I confirm, and my eyes drift shut just as she sings her tortured confession about missing a forbidden lover. "She's top five for me. Hands down."

"Tell me," he says, "what is it about her that makes you move like that?" And when I finally open my eyes again, he's staring at me so intently it steals my breath away.

Still, I manage to reply. Sitting up a little straighter, I square my shoulders and blurt out, "It's everything! Her tone. Her musicality and the almost electric sense of chemistry she has with her band. How expressive their artistry is when it's combined. How no one in the world sounds like her." I pump the brakes, feeling self-conscious about my intensity. I want Elliot to see me as an artist, not a fangirl.

But he surprises me with his response. His eyes flick over my face, drifting down to my neck and shoulders, caressing the swath of brown skin exposed by the blue strappy dress I'm wearing. "You remind me of her," he says. "Your style. Your voice." Then he wraps a tendril of my curly shoulder-length hair around his finger while staring deeply in my eyes. Chills instantly scatter across my skin.

More than handsome, Elliot Majors is what I'd call striking. He's got these dark, enchanting eyes that float like jewels on the elegantly sharp planes of his face. With the most buttery, flawless medium brown complexion, interrupted only by intricate tattoos that kiss the base of his neck and dance down his chest and arms. He's tall but super lean—like a man who considers the recording studio his gym, because he was once a kid who spent nights and weekends at home listening to records on vinyl and making beats on his Roland drum machine rather than at basketball or football practice.

Apparently it all worked out for him too. He's got over a decade of industry cred to his name and a string of platinum records to prove it. And when we walked in here, every head turned and some cameras even flashed. So now that I'm sitting here, practically in his lap, with Sade's sultry voice asking if it's a crime to want someone to want you, it's all so utterly intoxicating I can hardly believe it's real.

Taking me by surprise, he starts to sing. The tone of his voice isn't anything to write home about. But he's got perfect pitch and harmonizes flawlessly with Sade as she personifies her love—describing it as wide and tall, singing about how it dives, and jumps, and ripples like the deepest ocean. Elliot Majors is serenading me, and I feel like I'm on fire.

Then, as if doused in a bucket of cold water, I'm reminded of the self–pep talk I've been rehearsing ever since Elliot and I started fooling around after recording sessions. How I have to temper my hopes and expectations around him. How he probably sings like this to *all* the girls the first time he takes them out. How he probably says the things he knows will flatter them the most. How this is likely just Old Faithful for him—a tried-and-true feature of his repertoire. *Make me feel special. Like I'm the only one capable of being his true muse. Like I'm the only one who gets more from him than his musical genius.*

Drawing myself back into the present moment, I mentally shake those nagging thoughts away. Because despite what might have gone down with other girls, Elliot Majors is here with me now.

But he must have noticed my shift in mood because at some point during my mental tangent, he stopped singing. "Hey," he says now, after taking a sip of his whiskey and gingerly replacing the glass on the table. "What's spinning in that head of yours?"

"It's this song," I say, deflecting but not entirely shielding the truth. "I've always loved it . . . but I guess I just never really thought about how tragic it is."

He arches an eyebrow. "Tragic, you think?" He adjusts in the booth, squaring off with me like he's preparing to pose an argument. "I see it this way—she's presenting her heart to her lover on a silver platter, offering herself to him, telling him she wants him. Begging him to want her back." He pauses a beat, seeking agreement in my eyes. But all that's there is quiet curiosity. So, undeterred, he presses on. "Look at it this way," he says. "It's the kind of

love that's so vast and so willing that it can be molded and shaped."
Talking with his hands now, Elliot's eyes sparkle. He takes a sip of
his drink. "It's a love that can bend. If that's tragic, wouldn't you
call that tragically beautiful?"

I open my mouth to answer, but before I can, he's leaning in for
a kiss.

Now

GLITTER 'N DIRT:

After Months of Speculation That Elliot Majors Stepped Out on
His Marriage, Could It Have Been Ella Simone the Whole Time?

T HE LAST HEADLINE MAKES me lurch forward out of my plush
coffin of pillows. It's half past seven on the morning after the
awards show from hell—but you can't tell from the stringent dark-
ness of my hotel suite.

The blackout curtains and dead bolt have done their best to
keep the world at bay. But fifteen minutes ago, silly old me let it all
come tumbling in by turning on my phone. That rookie move un-
leashed a torrential onslaught of notifications—starting with an
impressive number of texts from Angelo, which coming from anyone else could pass for tame. But given how quickly I gave my
team the slip last night, shortly after leaving the stage, by hightail-
ing it out of the arena and calling up an Uber to my favorite hide-
away spot in Malibu, who could blame him for the endless barrage
of *Where r u, El*s and *Seriously*s?

As I kept scrolling, the guilt ratcheted higher, making my skin
prick with shame. But it was the *Even Miles is worried* text from
Angelo that stopped my thumb from swiping and made my chest
flutter. And the *Please. Just let me know you're alive* that got my
fingers moving again to tap out a reply.

ME: I'm sorry Lo. Had to get out of there. I'm here.

I dropped a pin to my location and burrowed deep in the covers to doomscroll the apps—and there I remained until bursting
forth a second ago. Seeing the worst of my fears come to pass, last

night's onstage gaffe turning into a messy media firestorm, has me upright and pressing call on Rodney's contact.

"Oh look! She has risen." He answers before the first ring cycles through, sounding harried—like he's both in motion *and* understandably tired of my BS.

I release a long, slow, and raggedy exhale. "I know. I know better than to go dark like that on you guys. I'm sorry."

"Mm-hmm," he shoots back. "Lucky for you I keep a grudge the same way I keep a secret."

Which is to say, not at all. I'd be relieved at Rodney's easy forgiveness if I didn't also hear an echo of his booming voice . . . and then a sudden knock on the door to my suite.

"You can't be serious right now," I mutter.

"As a stroke," he deadpans. "Now open up before I get Malibu PD called on me for being Black in a hallway."

I scurry out of bed, throw on a robe, and shuffle to the door. When I open it, my best friend is standing on the other side with a bottle of vodka, a tray of coffees, and a takeout bag of something that smells savory and divine.

"How did you find me?" I ask, stepping to the side to let him in.

Rodney's eyes scan me up and down in one long, assessing swoop. He shakes his head in the most subtle sign of disapproval. "That's for me to know and you to ponder," he says flatly. "This is cute," he muses, glancing around the suite as he sets down his accouterments on the counter of the kitchenette.

"So, we gonna talk about that little disappearing act you pulled last night first?" he asks. "Or would you like to address that kiss from Elliot onstage in front of five million viewers?"

I recoil at the memory. The shock that took over my body as I saw the prompter update in real time. Miles and I would not be accepting Elliot's R&B Song of the Year Grammy on his behalf after all. Because the man decided to make a surprise last-minute appearance at the show he'd sworn off not three hours prior, and accept the award himself. Never mind the fact that it takes more than eleven hours to fly from London to LA . . . which means this stunt was either meticulously plotted for maximum effect or undertaken on a "fly by the seat of your pants" whim. I don't know what's worse.

I'd been so caught up in the emotions, and wardrobe malfunctions, of the night that I'd forgotten he was even nominated for the award. But his pop-up presence in the arena meant that not only did I have to present my philandering, soon-to-be-ex-husband with a golden gramophone while millions looked on with rampant curiosity, but I also had to relax my face and body while he wrapped his hands around my waist and kissed me on the neck—only because I had the wherewithal to turn my head before his mouth landed on mine.

And worst of all, this went down while I was wearing another man's shirt. A beautiful, enigmatic man who happened to be standing *right there* radiating vibes I was far too out of step with my wits to read at the time. But now, after several hours of over-analysis, I've settled on *anger*. Miles Westbrook was positively fuming in that moment. Why? I'm willing to dedicate the next six hours to consider all the possibilities. Anything to keep from having to deal with the headlines.

"Earth to Ella," Rodney says, waving a mocha almond latte under my nose like it's smelling salts. "So, what's it gonna be, pumpkin?"

But a series of swift knocks on the door saves me from having to pick my poison. Assuming it's housekeeping, I eagerly accept the coffee while Rodney goes to answer it. But within seconds my assumption is proven wrong when what sounds like bickering in hushed tones can be heard coming from the entryway of my suite.

"You have some real nerve, Angelo. Showing up like this after—"

"Listen." My manager cuts my stylist, and best friend, off. "Can we not do this? Not now at least? And not *here*?" he begs of him.

I approach them cautiously, unsure of whether I should give them a minute to sort out whatever this is or nip it in the bud before it devolves. Figuring I could use something a little juicy and diverting to distract from my current state of crisis, I settle on the former. But just as I'm about to pad back into the bedroom and disappear beneath the covers, Angelo spots me.

"Well, would you look at that! Our vanishing princess!" he says, brushing past Rodney to make his way into the room.

He stalks toward me, not menacingly, but determined. I briefly picture him jabbing a finger in my direction and dramatically mouthing, *You!* and almost chuckle at the absurdity. But, shuffling backward, I hit the armrest of a plush velvet sofa and am forced to sit before I fall. Cornered, I deflate. "Look, Angelo. I'm really—"

"Spare me the apology." He cuts me off with clipped words. Hovering above me now, he raises three fingers to my lips and slides a glance over at Rodney. "Have you told her yet?"

"Told me what?" I ask, preempting Rodney's answer. His usually animated features sit hard and stern on his face like carved stone. My hackles immediately go up. "Okay. Somebody spit it out."

Rodney nervously checks his watch. "We'll have to explain in the car." He turns to Angelo. "Did you bring her change of clothes?"

Angelo tosses him a garment bag, while I look on in complete astonishment. "What's happening? Today's a dead day," I protest. "Angelo, you promised there'd be nothing on the schedule."

"Oh, honey," Angelo says, eyes pitying me. "That all changed when Janet Waterman called me before sunrise to request your presence at her home by nine a.m."

Rodney heads into the en suite to turn on the steam shower.

"So that means you've got half an hour to get it together, boo. That woman scares me, and I don't want to be on her bad side. So come on. Chop-chop!"

Obediently, I pad across the suite toward the bathroom. And when I step into the cloud of hot steam, I hope in vain that by the time I emerge, my life will be less of a hot mess.

8

JANET WATERMAN LIVES IN Brentwood, just on the border of Bel Air. The area, made up of jutting hills and sprawling canyons, is dotted with vast estates and their old money inhabitants. We may not be able to smell the ocean from the winding roads that snake toward Janet's tucked-back cul-de-sac, but we're close enough to Malibu that we can sense it. And when we arrive at what's sure to be an expansive property, I'd bet good money we'll be able to see the coastline from a scenic overlook.

When we pull up to a tall security gate, Angelo rolls down the window to his Model X and presses the call button on the little black box. Within seconds a disembodied voice crackles over the intercom. "Good morning. How may I help you?"

Angelo clears his throat. "Hi there. I've got Ella Simone, Angelo Espinoza, and Rodney Jenkins here for a nine a.m. with—"

"Very good," the voice cuts in. "You're our first guests to arrive. Ms. Waterman is expecting you, so please pull ahead." A buzzer sounds, and then the gates click and slowly begin to creep open.

"We're *first* to arrive," I ask, leaning forward between the head-rests. "Who else is she expecting?"

Angelo and Rodney both turn and look at me, simply shrug-ging. "Beats me," Angelo says. "I was only given an address, a time, and told to deliver the asset."

If Angelo hadn't once saved me from a short stint in an inter-national prison—long story—I'd have a lot more questions right now. If I didn't trust *both* of these men with practically my whole life, I'd think they were dropping me off at one of those black-site CIA interrogations with all this feigned ignorance. Then again, with the amount of bad press last night's gaffe has already gener-ated, going into witness protection might not be a bad idea af-ter all.

Once we've parked and exited the car, we head up to a grand white oak door, where we're greeted by a kind-eyed, middle-aged man who's dressed in smart casual attire. "Welcome to the Hernandez-Waterman estate," he says, and I know that voice from moments prior on the security intercom. "My name is Bruce, and I'm pleased to show you to Ms. Waterman's home office."

All three of us fall into step behind Bruce as he leads us down a long, brightly lit corridor. With walls painted in Chantilly Lace white and wide plank flooring in a light stain, our path is lined on both sides with ornate art pieces that stand in stark contrast to the otherwise neutral palette.

Rodney leans in close. "Did I just peep a Basquiat?"

"It's a dupe," Angelo whispers. "All her originals are on loan at the Getty."

"Mm-kay . . . so you're saying these are basically bougie post-ers?" Rodney asks, gesturing from one painting to another.

Angelo laughs. "In a criminally reductive way, yes."

Torn between feeling confused by their nonchalance in my

time of crisis and fascinated by this new dynamic I'm witnessing in action, I roll my eyes and focus the nervous energy on guessing the point of this meeting. When we reach an oval-shaped blue-green orb of light on a wall at the end of the hall, likely a James Turrell, I've come up with no plausible possibilities. Bruce turns toward a hidden door and knocks twice.

After a few seconds, a buzzer sounds, releasing the latch, at which point Bruce gently twists the knob and announces, "Ms. Waterman will see you now."

Between this, the long walk, and the light orb, I'm beginning to feel like we've come all this way to see the Wiz. But once inside, it's only Janet seated behind a sleek marble desk. She stands when we enter. "Ah! You've made it. Welcome," she says, her resonant voice booming off the walls.

Rodney leans over and whispers in my ear, "Gucci from head to toe on a Monday morning . . . I love her already."

"Before we sit down," Janet says, "can Bruce get anyone a drink? Coffee, tea, water? He can whip up a Bloody Mary, too, if you're in the mood for a little hair of the dog?"

I feel judged. But I mask the burn. I did hit it pretty hard last night, after all. Each of us politely declines her offer, and then we stand steeped in awkward silence.

"Well how about we sit, then?" she finally suggests, and we all follow suit. "I guess last night couldn't just be a casual evening with no headlines now, could it?"

Janet drums her fingers on one knee, like she's purposefully delaying whatever it is she called us here to discuss. Then I notice the way she's eyeing Angelo, as if gauging which of them should speak first. My skin tightens with renewed suspicion.

"It certainly was an eventful night," Angelo finally says, nervously rubbing his palms over his knees. And when he fails to follow it up with anything of substance, Janet's exasperation is clear.

"Okay, folks, I'll just come out with it. Since Plan A—and to refresh your memory, that was *supposed* to be you laying low and avoiding scandals—has jackknifed off a bridge, I think it's time we *lean in*."

"Wait. I'm sorry," I jump in. "Why do we have to abandon Plan A? We know how this works, it's one news cycle and people are bored. They'll move on! Besides, what is it exactly that we're *leaning in* . . . to?"

"Miles Westbrook." Her answer is very matter-of-fact, and she skips over everything else I just said. I should know by now not to ask her compound questions. Beyond that, if it's possible to choke on air, I'm probably doing it.

"The optics on that stage last night were, as you've no doubt discovered by now—less than ideal," she explains. "And whoever wrote your lines did you *no* favors—they were dripping with innuendo. Honestly, your publicist should have been more vigilant. Already this morning, TikTok is cluttered with Miles Westbrook workout videos set to your music. Not to mention all the memes of him looking ready to snap Elliot like a toothpick when he grabbed you. Or how the camera panned to his date's scowl in the audience. I mean . . . this is a feast the blogs can dine out on for weeks to come. If not months." Finally, she pauses for a beat. But only a brief one. "But enough of my babbling. I believe Angelo has something to tell you."

At this, my head swivels so fast I nearly throw out my back. I open my mouth to speak but he beats me to the punch.

"Before you rail at me," Angelo says, both palms raised defensively, "please just know that none of this was my idea and I am only the messenger."

"A messenger who pretends to know nothing, apparently," I add saltily.

"Mmm. Touché," Rodney says, and Janet and Angelo both cut him dirty looks. Rodney merely purses his lips and admires the ceiling.

Angelo takes a deep breath. "The label has cast—" He pauses, as if shoring up the strength to proceed. "Miles Westbrook for the lead in your next music video."

"Ha!" The laugh spurts out of me on a strong gust of air. Next, that's all I can utter. "Ha. Ha. Ha. You said *my* music video? As in . . . the one I fly back to New York to shoot at the end of the week?"

Everyone has the gall to nod their heads in confirmation. So I continue the manic chuckle as my gaze bounces from Rodney to Angelo to Janet, then back again.

"This . . . is a joke, right?" I am pleading as much as I am asking. Rodney shrugs. Now Angelo's become preoccupied with something on the rug. Janet simply looks at me with pity.

"Well, obviously Miles turned it down," I offer. Desperately. Then Angelo and Janet fix me with pointed stares, each wordlessly affirming that no, Miles did not turn the offer down.

"Okay. But we're all on the same page here that this *can't* happen, right?" I am standing now, without a plan for where to go or what to do. "It plays directly into the media's narrative . . . Elliot's too!" I've started pacing, arms flailing—am pretty sure I appear to be on the verge of a medical event, but could not care less. My processing continues . . .

"And just humor me for a sec, 'kay? What on earth is in this for Miles Westbrook?" Stopping in my tracks, I raise an index finger. "He can't be so hard up for *this* kind of press. Not after the last year *he* had."

At last, I'm off the soapbox. But when no one responds, I cast a wilting glance at Rodney, my perpetual lifeline. But even he says nothing and only returns a meme-able grimace in solidarity.

"Look. I understand your alarm," Janet says calmly—the kind of calm that makes me want to smash a vase just to see if it would get a rise. "But I've already confabbed with the label and also Miles's agent, who should be here shortly, by the way." She pauses when I reel back in shock. "Well, we certainly weren't all floundering in confusion when you went off the grid for twelve hours. Damage was done, and you pay us to control it." She shrugs.

"Also, touché." Rodney contributes another zinger, and now *I'm* cutting him a dirty look.

"Anyway," Janet continues. "I was made aware of the label's last-minute move to cast Miles in your video, and since they've got the final say, contractually, our hands are tied here . . . so we might as well parlay it."

Bzzzz!

"Well, that will be them." She clasps her hands together. "Give me a sec and I'll just have Bruce let them in," she says, heading to her desk.

I lean over and whisper to Rodney, "I'm sorry. Did she just say *them*?"

UNABLE TO HELP HIMSELF, RODNEY HAS THE NERVE TO SMIRK. "Didn't think you'd be seeing his fine ass again so soon, now did ya?"

I roll my eyes and ponder sinking into the floor like I'm in that scene from *Get Out*. At this point I'd wager the Sunken Place would feel like sweet relief from here. To say I'm not prepared to discuss a music video collaboration with the man I am being publicly accused of cheating on my estranged husband with is a major understatement.

"Ms. Waterman, I have Miles Westbrook and his agent, Gabriel Pearson, here to join your meeting," Bruce announces from the back of the room.

I am tempted to turn around and once again behold Miles's beauty, but something stops me from doing so. Instead, I stare at the floor like a petulant third grader who's been sent to the principal's office. Like the professional I am not, Angelo stands to greet Miles and Gabriel. Rodney follows suit. At the last second, a sliver of etiquette takes hold of me, and suddenly I'm rising and offering them handshakes too—but not eye contact. A girl in distress can only take so much.

In the next moment, we're all seated comfortably, and I'm wondering where two additional chairs sprouted from. But my preoccupation with the furniture layout is diverted when Miles's agent is the first to speak.

"Well first off, Ella, I just want to say that Miles and I are big fans of your work. And, Janet, thank you for welcoming us into your home," Gabriel begins. And instantly, I'm struck by his somewhat crooked but wholly sincere smile and how it seems to match the kindness in his eyes. I learned early on that you can tell a lot about a person in this business by the people they choose to represent them. And so far, Gabriel doesn't seem to fit the smarmy image of sports agents I'd built up in my head.

"That's kind of you to say," I tell him, with my eyes briefly flitting over to Miles, whose own haven't left my face since he sat down. I don't know this because I was looking. I know it because I can feel him.

"I'm glad you both could make it," Janet says, returning his smile. "Now to get down to it. We all know the train is barreling down the wrong track with rumors that Miles and Ella have been carrying on some clandestine affair. And trust me"—she pauses to glance over at me—"with reports of you half naked next to him backstage, neither of you are beating the allegations anytime soon."

Miles moves to speak, and Janet raises a hand for him to let her finish. He obliges.

"Gabriel, as you know, the label wants to capitalize on the attention this has drummed up. And, Ella, while we *could* play hardball with them on this one, I think we need to pick our battles and hold our punches for later. I say we lean into this in a *productive* way."

"But how is this productive for Ella, exactly?" Miles cuts in with the million-dollar question. And then he turns back to me. "If I have all this s-straight, things are contentious with y-you and Elliot right now? I'm really not trying to make it worse."

And while I'm grateful for his concern, I'm also *very* confused. Forgetting to acknowledge Miles, I glance over at Janet and Angelo. "Wait, I thought you guys said he was already in? And just so I understand this clearly," I add, "by 'productive' are you referring to some kind of PR . . . 'situationship' in addition to the music video or—"

"Ha!" Janet mock laughs. "I'm an attorney, not a pimp. I would *never*."

Angelo chimes in now too. "Exactly. Whether or not the two of you get involved beyond this video is none of our business."

"I honestly advise against it given the current climate," Janet says flatly.

"Agreed," Gabriel adds, with a bit more oomph than I personally find necessary. "In this case, you wouldn't be *dating* Miles," he explains. "Think of this more as an artistic collaboration . . . and better yet, it's for charity."

I pinch the bridge of my nose in mounting frustration at all the added layers of our situation. And in a lapse of self-awareness I blurt out, "Let me guess, the Boys and Girls Clubs of America?"

At this, Miles flinches, and I can tell the remark has rubbed Gabriel the wrong way too—instantly, I regret it.

"Cute," Janet says. "But no. Miles is actually founder of the Evelyn Foundation for the Empowerment of Women and Girls, and after a few strategic phone calls this morning, your next music video is primed to kick off their annual fundraising campaign."

"Look." Gabriel gestures toward his client. "To answer Miles's very good question. Our thinking here is that if we can tie the two of you together in a professional capacity and have it benefit a great cause, then we can add some credibility and context to the connection you two made at the Grammys. We'd start by releasing companion statements announcing the partnership . . . and the rest we'll take from there."

"I have to say, Ella." Angelo places a calming hand on my knee, which I hadn't even realized was bouncing rapidly. "In choppy waters, it's definitely not a rescue yacht, but it *could* be like a little life raft."

Figuring I've protested enough, especially in front of mixed company, I decide to hold my peace for now. Angelo and Gabriel spend a few more minutes discussing logistics like locations and scheduling while Janet returns to her desk to answer a pressing email. Rodney excuses himself to take a call from an important fashion house, which leaves me sitting here avoiding meeting Miles's stare from a few feet away.

"Hey," he says, leaning in. Perhaps he's had enough of my immature evasion tactics. "If this is something you're not cool with, we can forget the whole thing. The foundation means *a lot* to me. But we have other ways to launch the campaign if it's gonna be a major headache for you."

Beneath my cloud of stress and worry, I'd forgotten what it felt like to be on the receiving end of Miles Westbrook's undivided attention—like being lit up and warmed from the inside after shivering for hours. That might be more than just part of the reason why I'm reluctant to put myself back in this spot with him. I'm liable to want more than I should, or even can, have.

"Miles, you've been nothing but a gentleman in all of this," I tell him. "But I'm afraid I don't get a say in the matter. The label wants what it wants." I shrug. "At least this way, we're supporting your foundation."

He simply nods before offering me a measured smile. It's not the heart-pounding, showstopping one. Instead, it's one that says, *So, it's settled. We're doing this, then.* Next, Janet returns from her emails and we all rise to conclude the meeting. She escorts Miles and Gabriel from the office, briefly leaving me alone with Rodney and Angelo. The tension between the three of us could be cut with a wooden spoon. And apparently I'm the only one willing to say the quiet part out loud.

"Can we be serious for two seconds here?" I beg, while noticing the way they connect their gazes as if in agreement that I need a nap. They're not wrong. Except, it's hard to feel light and airy about this when the internet's most followed gossip blog has reduced your decade-long career to being a "jock chaser."

"At best, this whole plan will get clocked quick by anyone who gives up five seconds of their shrinking attention spans to this cheap gimmick. Worst case, it all backfires big-time and I get written off as the latest of *many* notches in Miles Westbrook's bedpost." I pause to breathe a weary sigh. "And the *best* that could come of this is I get pigeonholed once again. Just picture it now, we can name my next album *Ballers n' Bling*. But what do I know? I'm a female artist in the recording industry. I go where I am told.

I do it with a smile. So long as there's cleavage and a little leg showing, everyone's happy."

I glance up at them briefly, but long enough to see they're both eyeing me like a keyless grenade. I should stop while I'm ahead, but I've never known how to leave well enough alone. "Miles, on the other hand . . . he'll probably just *thrive* on this. He'll probably sell thousands of jerseys, get thousands of new followers. We might as well add image rehabilitation to my portfolio at this point."

That last line tasted terrible on its way out of my mouth. I don't feel good about any of what I've just said. But that doesn't make any of it feel less real, stiflingly so. And where there was a steady hum of energy in this office before, the atmosphere has since stilled. Now it's just silent. Too silent. After a second or two, I look up to find Rodney's face frozen like an ice sculpture with his eyes fixed on something behind me. Angelo looks like he's seen a ghost. I turn around and find out why. Miles is back. Standing in the doorway to Janet's office.

Looks might have the power to kill after all, because his eyes are boring into me now, and I think my heart just stopped. In them are emotions I haven't gotten from him before—definitely hurt, and possibly even mild contempt. I should have known. My skin started prickling with tiny electric sparks halfway through my rant, the same way it did when we were alone backstage. I dismissed the sensation, figuring Janet's AC was on full blast, and steamrolled right on ahead.

This day can go to hell.

Rodney mouths, *I'm sorry*, at me from a few feet away, like it's his fault I've stuffed my whole leg, foot first, in my mouth. Like somehow, he could have stopped this train before it went fully off the rails and careened over a cliff.

"Uhhh. Ahem." Miles clears his throat as Janet and Gabriel stand behind him in the doorway—the bluish green light from the Turrell installation forms a bright halo around them. Because of the glare it's difficult to make out his expression, which may be for the best. His posture, however, is as stiff as a statue.

"I uh. I—" His choppy words are cut off quickly. Not like he can't figure out what to say in this incredibly awkward moment, but more like his body is a dam, barring any words from coming forth. I look down, and sure enough, he's tapping his thigh.

Damn it. This is all on me.

"S-sorry to interrupt. I just forgot my k-keys right there." He points to the end table near where he was previously seated. Rodney moves quickly to grab and return his keys to him. What follows is a bit of a blur.

After an awkward shuffling of bodies at the door, suddenly both Miles and Gabriel are gone. Janet mutters something about us all taking a beat to process and regroup. And next thing I know, Rodney, Angelo, and I are cruising back down the hill.

WE ARE BACK AT THE HOTEL NOW, CUDDLED UP IN MY CALI-fornia king bed. Well, Rodney and I are *in* it and Angelo is techni-cally hovering, awkwardly so, on the edge at the foot. "Her methods are unconventional. I admit," he says as he runs his fin-gers through his uncharacteristically tousled hair.

"Oh good! So you *finally* admit that springing Miles on me like that was bad, bad form?" I ask, over a mouthful of the scallion ba-gel that Rodney brought me. "Remind me why you recommended Janet Waterman to be my divorce lawyer again?"

Angelo's shoulders drop, and he peers at the ceiling. "Because she's the best in the business!" he replies, waving his hands. "She got Kim disentangled *with* her billion-dollar skin-care line unscathed . . . she's practically a miracle worker."

"He does have a point there," Rodney chimes in. And I don't miss the swift but weighted glance between the two of them.

"Okay. What's going on here with you two?" I ask, before licking an escaped dollop of cream cheese off my thumb. Then I'm met with silence. "It's fine. Keep your secrets. Just know you're both irreplaceable to me. So if whatever you're doing goes south, no one's getting fired and we're all just gonna have to deal. Agreed?"

They each look up. First at each other, then at me. And something passes between the three of us that announces a mutual understanding without words.

"So look, Ella. That stuff you said at the end of the meeting, about this being a lose-lose situation for you either way you slice it," Angelo, says, pivoting back to business. "I understand where all that's coming from, and trust, I give absolutely zero credit to the public when it comes to how they treat women celebrities in situations like yours. But remember what I always tell you?"

"Every problem is an opportunity," I repeat, with the spark of a dying battery.

"Exactly!" he says. "So maybe just *try* looking at this as an opportunity to reintroduce yourself . . . this could be like your—your *Lemonade* era."

"Angelo is onto something," Rodney says enthusiastically. "You *do* realize that the storyboards for this music video are the textbook description of sexual and emotional liberation, right? And the fact that this single is a redux of one of Sade's most sensual hits. That the whole concept is about a woman finding love again after a toxic relationship."

"You guys," I say, "it's all so on the nose. It could be an absolute misfire."

"Or, it could be *exactly* what you need to turn this narrative around," Angelo offers up. "Think of it like planting a seed, then cultivating the image of what it would look like for your fans to see you blossom on your own, out from under Elliot's thumb. This could be your *Butterfly* era."

"Both of you have *got* to chill with the analogies," I say, before burying my head in my hand.

"But you know we have a point," Rodney says. "Elliot's been off doing his thing with Miss Thing for weeks, and he's hardly suffered any blowback for it. Don't get me wrong, I *hate* to see you playing the PR game. But if you're gonna have to do it anyway . . . might as well have some fun?"

At this, I'm instantly hit with a flashback of those moments in the wings just after my dress fell apart. The look of simultaneous shock and remorse on Miles's face when he realized what he'd accidentally done, and the chaotic blend of pure panic and forced productivity that followed. Then, finally, the expression of almost wonder in his eyes when he saw me wrapped up in his shirt. Without question, I looked ridiculous, but let his face tell it, and I was perfect. So yeah, this could be fun. It could also be my complete undoing.

9

PEOPLE

A representative from Ella Simone's communications team has released the following statement regarding recent headlines.

"Amid the backstage chaos at last night's Grammy awards ceremony, Ella Simone experienced an unfortunate wardrobe malfunction just moments before she was set to appear onstage to co-present the award for R&B Song of the Year. Ms. Simone and her style team are grateful to Mr. Westbrook for his generous assistance, with only seconds to spare, as the pair prepared to carry out their presenting duties. Mr. Westbrook and Ms. Simone look forward to collaborating again in the near future to benefit the Evelyn Foundation for Women and Girls."

Update: *People* received a reply from Miles Westbrook's representatives following publishing the above statement. "We echo and appreciate the comments made by Ms. Simone's team. Mr. Westbrook remains a fan of her music and looks forward to their future collaboration."

From: beverlyr@gmail.com
To: ellaelladee@gmail.com

Date: February 5, 2023

I've tried you several times to no avail. I suppose life is busy for you. It always is. But I'd think you'd take five minutes to answer a call from the woman who birthed you. I suppose it's all neither here nor there.

I wanted to ask you why my darling son-in-law didn't accompany you on the red carpet last night? Imagine my surprise when I turned on the television, eager to see what loud getup that stylist of yours had picked out for you this time, only to discover you sashaying down the line . . . alone. A married woman! I was surprised to say the least.

The performance was tasteful. You've always aspired to be like Mariah, so it's fitting that they gave you the tribute. I wasn't sure it was the best pairing, you and that Ariana girl. She has such a dynamic range that one. Such vocal agility. I must say, I was deeply disturbed by the whole presentation with the tall athlete. He is handsome, of course. But what was with the wrinkled shirt on you? Are pants offensive to you these days? A skirt even would have been a nice alternative to nothing at all. Regardless, your legs looked nice and toned. Compliments to your trainer.

And what was with that bizarre interaction between you and sweet Elliot onstage? I've gotten several texts from cousins inquiring about trouble in paradise. I get the feeling the two of you have been fighting again. That is a problem. The challenges of a marriage should never be displayed on Front Street. Elliot called me last week to check in. How kind of him.

Anyway, since you haven't answered, I suppose I've run out of things to say in this one-way dialogue. Call me when you can.

Mother

10

NEVER AGAIN.

It's what I told myself sixteen years ago, which was the last time I attempted organized sports. It was a class field trip to the batting cages that was "going to be fun"—they said. That was until Jimmy DelGiorno thought it'd be *hilarious* to switch the lever to *fastball* just ahead of my turn. Naturally, when the ball came hurtling toward me at warp speed, I froze. On top of that, my hand placement on the bat left a lot to be desired, so I went home with a broken metacarpal. This time around, a fresh round of torture has been set up by none other than my label publicist, Lydia Caplin.

"I hear the meeting ended up in kind of a rocky place," she'd said to me two days ago in her signature high-pitched, singsong rhythm. "Angelo and I spoke with Mr. Westbrook's manager, Gabriel, and we felt it might be advantageous for you both to get some one-on-one time together. You know . . . to break the ice a bit before your shoot."

She knows throwing Angelo's name in the mix is more likely

to get me to do *the thing*, whatever that *thing* may be. Even if he's lost some trust points for throwing me a major curveball the other day. Don't get me wrong, Lydia is good people. But she's also one of Onyx Records' people. And these days, that puts her squarely in the "smile and nod, but don't forget to stay woke" category.

Nevertheless, I haven't been able to shake off the ick from how I behaved toward Miles and Gabriel at the meeting. My shame quadrupled after I did my research on the Evelyn Foundation and discovered it was named after Miles's grandmother, Evelyn Garcia-Westbrook. In a GQ profile on Miles from several years ago, he talked about how she led after-school and weekend programs for teen mothers and their children in New York City. Eventually, with philanthropic sponsorship, she was able to expand her programs to service young moms and children across the five boroughs. And when she passed away six years ago, Miles launched the foundation in her honor to carry on that legacy. Now the foundation runs after-school programs as well as winter and summer camps, on top of providing scholarships for teen moms to continue their education.

So, after spending a few days scolding myself, I agreed to a get-together with Miles as a small way of making amends.

It's still the offseason, so I was supposed to meet "Mr. Westbrook" at a relatively deserted Dodger Stadium at seven o'clock. However, and because I'm a basket of anxiety, I arrived with thirty minutes to spare, hoping I could work the nerves out through a few rounds with the Calm app in my car. But after three guided meditations and one breathing exercise with a rainscape in the background, I'm just as jittery as when I parked. Only now I'm also in a rush to be on time.

Hopping out of the car, I grab my olive branch and quickly remove the tag. I figured it might serve as a nice gesture to wear a

Dodger blue baseball cap after I caught Miles off guard with my very candid and somewhat caustic remarks at what I now refer to as *the Cursed Meeting from Hell*. This way, by "committing to the bit," I can also signal that we're on the same team and I am not an evil monster risen from the depths. Apart from that, I'm in my signature disguise—natural curls, no brows, lashes, or concealer, and wearing gym shoes, leggings, and an oversized sweatshirt. In other words, I'm totally disarmed.

I wipe my sweaty palms down my front side and start trekking through the sparse parking lot toward Gate A exactly as Lydia instructed me to do. As I draw nearer to the main entrance that reads WELCOME TO DODGER STADIUM in bold, classic blue and white, a tall figure comes into clear view. He's leaning on one of the thick navy blue columns that support the iconic blue HEAVEN ON EARTH signage.

From a distance of several yards, it's apparent that he's not smiling at my approach. Instead, he just watches me—his eyes intently tracking my forward progress make every cell in my body vibrate with uncertainty.

When I'm two feet from Miles, he finally speaks. "So, you made it," he says, in a tone that suggests he thought I might flake.

In an effort to portray the enthusiasm he clearly lacks, I say, "I did!" And then add, "Couldn't wait, actually!" for good measure.

A line forms between his brows, and his mouth twists, suggesting he's not quite buying what I'm selling. Already, we're off to a less than desired start, and it feels like a good time for me to fall on my proverbial sword.

I take a deep breath and release it on a shaky exhale. Then, inwardly, I roll my eyes at myself because really, there's no reason for me to feel shy in front of this man when he's already seen me half naked and heard me mouth off about him. Still, there's something about being in his presence that knocks me slightly off-balance. It's not just that he's attractive, standing there in his navy joggers and a gray workout shirt that fits snug around his arms and chest. Or that he's tall and built like a walking Calvin Klein billboard.

"Uh . . . sooo you ready to head on in?" he asks, interrupting my mental sweep of his appearance. His words are brisk, like he might be in a rush to get this over with. I can't say I blame him if he's still offended or even annoyed by me. What I said was bratty and out of line, even if he wasn't intended to hear it.

"Ummm, yes." Now I'm the one who can't seem to get my words out. "But before we get started I wanted to—" *apologize*. I wanted to *apologize*, is what I mean to say. But, "say thank you" is what comes out of my mouth instead. "I wanted to thank you for agreeing to be in the video with me," I continue, trying to sound agreeable, normal—like my tongue isn't sedated.

Surprisingly, Miles smirks and crosses his arms. "Is that right?" he asks, with one thick eyebrow arching into the deep brown of his smooth forehead. "Because if I didn't know any better, I'd say you might want to apologize first?"

I'm so caught off guard by that, a laugh bubbles up from my chest. Then, and probably because though I have perfected it, I still don't like doing as I'm told, something stubborn and defiant begins to bloom inside me. And suddenly I don't feel so remorseful anymore. I feel like the games have just begun, a routine I'm all too comfortable with. "Oh really?" I volley back with some sass. "And what exactly is it I'm supposed to be apologizing for?"

All of a sudden, Miles sobers. His eyes shift across the planes of my face and he looks down. What felt playful and feisty a moment ago now feels heavy and uncertain, like rapidly changing tides. "I *am* sorry, you know," I say, rushing to get us out of this weirdness where I can't quite tell up from down, let alone how to act around him. "What you overheard me saying the other day. It wasn't me."

"It sounded like you," he says. And my attempt to hide the sting apparently fails. "I mean, it felt real," he explains. "Like you've been put in a hard spot and you were just saying how you really felt around people you've trusted to help you figure things out. I barged in on a private conversation and caught a few strays. Sucks, but I can't pretend I don't get where you were coming from." When he's finished speaking, the edge of a smile peeks through on his lips, and it feels like a pardon.

I sigh with relief and another errant laugh pops out of me. Even though nothing is funny. He's doing again what he did that night backstage at the Grammys—reading me with seemingly no effort at all. Despite all the ways I've tried to make myself a blank page for people, producers, managers, fans, to project their intentions, wants, and desires onto, standing next to Miles Westbrook, whether in a crowded room or alone on a stage, I feel like I've already bared my soul.

"Well, that may be so, but none of it was fair where you're concerned," I confess. "You've been nothing but kind and thoughtful when it comes to me, and I of all people should know what it's like to have the tabloids run wild with headlines and then to have everyone take it as Bible. For all I know you could be the opposite of a fuckboy. You could be a choirboy. You could be celibate!" I'm rambling now, as I tend to. So I quit before I dig an even deeper hole.

He smiles a big smile this time, and I feel it at the center of my chest.

"Apology accepted," he cuts in, totally sidestepping my last statement—which is probably for the best. It saves us from any awkward conversational detours we'd be liable to take.

He raises an arm to gesture toward the field entrance behind him, and my gaze catches on a long scar tracing the inside of his right elbow. I file it away in the memory box of my mind. "Now, if you don't mind, I think we came here to play some ball," he says, smirking.

I smile back at him and fall in step as he leads me inside the stadium.

"I HAVE BEEN TO EXACTLY ONE MAJOR LEAGUE BASEBALL game," I tell Miles entirely unprompted.

We're standing near the dugout now with the stadium beams on at fifty percent. It's more than enough light for me to feel the gravity of being here, at the center of a world-class baseball field with one of the league's ace pitchers.

"No way!" he says, with what looks to be genuine surprise. "That Yankees versus Astros playoff game in 2019?"

Now it's my turn to be shocked. "And how on earth would you know that?" I ask.

"Pfft. Easy," he says, flashing a dimple that makes my heart stutter. "You sang the national anthem."

"Ah. So you *have* googled me?" I cross my arms and lean against the rail.

"Was that in question?" he asks with a straight face. "I'm supposed to believe you *haven't* googled me?"

Touché. I simply shrug before sauntering over to the baseball tee he's set up for me at home plate. Perhaps I should be offended that he's so accurately clocked my aptitude, or lack thereof, by supplying a child's setup. But given my past injury and the residual trauma, I respect and appreciate it.

Miles has just fit me for a batter's helmet, which he's told me I can keep *as a souvenir*. And I'm trying to convince myself the only reason I nearly swooned at this is that I no longer know the difference between a genuine gesture of kindness and when I'm being *worked*. I have a strong feeling it's the first with him, but time will tell.

"So . . . what got you into baseball?" I ask, while winding up the bat, then lining it up with the ball he's just placed on the tee. "Wait! Let me guess," I say, halting the bat mid-swing. Miles flinches at my hasty change of course but recovers quickly. I keep talking. "It was your dad. And he gave you your first pitcher's mitt before your hand was big enough to fit even the smallest size."

For several seconds he simply looks at me with an unreadable expression. For a moment I begin to wonder if I've said something else to offend him. "What? Am I right?" I ask when I can no longer take the silence.

"No. Not even close," he replies, before glancing up into the stands. "I actually wanted to be a— I can't believe I'm telling you this." He palms his face and emits a deep chuckle. "I wanted to be . . . a t-tenor."

A small gasp puffs out of me, and I clap a hand over my mouth to suppress a half-baked reply. I wait a beat to see if he's joking, and when it's clear he's not, I say, "As in . . . Placido Domingo, Andrea Bocelli? *That* type of tenor?"

"Yes." He answers with a straight face and earnest eyes. "Go ahead. Laugh."

But I don't laugh at all. Instead, I stand across from him, beaming up with a goofy grin as he squirms under my amused gaze. "Come on, Miles. You've got me out here in a helmet, holding a blunt weapon, about to hit and miss a bunch of tiny balls. You owe me this. Let's hear it?"

I pass him the bat, and he looks at me with a creased brow.

Hands on my hips, I tell him, "That's your mic, Miles. And this is your moment."

Rolling his eyes, he raises the bat, knob side up, and proceeds to sing the opening lines to "Nessun dorma." It's not good—quite bad actually. But it's also . . . perfect.

After he warbles through the first few lines, his own laughter takes over, which forces him to stop. "Well, I said I *wanted* to be a tenor, past tense. Clearly, I didn't have the chops."

"But you did have the guts," I say, still beaming and in awe of what I just witnessed. "I will give you that."

"My grandfather was a custodian at a museum. He h-had this booming, resonant voice that just echoed through the halls on his late-night shifts," he tells me. "When I was a kid, I always wanted to sound just like that."

The faraway look on his face, the tinge of emotion in his deep voice—it all tugs at my chest. "I bet he's very proud of the talent you *do* have though," I say. "What was his name?"

"Reginald Westbrook," he says. And I don't miss the subtle rise of his chest—a small show of pride. "He's the one who helped me find baseball," Miles offers. "The summer I turned eight, he took me to visit his family in Kansas City, and we went to the Negro Leagues Baseball Museum. I remember looking at old grainy photos of these all-Black teams. Seeing their tattered shoes and weathered uniforms. Learning how they'd play for days on end without being able to stop for food or rest because of sundown towns. How they were barely paid enough to send some money back home to their families. All of this for either the love of the game, or because they were so good at it their talent couldn't be denied. Then I get home to my great-aunt's house and I'm so lit up by the experience that I'm *begging* to use her computer so I can find out more about Jackie Robinson. And that's when I stumbled across Roberto

Clemente. He was Puerto Rican, just like my grandmother. And I don't know . . . it just kind of felt like baseball was gonna be *it* for me after that."

"You kind of look like him. Clemente," I say, and it draws out a big smile.

"I've been told," he replies. "So yeah . . . I went to bed that night asking my grandfather to sign me up for Little League when we got back to the Heights."

"I take it you were the best on the team?"

Miles sucks air through his teeth as his head teeters side to side. "To be honest, I had a rough go at first. I started in the outfield, trying to force it and be like my hero, Clemente. But my JV coach—he pulled me out of my comfort zone and put me on the mound," he explains.

Then it dawns on me that while telling me all this, he hasn't stumbled over his words once. Or at least not that I've noticed. And while I've listened intently, I've also felt lulled by the current of his gaze, his words, and his attention. All the while, fighting the feeling that I'm being pulled out to sea.

"And the rest is history?" I ask.

"And the rest is history," he says. "Now." He claps his hands. "You ready to learn how to bat?"

"Not at all," I tell him, and he laughs.

"Don't worry, we'll go slow," he says with assurance.

I don't tell him that I'm afraid it might be a little late for that.

11

HAVE A QUESTION FOR you." Miles is seated next to me in the dugout, seemingly unbothered by the amount of Dodger Dog I've just stuffed into my face.

Upon my arrival, I assumed he'd been anticipating our little publicist-issued "playdate" as one might look forward to traffic school. But to my surprise, and my stomach's delight, he arranged a picnic of sorts.

You really didn't have to go to all this trouble were the words that came out of my mouth when I saw the gooey nachos drizzled with jalapeños and world-famous Dodger Dogs wrapped in foil. But if I could hear my eyes, I'm sure they'd have been screaming, *Get in me now!*

"Growing up, I was taught young to make sure a woman always had food options nearby . . . if she wants them," he explained. And *want them* I did.

"Well, are you going to ask that question?" I ask now, before licking an escaped dollop of mustard from my mouth.

Miles shifts somewhat uncomfortably on the bench. "Do you

like what you do?" he asks. "Your career I mean. Do you love it as much as you did when it was just a dream?"

I bristle a bit. Mainly because it's a heavy topic to delve into while chewing a footlong. Also, because I try my best to avoid thinking about the answer. But something about the novelty of this thing happening with us, how after the video shoot we'll probably never see or speak to each other again—it breeds a sense of freedom. Like, for once, the stakes here could be low. So this time, instead of thinking, I just speak.

"No." The truth is out there now, irrevocably so. And suddenly, I'm rushing to catch my next breath—like I've taken even myself by surprise. I lock eyes with Miles, a veritable stranger to whom I've just confessed a point of deep sadness, and heat flames across the surface of my face. I have the odd sense that I might cry.

"I'm sorry," he says, inching down the bench, then stopping himself mid-scoot. Probably thinking better of getting closer to me. "I shouldn't have—"

"No, it's okay." I cut him off, figuring now's a good time to set down the hot dog. Turning away from him to face the lit-up field, I wrap my fingers around the cool edge of the bench. "When I was a kid, I used to go around telling people that music was my first language," I say, laughing at that little innocent Elladee. "Kids my age were either confused by the statement or they could not care less. Most adults thought it was cute, maybe mildly odd. Eventually, after telling me in no uncertain terms that it was *not* the case—my first word was 'Barbie,' go figure—my parents would just roll their eyes or change the subject.

"Well anyway, I spent so long loving this, this *thing* that everyone around me seemed mostly ambivalent about. I mean, sure, who doesn't love music? But for me, it was a first love and a best friend all in one. So I went off to a college on the other side of the country where it seemed every single person around me was the *opposite* of ambivalent about this thing that I loved. You'd think I'd finally found my place, right?" I glance over now at Miles, who's watching me so steadily I nearly lose my train of thought. Clearing my throat, I continue. "But it was like a holding pen—so stifling. I just wanted to get back here and *do* the thing. So I did come back. Then I met Elliot. And, as they say, the rest is history."

It strikes me now that in a way, falling out of love with Elliot coincided with my falling out of love with being an artist. It also strikes me that I've basically just recited chapter one of a memoir to a guy who simply asked me if I like what I do. If it was in question before, it's clear as day now that I am *so* not ready to get back out on the dating scene.

"I am . . . *so* sorry for dumping all of that on you," I say, face flaming again. "Scratch all of it. Yes! I *love* what I do. I am . . . so . . . lucky. So . . . so privileged! *Blessed*, honestly. Won't He do it?"

"Ella. Ella." Miles cuts off my meltdown. "It's okay. I was aiming for honesty, and that's what you gave me. Doing what you love for a living has its own way of sucking the joy out of it. I can only imagine what it's like when that love is tied up in someone else."

For a second, it appears as if he's got more to say on that train of thought. But he backs off it.

"I have to imagine it was that way for you to an extent, right?" I ask, feeling a little like I'm out on a ledge. "With your ex?"

"You could say that, I guess," he says after a beat. "Baseball practically runs through Monica's blood. Her dad, uncle, brothers . . . all of them at one point played in the minors or majors. In some ways she seemed more at home in a stadium than I am. But it's not easy being the wife of a player. So, I can't pretend it was all a walk in the park for her either."

Even though I'm sure it's entirely true—I *have* seen my share of

WAGS episodes after all—to speak this way of the ex-spouse who carried on an affair with your teammate strikes me as . . . generous, to say the least. Especially after all the punches life threw Miles's way in the aftermath of the big reveal. But here he is a year later appearing to be—dare I say, healed? And here I am, right in the thick of it, trying to fathom a day in the distant future when I'll think of the years I spent with Elliot as anything other than stolen time I'll never get back.

"You're not angry anymore," I say. And I'm as shocked that these words have escaped my thoughts as he seems to be, with the way his eyes spark in surprise.

He recovers quickly, though, shrugging it off. "I was never angry for the reasons people seemed to think I was."

Thankfully, Miles fills the silence. "Can I ask you something kind of personal?"

My shoulders immediately tense. But I like talking to him, so I nod anyway.

"What was that? Onstage, with you and your—" He gets stuck just slightly on the last word, and I glance down, noticing him subtly tapping his leg.

Clearing my throat, I meet his eyes again. "That kiss from Elliot was a performance," I provide. "He and I are getting a divorce. It's just a lot of red tape and lawyers and . . . drama. I'm sure you get it."

"Maybe a little too much," he says, seemingly satisfied with my explanation. Then his face clouds over, like the memories of his own lengthy, very public divorce battle still linger too close to the surface. "They'll tell you it gets easier," he says. "But what they won't say is that it gets harder first. This person you, at least at one point, vowed the rest of your life to suddenly starts acting like your enemy. Up is down."

"But you're used to that though," I say. "Facing opponents."

"You'd think so, yeah," he replies. "But it's a whole new ball game when it's someone you thought you'd spend the rest of your life with. Someone who knows you better than anyone." He laughs now, but without humor. "And to think for a minute I thought we could make it work."

This makes me rear back a bit. I swallow my judgment, though, because I can see he's judged himself enough.

"Foolish. I know." He pauses, rubbing his forehead. "Anyway, I didn't mean to make this about me. I just wanted to let you know I've been through what you're about to go through and that you'll get to the other side."

For a few seconds I try to picture exactly that—*the other side* of all of this. But it's too overwhelming. Because for the first time in a while, sitting here in this dugout, with this Dodger Dog and these fake cheese nachos, I'm not in a rush to be anywhere else.

12

F THERE'S ONE THING for certain about me and the glam team when we're tucked behind closed doors, it's that subtlety doesn't exist between us. My trailer is our cone of silence. In this hallowed space, we can think and feel things out loud—even if that means being loud and wrong. It's quite fitting, too, seeing as none of us seem to know how to bite our tongue . . . at least not for long.

"Mm-mm-mm." Sheryl's grunts of disapproval come in as if on cue while she pin curls my long silky tresses. "Can't believe they have me putting in all this good work just for them to go and ruin it by the end of the day," she scoffs.

Sheryl's referring to the dramatic effects my music video director, Laurel Chevalier, has planned for the final scene of today's shoot. She finishes her mini-rant by sucking air through a slit in her teeth, and the resulting sound mimics a whistling tea kettle.

"A little fake rain never hurt anybody," Rodney chimes in helpfully from across the room, where he's steaming my last look for the shoot—a slinky maroon dress that hangs off the shoulder, falls to my ankles, and fits me like a second skin. "Besides, I thought we all understood the assignment as given," he adds. "The Ice Queen said *lean in*. So that means we gotta pull out all the stops!"

Unfortunately, Rodney's enthusiasm isn't contagious. The team's plan for wrestling back control of the unraveling media narrative might be well underway, as we are on the first day of my music video shoot for "No Ordinary Love." But I have not so much *leaned in* as I have disassociated, while I sit staring blankly at my e-reader, sipping from a mug of hot tea.

Only a week has elapsed since Elliot, Miles, and I maneuvered awkwardly like an unwitting throuple in front of a million eyeballs at the Grammys, and I have been taking a beating online ever since. This morning I caved and deleted the social media apps from my phone—but only *after* I spiraled and spent an hour watching all those TikTok videos of Miles working out to my music that Janet had alluded to.

I'm not proud.

There's a great gulf between indifference and obsession when it comes to minding the masses and their opinion of me as a public figure. I've always fallen somewhere smack in the middle. But whenever I find myself careening further toward either extreme, I shut it down. Total social media cleanse. It's never been more necessary than right now.

For Elliot's part, with his intended message sealed and delivered—that he's not letting go without a fight—he's already traipsed back across the pond with Miss Thing in tow, but not before having his lawyer serve me an amendment to the divorce papers.

"Has he lost his damn mind?" I recall whisper-shouting at the rectangular device clutched in my palm in the back seat of Rohin's Escalade on the way to the airport. "Elliot's threatening to revoke my fifty percent split of the performance rights? Is that even legal?"

"There's a clause in the prenuptial agreement you likely missed given how deep it was masked in jargon," Janet went on to explain in her signature calm, clipped competence, "but it details how those rights were *always* tied to a contingency."

My heart dropped to my stomach. "What kind of contingency?" I still managed to squeak out.

"One that occasions any public embarrassment of a significant scale . . . essentially Elliot's lawyers embedded a one-way morality clause that could be exercised at their client's discretion."

"So, you're saying he doesn't even have to provide evidence of my wrongdoing? He just has to tell the judge I hurt his feelings?"

Then Janet drove the nail into my coffin. "Honey, the headlines *are* the evidence." And that's when my heart fell to my ass. "I see this often, particularly with men," she continued despite my distress. "When their egos and emotions get behind the wheel, it's *buckle up everybody*! No one's safe. And since I doubt we can rely on logic or reason to take the keys back anytime soon, we'll just have to add this to the list of things we aim to challenge in court."

Normally, I'd be content with the tried-and-true PR strategy of lying low and praying it all blows over with a quickness. But with so much at stake, I can't risk any more control slipping through my fingers. The court of public opinion packs a mighty punch, and if the blows keep coming at this steady clip, my chances at winning in *actual* court against Elliot only diminish with every new scandalous headline.

Before I did the app purge, notorious celebrity gossip account Glitter 'N Dirt had posted a series of anonymous tips from followers claiming to have insider knowledge of my pattern of stepping out on Elliot over the course of our eight-year marriage. Apparently, these "sources" could credibly link me to a string of B-list actors and professional athletes. In GnD's posts, account owner and soulless Hollywood gossipmonger Rick Fenway had started replacing references to me as Ella Simone with TWW. One quick Google search led me to a cursed Reddit thread explaining that, in my case, the acronym stood for "The Wannabe WAG"—my left eye hasn't stopped twitching since.

I was already high-key dubious of Janet and Gabriel's Plan B strategy to give professional context to my relationship with Miles Westbrook *before* this new development. But now, you could light a match in my vicinity and probably incinerate a city block with the way I've been fuming over this whole ordeal.

"Ella, you okay, girl?" Jamie asks, and it stirs me out of a daze. "'Cause if that eye keeps twitching, this lash is going to end up glued to your retina."

Suddenly, the levee breaks, and a dam of unshed tears bursts free. Perhaps I could have kept it together, if only Jamie hadn't uttered the words *you okay, girl?* Like the wound that only hurts if you touch it, most days I'm *fine*. Perfectly fine actually—so long as no one pokes below the surface. But something about today, and everything leading up to it, has me feeling rubbed raw, utterly exposed, and totally in over my head. Not to mention the fact that in T-minus two hours, I've got to convincingly fall madly in love with Miles Westbrook, while still coming to terms with how I've spent the last several years slowly falling *out* of it with Elliot Majors.

"Oh hell, here we go." Rodney groans from across the room before rushing over with a box of Kleenex. Sheryl and Jamie both stop their prep work and crowd around me as I crumble in The Chair.

"Go on and let it out," Sheryl says. "This is what we're here for, girl. You know we've got you."

"Mm-hmm. Speaking of," Rodney cuts in. "You may need a shot. Jamie, where's the tequila?"

This makes me laugh. "Rodney, it's nine in the morning. You can't be serious?"

Out of seemingly nowhere, Jamie produces a bottle of reposado. "As a heart attack," she says, after brandishing four shot glasses.

13

C AN WE GET SOME *wind on the lovers before my Botox wears off? Please and thank you!*

Laurel Chevalier has more than likely never turned down a cigarette. You can tell from the almost painful authenticity in her vocal fry. It's not an affect, she earned that singed larynx. This is also evident in the faint odor of tobacco that announces her presence in any room. Vices aside, I've been counting my lucky stars since Lydia told me we'd finally booked her for a shoot after years of failed attempts at doing so. Not only is she a legendary videographer who's held her own as a woman artist in a male-dominated industry, but she's directed some of the most iconic music videos of the past three decades.

Laurel's just requested wind, if not for practical reasons, then at least for *artistic* ones. With only a shiny metal pole between Miles and me, I'm trying not to squirm under the intensity of his unbroken gaze. We're on the first scene of the video shoot and so far, it's been a whole lot of "hurry up and wait" while Laurel's director of photography sets up the shot. Along with about a dozen extras and a handful of dancers, Miles and I are on a soundstage crammed into a replica of the 4 train. Within seconds, that implausible gust of wind kicks on in the interior compartment, and a shiver runs up my spine.

"You cold?" Miles asks as his eyes skate over the goose bumps that are now peppering the exposed skin of my shoulders and arms. Because of Laurel's tight schedule, a video that was supposed to be taking place on a hot summer day in New York City had to be scheduled way out of season. It's February in Midtown Manhattan, and I'm wearing a ribbed tank top and cutoff jean shorts. We may be on a heated soundstage, but it's still frigid.

"Always," I say, swallowing hard. I haven't been nervous for a video shoot since my first one more than eight years ago. But the stakes have never seemed so high. I also haven't truly had to *act* out a part like I'll be expected to do today. Usually, I just have to nail the choreography while striking the right balance between confident and sexy, all while lip-synching to vocals I laid down in the studio. But today I have to convince people I'm in love. Something I probably should have perfected over the past few years.

"You mind?" Miles asks, before placing his hands like brackets on either side of my arms. He's left about a two-inch gap so that we aren't quite touching yet. But it feels like we are. Heat radiates from his palms, warming my skin from a distance. I nod yes without thinking much of what granting my permission means. And then his hands are on me, and a full-body shudder rolls from my feet up to the top of my head. I fight the urge to let my eyes flutter closed. But then I give in.

"Speed!" the DP calls out to indicate that the cameras are now rolling.

We aren't recording sound, so Laurel calls out, "Action!" next.

"Roll music!" the sound operator shouts, and any chance I had to savor the moment melts away.

Like I've been snapped out of a trance, my eyes shoot open. Miles's touch quickly drops away, and all that gooey warmth goes with it. We practically snap apart to take our places on opposite sides of the train, while the seductive drumbeat and percussive guitar intro to "No Ordinary Love" fill the space around us. The camera slowly tracks toward us from the back of the train, making its way past the extras and dancers, which gives us a few seconds to get on our marks. On my way, I rehearse Laurel's notes in my mind.

We're filming the scene in one long take, so once I reach my mark with my back to the train door, just like we'd rehearsed, I begin by checking my phone and swiping open a text message from my imaginary ex-boyfriend. I pinch my brow and release my neck so that my head thuds on the grimy window behind me. We're rigged up on a fake track so the train rumbles and shakes as if we were coursing speedily through the tunnel. Humidifiers pump moisture into the air, so despite the aesthetic wind, it starts to feel muggy and damp—like a true New York summer underground.

I haven't looked over at Miles yet, though I know he's standing directly across from me. And tension coils in my stomach because I know—per Laurel's notes—that after I toss my phone in my bag, massage my temples, and groan, when I look up, I'll lock eyes with a tall, handsome stranger. And from that moment on, our imaginary love story will take flight.

First, you'll just look at each other until I give my signal. Then, like magnets, you'll both step forward to the center of the train, with only the balancing pole between you. At this point, I just want you

*to talk to each other. Chitchat. Make each other smile and laugh.
It doesn't matter what you talk about really, because the conversation I want to capture is the one that happens every time your eyes
meet.*

I glance up, and sure enough, Miles is there with his eyes boring into me. A small half smirk on his face takes me by surprise,
and a nervous burst of laughter floats out of me. Can it be possible
I've been out of the game so long that I don't even know how to
pretend to flirt with a man I'm insanely attracted to? I immediately kick myself for already breaking character, then remember
Laurel's number one rule for this first long take—*No cuts! No matter what, we keep rolling.* With my head back in the game, I focus
in on his face. In response to my awkward laugh, Miles's smirk has
stretched into a wide smile. And something like a hunger pang
has settled low in my belly.

His gaze falls to my tote bag, and something serious briefly
clouds his features, like perhaps he's wondering what on the phone
could have upset me just now. I make a mental note to compliment him on his acting chops later on during our break.

I allow my eyes to free-fall and run the length of him, drinking
him in. At the same time, I am keenly aware of the multiple cameras strategically positioned to capture our every move. I find
their presence comforting—like a safety net. As long as the cameras are rolling, I know I have the creative freedom to let go and
enjoy the intensity of this attraction, to give in to this magnetic
pull. Because after all, it's just for show.

OKAY, EVERYBODY, TAKE FORTY-FIVE!

Laurel releases us for our first break of the day, and Rodney
scurries over to me with my trusty fluffy robe—the one I always

make sure to carry with me for long days on drafty sets. After helping me bundle up, he brandishes my cozy Ugg boots, assisting me as I slip them on. It occurs to me in this moment, as it does at odd times throughout any given day, just how much of a lucky fool I am despite all the mess I've recently found myself in.

Without thinking, I reach out and pull my oldest friend into a tight hug.

"Don't wrinkle me, bitch! You know I hate creases," he demands, returning the tight squeeze. "What's this for anyway?"

"I couldn't do any of it without you. You know that, right?" I tell him, because I'm certain I don't say it enough.

"Trust, my love. I am well aware," he replies, with a gentle pat on my cheek. "Besides, I get paid for this."

I roll my eyes lightheartedly and stalk off to survey the cornucopia of meal options and snacks at the crafty tables. After a meticulous perusal, I opt for a bag of Doritos, a massive chocolate chip cookie, a turkey pesto wrap, and my favorite fizzy beverage. On most days I keep a pretty bland diet. When life and schedules are chaotic and you're never quite sure which city or time zone you'll be in, having consistent meals at the ready that are satisfying and healthy is clutch. But the craft service tables are my favorite location on a set—all my favorite creature comforts gathered in one place.

With the rest of the crew dispersed, I am left to my own devices—my version of heaven. I'm humming, swaying my hips from side to side, imagining locking myself back in my trailer and scarfing down my spoils, then stealing at least fifteen minutes to recharge with a catnap.

"Foraging for a long winter?"

That deep, gravelly voice makes me jump, gracelessly tossing all my goodies into the air. Each one hits the floor with a prominent thud. Then the top to my can of soda water pops open, releasing a steady stream of liquid directly at Miles.

I hold back a shriek as he crouches down to pick up the mess.

"I'm so sorry!" I shout. "You're soaked." I begin frantically searching for a towel to dry him off.

"It's fine," he replies, standing up to go toss the now-warped items into a large trash bin. "I should know better than to creep up on a lioness while she's grazing," he jokes, peeling his damp shirt from his chest and stomach.

Briefly distracted by the visual, I clear my throat. "You really should," I reply. Then, eager to help the situation, I grab a handful of napkins, and without thinking I start pressing them into his damp shirt—against his very firm and well-formed torso. Suddenly, I fear I've made a grave mistake. I retreat as if I've been burned, thrusting the napkins at him so he can finish the job. He chuckles.

"So, you just happened to have the free time to come out to New York right before baseball season to be in a random pop star's music video?" I ask cheekily, both desperate for a change of subject and genuinely interested in his response.

After dabbing himself off, he makes a wad of the napkins and tosses them into the waste bin with perfect aim, making me wonder if basketball is in his repertoire as well.

"Would you believe me if I said I've got n-nothing going on till we ship out to Camelback in a few weeks?" he asks, and a glimmer in his eye makes me blush.

"First, I'd have to know what on earth that means," I reply out of honest confusion.

"You're funny," he says, smiling but not laughing. As with all of our interactions to date, I notice him notice my every move, like tucking a lock of hair behind my ear, or tightening the belt on my robe—like he's studying me for a portrait. It's unnerving and elec-trifying all at once.

I scrunch my nose before taking a swig from a fresh can of blackberry-flavored sparkling water.

His breath hitches, like he's remembered I'm still waiting for an explanation. "Camelback Ranch is where the team holds spring training. It's basically the start of our season," he says plainly, be-fore answering what I'm really asking him. "So, we have this kinda fun, kinda weird night at the Grammys. Next thing I know, my agent's calling me with this random request to be in your music video. He sets up a meeting. I go. You insult me. I consider pulling out. Then you show up to the stadium and—" He pauses, a slow smile curving his lips. "Let's just say, you surprised me. So, I thought . . . maybe this could be fun?"

"Huh." I realize too late that I've been mindlessly worrying the tab on the can of my drink back and forth between my thumb and forefinger when it suddenly snaps off. Quickly, I pop it in my pocket. "Is that so?"

"I wouldn't lie about it. I've got nothin' to hide from you," he says. "Also . . . y-you're not a random pop star."

And because I don't quite know what to say to that, I settle for saying nothing at all.

Then we're silent for a few beats and a layer of awkwardness falls over the exchange. Miles breaks the ice, though, with a safe change of subject.

"So, what are your plans for when this never-ending shoot eventually does end?" he asks.

I'm not foolish enough to think the question is anything more than small talk. Needlessly tousling my hair I say, "Ohhh . . . I'll probably hole up in my hotel with way too much takeout and watch *You've Got Mail*. It's my evergreen comfort watch."

"Huh. Never seen that one," he says, with his chin slightly lifted as he eyes me through the bottom of his lashes. "I'll have to check it out sometime."

"I expect a thorough review."

He laughs. "You got it, Coach."

14

STREAMS OF DANCING DUST and sunlight paint golden strokes over an otherwise stark and unmoving space. For this day of make-believe, the tall and handsome stranger who charmed me on the train has now whisked me off to the Met, where he's been given strict instructions to up his woo game.

Long curving tracks have been laid on the marble floor so the cameras can seamlessly follow me and Miles as we explore the light-filled entry court to the Met's American Wing. The grand space is temporarily roped off for the shoot, and this time around, there are no dancers or extras—just us and the statues. Right about now I feel like one of them—cold and hard and disconnected from all the hustle and bustle around me.

Crew members mill about, fast at work with their respective tasks. Rodney and Sheryl are huddled together over in a corner on a bench engaged in deep conversation. Jamie's dabbing a beauty blender on Miles's forehead, her jaw practically unhinged with laughter at something he's just said. For the past ten minutes or so, Laurel's been meticulously eyeing the shot list with her AD,

Sam. But now she's walking my way, determination furrowing her brow and tightening the few lines left to frame her mouth. I have the sudden urge to evaporate into thin air just to avoid whatever vibe modification she's about to attempt on me.

Laurel approaches, arms lifted as if she's coming in for an embrace. But when she arrives, instead, she clasps my hands in her cool, smooth palms—a gesture probably meant to disarm or comfort me but that does the exact opposite.

"How are you feeling today? You feel good?" Her words stretch unnaturally soft and sweet, like she's cooing at a troubled toddler.

Clearing my throat I say, "Great! I feel fantastic!" trying to muster the emotions with the words. At her disbelieving stare, I deflate. "Why do you ask? You're getting what you need from me, right?"

Waving her hands, she makes an exaggerated show of shaking her head. "Oh no! You're perfect! Not a hair out of place!" She pats me on the head as if to emphasize her point.

Laurel then extends a hand to tuck a long curl behind my ear, and when she leans in farther, her voice drops low. "Listen. Some of your takes are coming off a bit—" She pauses, teetering her head back and forth, really grasping for the words. "Well, let's just call it *frigid*. And maybe a little scared too. It's almost like you're afraid to touch the man."

Laurel releases a pent-up breath and her shoulders relax, like she's been holding that in all day. Then she just looks at me square in the eye—as if she's actually asked me a question and wants her answer.

At a loss, I simply utter a muffled, shameful "Oh-kaaay." My face flames, and for probably the fifth time today, I contemplate another disappearing act.

"Look, I get it," she continues, having apparently laid all pretenses aside. "I know things are probably a mess up here." She points to my head, then to my chest. "And in here. But today, let's not be people. Let's just be artists. Let's just . . . push all that stuff out *there*. You know?" She motions to the windows with both arms gesticulating widely. "And come on, Ella, look at that man. I mean for real . . . Look at him!" With a bold forefinger she points over at Miles, a movement that naturally, and unfortunately, commands his attention. I fight back the urge to drop my face into the palm of my hand—but heaven forbid I ruin Jamie's immaculate beat.

"What can we do for you?" Laurel asks, interrupting my inward spiral. "There's a mental block in there somewhere. So tell me. How do we get you over that hump?"

I open my mouth to assure her that there will be no need for extra measures. Her notes are taken and I can, and will, do better. But she cuts me off. "I know!" she practically shouts. "I think I've got just the thing."

LAUREL'S GRAND PLAN IS TO LET MILES AND ME PLAY DJ, GIVE us our choice of mood music to play for the next scene with my selection coming up first. Since we're shooting B-roll and there will be no choreography or lip-synching involved, all we're really using sound for is to set a vibe. So in the spirit of the remake, I've asked for "The Sweetest Taboo," one of my all-time favorites.

Back on in five, four, three, two . . .

Speed!

Roll music!

Action!

When the song starts, the sound of rain followed by syncopated drums fills the space around us, bouncing off all the marble, bronze, and brass surfaces. And just when Sade begins to wonder what will happen if she tells her lover how she really feels, Miles surprises me by first brushing his fingers against mine and then interlocking them all together.

Laurel's choice word reverberates in my mind . . . *frigid*. But with his hand in mine, that intimate, overwhelming touch gives me more than chills. It makes me quake on a cellular level, converts the rigid, sure parts of me to raw energy. I haven't been afraid to touch him, so much as I've been practically *burning* to do it. But that alone is terrifying.

Seconds pass with us simply standing there holding hands before Miles leans down so that he's mere centimeters from my ear. "I know we're probably supposed to walk around and look at all this art, but I really want to dance with you."

I glance up at his smiling eyes, and without questioning it, I nod *yes*. Swallowing hard, I face him just as his free hand briefly brushes past my hip bone to find its place at the small of my back. The heat from that compound touch sends my senses into overdrive. Anyone feeling the crush of sensations coursing through me right now might think I've never danced at all. Of course I have, just never with Miles Westbrook.

Thank God for muscle memory.

I place my left hand at his nape, where the smoothest swath of warm skin meets the crisp fade of his hair—a delicious contrast, like water approaching a shore. Miles raises our clasped hands to his mouth and brushes my knuckles across his lips. I have to actively remind myself that we're pretending—merely putting on a show.

"I take it you've been here before?" I ask, figuring a little small talk will ground me in the reality of what we're doing—making a video.

"Oh yeah," he says. Then a small laugh spreads into a beaming smile that takes over his whole face. "My grandparents . . . they retired here together. After school most days, I was either out on the diamond or here, bothering them on the late afternoon shifts."

"So, that 'museum' you said your grandfather worked at . . . was the Met?" I ask, unable to mask my surprise.

"Mm-hmm," he confirms, before taking me for a spin and then pulling me back into him. "My abuela spent thirty-five years as a seamstress at the Costume Institute. And my grandfather, the one with the voice"—Miles tilts his head to meet my eyes—"he eventually worked his way up to head of security here."

"Let me guess," I say. "Your favorite part was helping him patrol the hallways?"

"Nah," he says with a chuckle, and we're pressed so close I can feel it rumble through his chest. "I actually was blown away by all the garments and textiles my grandmother got to work with. Some of that stuff was like . . . centuries old. I mean . . . don't get me wrong, running around with Pop was fun as hell." He pauses. "I miss them both."

"I'm sorry they're gone," I say. But it feels like a woefully inadequate response for such a massive loss.

"Don't be," Miles replies. "I've committed so much of them to memory." He pauses for a moment. "It's like they're with me everywhere I go."

I let his words sink deep, roll them over in my mind. The overwhelming urge to rest my head on his chest so I can feel if his heart is beating as hard and fast as mine hits me like a train. But the song changes and with it, so does the mood. Because if I'm not mistaken by the opening chords, Miles has picked for his choice "All the Things (Your Man Won't Do)" by Joe.

I stop moving and look him squarely in the eye.

"You did not," I say in utter disbelief at his very on-the-nose song selection. A song in which a man vows to do "all the things" his conquest's boyfriend has neglected to do, both in *and* out of a bedroom. It's the quintessential throwback to that soulful late-nineties and early 2000s R&B, when crooning and wooing was the name of the game—*baby-making music* as Sheryl likes to call it.

Miles simply shrugs with a wicked sparkle in his eye. "Laurel told me to up my game." He swipes his thumb across his chin beneath a boyish grin. "And I like a challenge."

"Miles," I deadpan, stifling the urge to step back and place my hands on my hips. But with the cameras still rolling, all I can do is laugh. I peek over at Laurel, who is beaming from ear to ear and giving us two thumbs up. *You're doing great*, she mouths.

Miles beckons for me to come back to him so we can finish our dance. One part embarrassed and all parts turned on, I go willingly. "Not gonna lie, this kind of feels like ninth-grade homecoming when you finally score a dance with your crush and the whole time you're fighting a massive erection," he murmurs in my ear.

At this I can't help but burst out in laughter as I pull away.

"It's a joke! It's a joke, I swear," he assures me. He playfully draws me back into him, and I am like putty in his hands. But instead of dancing face-to-face, he spins me so my back is to his chest. Miles wraps his arms around my waist and clasps our hands together over my stomach. And then, we just sway. We're directly in front of the golden statue of Diana, the archer. She balances gracefully on one foot with her bow and arrow raised, eyes on her target.

"She reminds me of you," he says. "Strong. Purposeful."

Gently, we step out of the embrace to stand side by side. With our shoulders pressed together, we both look up in wonder at the iconic bronze statue. "Why are you so kind to me?" I ask. "Why say all these nice things when we hardly know each other?"

"I'm not tryna tell you nice things, Ella. I'm just telling you the truth."

This time, it's my hand that reaches for his.

MILES WESTBROOK IS NOT JUST EYE CANDY, HE IS A WHOLE problem. An emotional wrecking ball with the potential to make me crumble to pieces in the palm of his hand, to be exact. If I'm not careful, I'll be doodling our initials in my gratitude journal and searching Google images for him in my off time. Can't have that. Thankfully, we're on the last leg of what has felt like a marathon, and I'll be out of the woods and back to regular beat-my-ex-in-court programming soon.

We press on at a breakneck pace. Across various locations and expensive soundstages, Miles and I have braved the pseudo-sweltering summer heat of the pseudo-subway, wandered hand in hand through the American Wing of the Met, fed each other pastries in a plush red booth at the Russian Tea Room, and even shared a paddleboat in Central Park—the green screen version, that is.

Now, it's well past ten p.m. and we've finally made it to the last shots on the list—a soundstage made to resemble a rainy rooftop on the Lower East Side.

"I'm just saying, you might need to own this dress when it's all over with," Rodney whispers conspiratorially while stripping off my fluffy robe and, along with it, the warmth it provides. "Don't worry, I'll just tell the rep at Cult Gaia it fell off the truck," he whispers, winking with practically his entire face. Then he darts off to join Sheryl and Jamie at the edge of the roof, where they'll watch and no doubt reserve all their well-meaning but shady observations for later.

Laurel was right about me. I've been an anxious ball of frigid nerves all day. But this final scene is the one I've feared most. And even though Miles got me to loosen up a little with our dance among the statues, I haven't been able to get my mind off the thought of kissing him. Will we? Won't we? Can we even? Would the world explode?

All our scenes leading up to this point have felt akin to playing with fire or dancing at the edge of a waterfall. Every heated glance, the brush of our hands, even the gentle press of our bodies as we moved so effortlessly to lyrics that confessed things we'd never dare say out loud. Because if between takes, we did say those things—if I told the truth, that *it's never felt like this before*, it would mean admitting that for me, today wasn't just a day of playing pretend after all. Today was a wake-up call.

"Do we have them kiss?" I hear Laurel ask Lydia in what I'm sure she mistook for a discreet volume.

Both of them eye me from about ten feet away, then turn back to each other before Lydia whispers, "What would Majors think?"

Turns out, reading lips is a secret talent of mine.

Before I can think better of it I find myself shouting, "Majors isn't here!"

Miles's eyes go wide with surprise and a little spark of mischief—kind of like he's both in awe and scared of me right now. He steps closer, leans in then just slightly, and with a low rumble, says, "Careful. This zero-fucks attitude looks good on you."

SPEED!
  Cue rain!
  Roll music!
  Action!

Hand in hand we burst through the fire escape door, onto the roof and into the pouring rain. We laugh and spin, basking in the water until, as we've been directed, Miles backs me up against a brick wall, where things are supposed to really heat up. By now we're both totally soaked. Unlike real rain, which gradually dampens your clothes, fake raindrops are three times the size and land with a heavy thud, seeping through your layers fast. That maroon dress that already hugged each one of my curves is glued to me now. And not for the first time today, I'm grateful to be on a heated soundstage.

A violent shudder runs through me and, perhaps emboldened by the rain or this wild thundering in my chest from the kick drum that has become my heartbeats, I clutch at Miles's shirt and tilt my face up to his. In turn his hands gently cradle the back of my head and his eyes bore into mine, questioning, almost pleading for an invitation to venture further.

"Yes," I say, nodding with a smile. "Yes." I repeat the word. The second time as more of an affirmation to myself that I really want this.

The next moment becomes a starburst of connection, and suddenly, nothing else exists beyond the slide of our lips, and hands, and the breath that passes between our open mouths.

Cameras be damned.

Miles Westbrook is kissing me and I'm responding in kind. Half in shock, half ecstatic from the feeling of falling without care or thought of a safety net. For the first time in a long time, I'm not worried about the script or the blocking. I am strictly feeling.

Speaking of, Miles has just lightly sucked on my bottom lip, and I think I just moaned. I don't know because my song is playing at full blast. I can hardly hear anything but my own voice and the music, or see anything but the man who's pressed against me, whose body is holding me up against this wall, moving with intention against mine. Whose hands have molded against my curves and left fire in their tracks.

If she's not careful, a girl could get irrevocably lost in this.

"And cut!" Laurel shouts. "That's a wrap on Ella and Miles!"

Then, just as fast as we started, we stop. The rain suddenly abates.

The crew applauds. Miles gently extricates himself from my grasp, and without his weight against me, I lose my balance. He steps forward to catch me, and our eyes meet only for a moment before his dart away.

15

[MAJORCHORD413 VIA INSTAGRAM]

It's never like me to comment publicly on private matters. But there's something I need to get off my chest. It is with a heavy <3 that I share with you today that my relationship with Ella Simone has come to an end and we will be divorcing. Without question, launching her career and supporting her dreams for the past 10 years has been one of the top accomplishments of my life, second only to being her husband. But as the saying goes, all good things must come to an end. At a time like this, it's the love from every one of you who have rocked with me over the years that's gonna get me through. All I ask is that you understand and give me some time and space to process and heal. Then it's back to the hits! Peace and Blessings. —Elliot Majors

GROUP TEXT: The Glam Squad

SHERYL: Now ain't this some bullshit.

[IMAGE OF MAJORCHORD413'S IG POST]

JAMIE: Anybody else get the feeling Majors would be on the bad guy's team in Stomp the Yard?

JAMIE: Some folks are just born lookin like villains.

SHERYL: Mhmm. Yeah. I see what you mean. Very Jafarian.

RODNEY: I just know Coco had to write this statement. Majors don't know how to place a comma to save his LIFE.

SHERYL: The man's a musical genius, not a grammatical one.

JAMIE: Majors just wanted to upstage the 🔥 you and Miles made on the internet . . .

JAMIE: Couldn't give you one day!

RODNEY: Ella. Girl. You okay?

From: beverlyr@gmail.com
To: ellaelladee@gmail.com

Date: February 14, 2023

Ella, please pick up the phone when I call. This is getting to be ridiculous. I just heard the most upsetting news. I know it can't possibly be true. But I would like some assurance from my own daughter. I deserve that much. Cousin Ada tells me that Elliot has announced your separation? Publicly? On social media? This is absurd. How could you allow this to happen? After everything he's done for you. Everything we've sacrificed. Please tell me this is nothing more than salacious and misguided tabloid gossip and that I have nothing to worry about. And for God's sake please answer the phone, Ella. It is unacceptable to keep me in the dark like this. What am I to believe?

Mother

16

ANGELO BOUNCES THE TINY red ball, scoops up three jacks, but fails to catch it before it connects with the floor. It's clear he's distracted, but I'll take the advantage. Giggling to myself, I prep for my turn while he mouths an expletive.

"Roxy and her team got the memo," Angelo says, switching back into manager mode. "She mentions any word that comes close to rhyming with Elliot or so much as alludes to that IG post, and we're out of here."

Half listening and fully focused on the game, I'm successful this go-round and score three jacks for my stash. "Roger that," I say, punching the air in victory.

We're killing time in the greenroom of New York's hip-hop and R&B radio station Power 103 before I go on the viral morning show with legendary host DJ Roxy Dee. By now, I know Angelo well enough to know he means business about Elliot being off-limits. I'm sure he's studied a map of the building and pinpointed the exact location of the signal booster. Wouldn't put smashing the transmitter past him, either, if Roxy steps out of bounds with her line of questioning.

It's my first interview since the video premiered at midnight eastern, and ever since then I've been steadily trending on pretty much every social platform right next to Miles, and unfortunately Elliot too. Apparently, he wanted in on the fun and games and decided to announce our divorce on Instagram of all places.

Angelo scoops up an impressive four jacks this time around. "But you know what this means, right?" he asks, voice taking on a more serious note. "To make this worth her while, she's gonna go hard in the paint on the video. Try to trip you up and get a viral sound bite on you and Miles."

At the mention of his name, I completely fumble my turn and drop the few jacks I'd managed to grasp. "Thanks, Lo. I think I can handle it," I say, sounding a bit sharper than I intend to.

"I know you can." Angelo sighs, before bouncing the ball and clearing the remaining jacks in one fell swoop. "I'm just saying . . . stay woke." He winks at me, and I playfully roll my eyes.

"GOOD MORNING, GOOD MORNING TO ALL MY BEAUTIFUL people out there listening! You know me, I'm DJ Roxy Dee. It is a sunny Tuesday morning here in New York City, and I am pleased, as always, to be back rockin' the airwaves for you on your morning commutes. But before we get to spinning those hits, we have a very special guest with us today . . . one of our favorites here at Power 103. So, without further ado, joining us after the worldwide premiere of her latest music video for the *Billboard* top one hundred hit 'No Ordinary Love'—which broke the internet, might I add—is the pop, soul, R&B princess herself, Miss Ella

Simone. Yes, everybody in the studio, please give her a warm welcome!"

"Thank you. Thank you all so much," I say, adjusting my headset. "You know I always love coming to visit you guys here at
Power 103. This really feels like coming home to me."

"You know it's all love. But, *girl* . . ." The word lands with a thud.
Like a full declarative sentence, and one that you know will be
followed by either an interrogation or an accusation. "We wouldn't
be family if I didn't come at you direct. Now, you got some
'splainin' to dooooo!"

Inwardly, I roll my neck and shoulders. *So it's like that? Already?* I think to myself. Angelo was not exaggerating. But like the
consummate professional I endeavor to be, I plaster on a trained
smile. The one that says I'm unbothered. No matter what question
Roxy's got locked and loaded, she won't see me sweat.

Besides, I know where the door is.

When Laurel sent over her final cut, I knew I was in for some
mess—even before the frantic calls from my team started to roll
in. There were even questions of scrapping the whole thing and
starting from scratch. Surprising myself, I reminded them that
despite my own expressed doubts, casting Miles in the video happened at *their* urging and that now perhaps it was their turn to
lean in to the public's response.

For me, something about that day spent traipsing around the
city loosened a knot I didn't know existed inside of me. Something
about spinning around in that fake rain, kissing a man who is *not*
my ex with reckless abandon—cameras be damned. By the end of
the shoot, I felt the opposite of afraid. I wanted more. Headlines
be damned too.

Snapping back to the present, I reach into my bag of tricks for
disarming the media and select flattery. "Oooh, look at you hold-

ing out that note like a soprano, I see you, girl!" I playfully tease Roxy in response to her thinly veiled ambush.

"Coming from you," Roxy says, her eyes narrowed, having likely clocked my game, "I'll take the compliment. But it won't distract me! I have a one-track mind this morning because I, like five million other people, have streamed a little video for a little ditty called 'No Ordinary Love' about five times since it dropped at midnight and, miss ma'am, you have given the people some food for thought! So, let's get into it."

"Okay. Okay. But first, I need to issue a disclaimer," I interject, hoping to redirect the locomotive before it runs off the track. "I recently picked up an acting class or two, so this was really a way for me to exercise those chops—"

"Nah! Nope!" As suspected, Roxy's not having it. "I'm not letting you off the hook that easy, little lady. We need to talk about the electric chemistry between you and your leading man. And for those of you living under a rock, I'm talking about starting pitcher for the LA Dodgers Miles Westbrook. So, you're telling me that was acting? You tryna win an Oscar? Be a triple threat? Because that rain-soaked make-out session at the end of the video almost cracked my back *and* my screen apart!"

"Ha! No. It's not like that," I reply, my cheeks aflame from her directness. "I'm just saying, we committed to the roles we were playing. And the end result was *clearly* effective." I gesture with a hand in her direction. "Hope your back's recovered," I add cheekily.

Roxy seems poised to push back with another snarky barb, so I reach for my next trick . . . politely overtalking to take control of the conversation. "I think people may be reading a little bit more into this than what it really is. It's a music video. And sure, it's a departure for me. I'll admit that given the news about my personal life lately, I can see why fans are having such a strong reaction. But this video was purely about creative expression. Nothing more."

Roxy doesn't appear to be convinced. "So, you're telling me, on the record, that there is nothing going on behind the scenes between you and Mr. Westbrook?"

"Yes. That is what I am telling you," I declare firmly as I imagine getting booked for an interview where I get to talk about my music for once. "Miles was a perfect gentleman on set and a phenomenal sport on a grueling day. I'm also honored that the video streams are helping raise funds for a foundation he started and named after his grandmother Evelyn, which provides support to women and girls in tough situations. It's my small way of thanking him for helping me out on the night of the Grammys with my little wardrobe snafu. That's what I'd like to direct our focus on. Because beyond that, there's really nothing to see."

I can see the moment it clicks for Roxy, that this is a losing battle. She's not getting a viral moment out of me. By her show's standards, this segment has been "a dud." Now, there's nothing left to do but play the song. Thank God.

"Well, folks, you heard it here first. Nothing to see here," Roxy says, with about as much energy as a milked-out baby. "How about we give it a spin, though, because it's a certified banger. In my humble opinion, you gave the inimitable Sade Adu a beautiful tribute. You wanna top it off for us?" she asks.

"It would be my pleasure," I reply, relieved to have the finish line in sight. "To the beautiful listeners of Power 103, I'm Ella Simone, and I'm pleased to share with you my latest single, 'No Ordinary Love.'"

THANKFULLY, JANET WATERMAN'S SATELLITE OFFICE IN CHELsea is far more discreet than her main setup in Century City. Angelo was able to drop me off with nary a paparazzo or a pinstripe suit in sight.

I've got good news and bad news to share with you, Janet texted about five minutes after I wrapped my segment on Power 103. Care to swing by the office for lunch?

That was an hour ago, and now we're perched across from each other on dueling mohair sofas with a sleek black coffee table topped with rare books and collectibles between us. "Lunch" in her mind apparently meant hot beverages, so I'm cradling a frothy cappuccino and hoping she can't hear my stomach growl.

"I'm glad you could make it on such short notice," she says with her signature, all-about-business rhythm. "I figured since I'm in New York, we might as well have a face-to-face."

"Could hardly get here fast enough," I reply. "You said there's good news and bad? Lay it on me!"

"I got the prenup tossed out in court," Janet says, while primly sipping from her coffee, like she's just informed me she closed a ring on her Apple Watch—slight work in her book. "Congratulations."

Shocked, I nearly do a spit take. Since covering a thousand-dollar silk blouse with mocha cappuccino mouth spatter is *not* the proper way to thank one's attorney for winning a case, with some effort, I manage to choke it down. "I'm . . . I'm sorry," I stammer over a scalded tongue. "But . . . how? I thought we'd have to . . . argue something? Present some evidence . . ."

"Elliot's attorney probably thought he was slick," Janet says with a subtle one-shouldered shrug. "But all he accomplished was to delay the inevitable when he neglected to include the final page of the contract, which showed the signatory lines. As if I wasn't going to catch that," she says. "He knew that doing so would make clear to me that you, in fact, as an impressionable young woman, were not availed of legal counsel upon entering into an agreement with an older, more powerful man."

Suddenly, the urge to defend my past self crashes down on me like a wave. Setting down the coffee and clearing my throat I say, "I . . . I was twenty. I was an adult." The words are feeble sounding even to me. "And Elliot assured me that Larry was looking out for both of us."

Janet tilts her head, and her mouth draws into a flat line. An expression that says, *Please keep up*, without words. Because after all, we both know everything Elliot told me was a lie.

"Anyway," she continues, "when one party is railroaded into signing away rights without legal counsel, the court may deem that resulting contract 'unconscionable.' I was able to make a compelling argument to that effect. So, the prenup is dismissed."

All I can manage to say is "Wow."

"So that's your good news," she replies. "But we're not out of the woods yet. Not by any means."

This is like a record scratch.

"There's still the challenge to your recording contract with Onyx Records. Extricating you from this won't be so cut-and-dry I'm afraid."

"I take it this agreement can't be expunged on the same grounds as the prenup?"

"That'd be too easy," she says. "Larry Spradlin's signature is listed beneath yours as legal counsel on this contract, which is dated two months after the prenup."

"*Elliot's* Larry," I say with a sigh of defeat.

For several moments we sit in silence as Janet lets me process what this all means. The prenup was always about mind control. Elliot never intended to enforce it—probably always knew he never could. But the recording contract I signed months later, that's what truly backed me into a corner. He knew I'd been put through the paces after a whirlwind couple of years, having dropped out of school, been cut off from home, and trying and failing to break through in LA. All those losses made him look like a major win. And in almost every sense of the word, he was. I have the career nineteen-year-old me *dreamed* of all those nights she spent chasing pavements. But what they don't tell you is that sometimes our dreams look a little different when they become a reality.

"There's a reason I only take on women as clients," Janet says, breaking the weighted silence. "We're not expected to fight. They assume we either don't have the will or we can't find the resources."

I let her words sink in, and when I don't respond, she shifts in her seat. "Mind if I tell you a story?"

"Of course not," I say.

She replaces her coffee on the table between us and settles back into her cushions. It's the first time I've seen her assume anything resembling a casual posture—like she's removing a mask of sorts.

"When my maternal grandparents emigrated from Mexico, they came here with two little boys, my uncles Tomas and Eugenio. My mother was born a few years later, after they'd gotten settled in Southern California. But my grandparents and the boys spent those first years without documentation. Naturally they found jobs and got by, and eventually, my grandfather went through the naturalization process. After a while he got his boys set up too. Then, of course, being born here, my mother was a citizen. She was good. But my grandmother, her mom . . . my grandfather refused her every time she asked. He knew that without papers, she could never truly leave him."

At this point I feel a strange heat take over my body, a fury for a woman I could never know, but who feels so familiar to me at the same time.

"And so," Janet says, subtly swiping a tear from the corner of her eye, "you're probably thinking, 'Now, why is my divorce lawyer telling me her family's backstory?' I'm telling you for this reason— and I need you to understand me plainly—there are *many* ways to abuse a person."

Her words sink into me like stones. And her gaze pins me in place. Like she hopes I have heard her. Like she needs me to know that she's not just talking about her grandmother, in the same way she's not just talking about me. She is talking about all the many women and people like us who have found themselves struggling to figure out why love sometimes hurts, when the truth is, it wasn't love to begin with. It was control.

17

Eight years ago

THIS WEATHER IS A flagrant foul! If I wasn't *very* aware of how broke you are, I'd sue you for damages," Rodney bleats against the bitter cold and razor-sharp wind.

"Oh, hush," I shoot back with considerable effort, given the fact I can hardly feel my own lips. "You live in Boston, don't act brand-new!"

From my East Village apartment, we walk westward on Eighth Street, arms linked, toward Electric Lady Studios. I'm nervous and giddy as all get-out because my best friend in the whole world is about to meet my new husband—and he has no idea.

No one does.

Elliot and I eloped last week in LA, and I haven't even told my own mother. It's been such a whirlwind, that I have yet to officially move into Elliot's sleek penthouse in SoHo. Since Rodney's flight landed this morning we've been holed up in my studio in Alphabet City. Unlike me, Rodney chose to stay the course at Berklee and is now spending a week with me in the city for his winter break.

"Well, in Boston I don't walk around aimlessly in subzero

temperatures," he replies. "Remind me why we didn't call an Uber? Better yet, why didn't the label send a car for you?"

Good question. Elliot hasn't answered my last three texts inquiring about the same thing. But today is supposed to be a *happy* day, so I bite back the irritation and creeping concern that something's not right.

We stop at the crosswalk. "I *wanted* us to take the scenic route," I insist, fudging the truth a little. "Figured it'd be fun to show you around the Village."

I spread my arms like Willy Wonka opening the doors to his chocolate factory. Rodney's eyes go wide with suspicion. But still, he humors me by taking a quick scan of our surroundings just when a massive rat with a condom wrapper in its teeth scampers between us. Squealing, I jump back about a foot and almost bust it on a strip of black ice.

"Very cute," he deadpans, reaching to help me regain my balance.

"Well, someone's practicing safe sex at least?" I offer, attempting to catch my breath and steady my pulse.

"Since when do you make jokes?" Rodney asks.

"Since when are your eyes blue?" I tease, clocking the new color contacts he's acquired since we last FaceTimed each other.

My best friend rolls his ocean eyes while straightening my beanie. "Promise me this won't change," he says, gesturing between the two of us. "I know you're about to be *a star* and everything." He makes little quotation marks with his gloved hands. Then soberness seeps into his eyes. "But promise me you'll remember this version of *you*." He taps my chest. "And take care of her too."

My eyes are stinging suddenly, and not just because it's seventeen degrees outside with a windchill of minus two. When I told my parents I was dropping out of Berklee, they cut me off. Not just financially, but entirely. Apart from a birthday card they still sent me last May, we haven't spoken in more than a year. And all the emails I've sent them with updates about my progress with music have gone unanswered. Even my short stint on *The Voice* barely registered a blip from them.

Rodney and his cousin Frank, along with a random crew member, were staged as my "family and friends" who watched from the wings during my televised audition. And when the performance resulted in a four-chair turn from the judges plus a spotlight the next morning on the *Today* show, only then did I get a snippy email from my mother wondering why she and Dad hadn't been mentioned on camera.

I was eliminated several weeks later at the start of the live performance rounds, and as I packed up my lonely hotel room, I could practically hear her voice in my head telling me *I told you so.* As for my dad, all I heard was what I've come to expect from him . . . radio silence. Somehow, that was worse.

Everyone needs someone in their corner. I'm lucky enough to have finally found two someones—Rodney and Elliot. And they're about to meet each other for the first time.

"Mark my words, Rod. *When* I become a star," I say, "I'll be taking care of *us.*"

WE FINALLY MAKE IT TO ELECTRIC LADY AND GET BUZZED IN BY security. Sonica greets us when we enter. Her shock of bleached blond hair, kaleidoscopic tattoos, and signature black lipstick pay perfect homage to the scores of punk and rock groups whose legendary music made these hallowed walls vibrate with energy. The place was founded by Jimi Hendrix in 1970 and has been a famed workshop for the likes of Stevie Wonder and David Bowie to Beyoncé and Jay Z.

By now I have been here so many times that Sonica recognizes me on sight. Still, I pinch myself each time I cross the threshold. But this time, when her eyes land on us, they dart around with a slight sense of panic.

"Ella! What a lovely surprise," she practically chirps with a quick recovery. "We weren't expecting you today." Her voice is a bit higher and thinner than I remember.

"Heeeyy, Sonica," I reply, keeping my words bright and steady, like I do this all the time. "I'd love you to meet my very best friend in the whole wide world, Rodney Allen Jenkins."

"Girl, you ain't have to give her my whole government name, did you?" he whispers in my ear as we approach her desk. He leans forward to shake her hand. "It's lovely to meet you."

Sonica gives Rodney a brief shake and a genuine smile while swiftly donning her headset and dialing a number. "One second," she says, winking. "Elliot's in with an artist. I'll see if he's got a break coming up in the session. In the meantime, how about we set you up in a private room?"

She must sense my unease at her suggestion because she adds, "If that's all right?"

"Ooooh, a *private* room," Rodney coos, with a subtle shoulder shimmy. "Don't threaten me with a good time."

At this point, the growing unease from Elliot's earlier unresponsiveness is full-fledged. I knew he was working today. When Elliot and I spoke this morning before Rodney's flight landed, he told me he'd be in the studio workshopping some arrangements for the songs he and I have been writing together and that he'd send a car to pick us up to join him later. I've been so excited for Rodney to finally see me in the booth with *the* Elliot Majors be-

hind the mixer. Finally, someone who was in my life before everything changed was going to witness me living the dream I'd been
talking up forever. But it seems like Elliot had other plans.

But for Rodney's sake, right now, I am a swan—calm up top,
but scrambling like hell with worry under the surface.

Once in the meeting room, Rodney and I preoccupy ourselves
with catching up on his dating life and the epiphany he's had
since pursuing a degree at Berklee in music business and management.

"So, turns out I don't think I want to be an executive after all,"
he tells me.

At this, my head tilts to the side like a confused puppy. "I'm
sorry. This coming from the guy who idolizes Clive Davis like
most people do Michael Jordan? I mean you've stalked clips and
photos from his pre-Grammy party every year since you were
eight."

"Oh, imma finish this degree and do all the internships, don't
get me wrong," he says. "But I'm starting to see that what's drawn
me to the industry, more than even the music, is just the open avenue for creative expression. And I'm into it in a big way. The photography, the fashion . . . I simply don't care as much about deals
and the contracts."

Watching him explain this is like watching the clouds break
after a storm. My friend is practically glowing with excitement,
and it's the brightest spot of this so far very dreary day. I'm about
to tell him how happy I am that he's found this new direction
when suddenly the door bursts open and in walks my very tardy
husband.

"I guess I'm here to meet the man of the hour," Elliot says, voice
booming as he enters the room. He carries along with him an
indica-laced aura and two men I've never met. Heading straight

for Rodney and drawing him into a hug, he nearly jumps upon spotting me next to him.

"Oh! There you are, babe," he says, before leaning in for a kiss. "Sorry, it took me a minute. Had a session run long. You tell your friend the good news?" I don't miss the faraway look in his eyes or the very concerned one in Rodney's.

"What news?" Rodney asks, trying to hold on to a precarious smile.

I smoke from time to time. It shouldn't be a crime. But then again, why do *I* feel like crying? Instead, I clear my throat and wrap my arm around my husband's waist. "Elliot and I—" I say, but then pause. And for some reason the words are jammed in my throat, like they've been dipped in concrete and I've got to force them out. "We . . . got married!"

Elliot's two friends start clapping him on the shoulder and dapping him up, and Rodney just stares at me in blank shock. But he must read my unspoken plea, because it only lasts for a second or two before the shade lifts, and gradually, he's smiling and cautiously congratulating us too. Then, as promised, Elliot brings us into the studio, where for the next four hours, he proceeds to dazzle us all with his virtuosic command of the soundboard.

"DON'T LOOK AT ME LIKE THAT," I TELL THE BACK OF THE DRIVer's seat of the sleek SUV that my new husband arranged to bring Rodney and me to "anywhere our hearts desired" after we left the studio. And while we're on our way to Sylvia's in Harlem—Rodney's pick—my best friend's eyes are currently piercing my profile with ice beams of judgment. And like a coward, I'm staring ahead, unable to meet his eyes for fear that doing so might threaten the last fragile shards of confidence I have left in my big decision.

"Look at you like what?" he responds softly, feigning ignorance as he turns back to his window.

A long, slow exhale whooshes out of me. "Don't look at me like I just got a face tattoo," I say. "I mean I get it. On the surface, this feels fast, I know. But there's so much more to Elliot. You just have to get to know him."

"Do you though?" he asks, and at this I turn to wordlessly stare at him in confusion. "Know him. Do you *really* know him?" Rodney clarifies.

I sit with Rodney's question for a minute, turning over the length of time I've "known" Elliot in my mind—roughly five months at this point—which isn't *so* far off from shotgun wedding territory that it won't continue to raise eyebrows as more of our loved ones, and the world, catch wind of it. But my parents got married after less than a year of knowing each other. And my grandparents had an even shorter runway than that. While I wouldn't consider either relationship to be enviable, they each stood the test of time.

"I don't fully know him yet," I admit. "But I think that it's impossible to truly know a person anyway until you've done some life with them. And that's all we're doing here, committing to doing life together, and learning about each other on the way." I can practically see the question churning in Rodney's mind: *Doing life together, is that what you'd call what I just witnessed at Electric Lady?* Because it's the same question on mine. But at this point I'm merely working my theory out loud, hoping it sounds as solid to Rodney as it does in my head and heart.

"But El, baby. Marriage is big. You couldn't have just . . . I don't know, moved in with the man?" he asks, and this is the moment the spark of hope that my best friend would cheer on my latest rash adventure begins to wither. It must be apparent on my face, too, because next, Rodney's rushing to walk it back. "Look. I'm wrong for that, okay?" he says, flustered. "Ignore me, please. Come what may, you've got this. You always do."

Then he grabs my hand on the middle seat, and our eyes meet as gradual smiles, mine tentative, his reassuring, reflect on each other's faces. "Besides, if he fucks it up, I know a guy."

18

Now

"HELLO." I SPEAK INTO the receiver, surprised at the steady resolve in my voice. When more than a year has passed since you last spoke to a certain someone on the phone, you start to wonder if perhaps you've forgotten how. But despite my efforts, silence greets me on the other end of the line.

"Hello?" I say again, confused and quietly regretting my decision to answer.

"H-hi." A response comes through finally. It's shaky and thin but unmistakable. A total shock to the system, hearing again the voice that once sang me to sleep with lullabies. The same one that eventually called me her greatest disappointment.

"I'm sorry, I—I guess I'm just shocked you actually picked up is all," my mother finally says.

I reply with a listless "Yeah," thinking of how I surprised myself, too, but not saying it.

A tension headache blooms at my temples, and I shift uncomfortably on the plush velvet accent chair in the quietly luxurious hotel room I've called home since moving out of the penthouse I once shared with my ex. It's past ten p.m. and I should be in bed. With a four a.m. call time, I'm already running on fumes. But I am getting divorced, and now the whole world knows. It feels like one of those moments in life when you pick up the phone simply because it's your mom who's calling. So this time, I did.

But now there's more silence—so still and prolonged that for a moment I wonder if the call dropped.

"So," she says, piercing through the quiet and making me jump. "Is it true? What I'm reading in the blogs about you and Elliot. He's divorcing you?"

I shouldn't be surprised she got straight to the point. No *how are you?* No *I'm sorry.* No, *I'm proud of you.* No *are you eating?* And I'm not surprised. But it's jarring each time I'm faced with this version of a mother that's so vastly different from the one I need in the moment. I swallow past the lump in my throat, the one that always forms when I think of her and all the ways things could be different for us.

"We are divorcing," I reply, angry at the stinging threat of tears behind my eyes and opting not to correct her framing. It was me who decided to leave Elliot. He'd have been content to keep our rings so long as I agreed to keep pretending everything was fine.

"I—I don't know what to say, Elladee," she replies. "Your father and I were hopeful this could be the year you finally gave us a grandchild. I know it's something Elliot wanted too."

At this, I nearly choke on my tongue. "Well," I say, with a puff of humorless laughter. "I'm sure the three of you can still accomplish that together if you *really* put your minds to it."

"This isn't funny, Elladee." The words drop like weights, like I'm a teenager again, being disciplined for missing curfew or failing a test. Except that's not what this is. This isn't Parenting 101. It's something else entirely.

"I'm sorry to keep disappointing you, Mother," I say. "But our relationship was toxic. He wasn't faithful. I wasn't happy."

"Please tell me you're not planning to drag this out and let things get messy, Elladee," she begs, sidestepping everything I just said. "I'm assuming there's a prenuptial agreement in place, and honestly, you owe that man. Who knows where you'd be right now if he hadn't taken a chance on you."

I can hardly believe my ears. But at the same time I can. After all, hers is the voice I hear whenever I doubt myself, or question my own instincts.

"Mother, I have to go," I say.

"Of course you do," she says bitingly. "Our first conversation in over a year and there you go, running away because I've told you the truth. *I'm* sorry I'm not one of those 'yes' people you're sur-rounded by all the time."

"Have a good night, Mother," I say before clicking off the line. Then I block her number. I'll probably unblock it tomorrow. But for tonight, it gives me peace knowing she can no longer invade my bubble.

IT'S POSSIBLE I'VE BECOME A CLICHÉ—THE FRAGILE POP STAR who's finally starting to crack under all the pressure.

After a decade in the business, I'm still waiting for that tough outer shell everyone says is coming. The one that's supposed to somehow shield me from the industry's sharp edges. But what they don't tell you is that it's the inside stuff that'll get to you first. Because whenever it's quiet and I can manage to sit still long enough, all the overwhelming fears that were embedded in me early on in the game start to compete for their turn at the mic. Is Elliot the only reason for my success? Would I have a career without him? Will I have one after him?

Eventually I reach my boiling point. I might get snippy or impatient with my team, then apologize profusely seconds later. Or I might pull another adolescent disappearing act. On the very rare and very private occasion, I might dissolve into a puddle of tears.

Apart from now, I actually can't remember the last time I let myself indulge in a really good cry. The kind that leaves you feeling dehydrated, puffy, and hoarse. At this rate I'll be all those things by tomorrow. Things I can't afford to be on *Good Morning America*. It's why I usually tend to avoid tears at all costs. But after pressing end on the call with my mother tonight it was pretty much a losing battle.

Most days I'm surrounded by people, a dozen or so of whom are at my beck and call. And if they aren't nearby, I can just ring them up. Like now, for instance, I could call up Rodney or Angelo. Chances are they'd catch the quiver in my voice and invite me on as third wheel for their date night. Or I could try to crash Sheryl's Sunday night family dinner. Or play the world's worst wing woman for Jamie out at the bars. But then I'd just be an extra in their lives, a seat filler. One who's liable to suck the air and attention out of the room the moment I step into it.

Nobody wants to attend the pity party for the girl who has it all anyway. So, I'll settle for alone. I'm headed to the en suite to fill up a hot bath when—

Ping!

A notification on my nightstand makes me jump. With my work phone on do not disturb and everyone with my private contact info otherwise occupied, I'd expected a quiet night of merlot and a moderate mental breakdown. But when the phone pings a second time, I jump to see who it is. Padding over to the nightstand, I pick up the phone and turn it over.

UNKNOWN: Don't cry. Shop girl.

I arch an eyebrow because only about a dozen people have this number. Then a chilling suspicion creeps in that maybe it got leaked on Reddit and I'm about to have an influx of prank calls and dick pics. Who on earth would be texting me a quote from *You've Got Mail* out of the blue? But despite the apparent risks, curiosity gets the best of me, and before I can stop myself, I'm typing a reply and pressing send.

ME: Who is this?

UNKNOWN: Shit. Sorry

UNKNOWN: It's Miles

UNKNOWN: Westbrook

My heartbeats gallop in my chest, like syncopated thunder. Biting my lip, I think of the headlines and the very real chance that this could be some prepubescent kid having a razz at me.

ME: Not buying without proof.

A minute later, a slightly grainy image that is unmistakably a selfie of Miles Westbrook comes through. In it he is wearing a plain white T-shirt with a thin silver chain around his neck. He makes eye contact with the lens and smiles while holding a Blu-ray copy of *You've Got Mail* with a Post-it note that reads *Hi, Ella!* stuck to the front of it.

He couldn't possibly know I was crying, but his timing *is* uncanny . . . perfect actually. Because I'm not anymore.

ME: Did you just send me a selfie?

UNKNOWN: Depends.

UNKNOWN: Did you like it?

A laugh bubbles up from my chest as I plop onto the bed and lean back against the headboard. This boy. This *man.* He's a complete surprise from one day to the next. And the worst part is that I have no idea what he wants from me. For all I know, he could be reaching out to express his deep regret for being in my video now that his face is on the landing page of every digital tabloid with spring training starting so soon and a lot of pressure to lead the Dodgers on a redemptive season—I might have spent some time reading up on Google in recent days.

ME: Miles. How did you get my number?

ME: And what exactly is happening here?

UNKNOWN: I thought that was obvious.

Nothing about Miles Westbrook is obvious. Except for the part where I'm painfully attracted to him. And the other part where that attraction could potentially spell a whole lot of heartache for me, and a major headache for both our teams.

UNKNOWN: I'm trying to flirt text with you.

UNKNOWN: Flext. If you will . . .

A flurry of questions bounce around in my head like . . . Did I just giggle? When did all my tears dry? What grown woman sits like this, curled up on a bed in a ball like a giddy schoolgirl grinning from ear to ear? While I'm in the middle of interrogating myself, a string of texts comes through from Miles.

UNKNOWN: Jamie gave me your number btw.

UNKNOWN: I hope that was okay.

UNKNOWN: I was thinking about you.

UNKNOWN: Quite a bit.

I sit frozen. Chewing on my manicure. The ability to think of words beyond *I was thinking about you* and *quite a bit* completely evaporates. I have a decision to make in this moment. A "red pill, blue pill" kind of thing. Sink or swim. I decide to jump.

ME: Me too.

Miles's text bubble pops up, does a little dance, then disappears again. Sweat has broken out at my temples and I am practically panting, in shock at what I've just admitted—and in writing. That's when the panic sets in. What if this *is* a scammer after all? What if that cute af selfie was a deepfake? What if screenshots of this conversation are going to be plastered all over the internet tomorrow? Before I can register the decision, let alone stop myself from doing it, I'm calling *Unknown*.

"H-hi, Ella." He answers on the first ring and his voice is like dark silk. Immediately, my pulse slows and my breathing calms.

"I . . . I'm sorry, I just, kinda panicked there for a second and called to make sure it was really you," I admit in a cluster of word vomit.

"It's okay," he says, laughing a little. "I probably should have done that to begin with. I just do better with texting sometimes for . . . reasons. I'm sure you understand."

"Oh!" My face drops to my hand. "Right. If you don't want to talk this way, it's fine I—"

"No! Don't get me wrong. I *want* to talk to you," he cuts in. "I *like* talking to you."

"Oh?" A warm feeling blooms in my chest. "I like talking to you. Too."

"Well, I actually reached out for a reason," he says. "I w-wanted to ask what you were doing next weekend?"

Absurdly, I'm grinning so wide my face hurts. "Are you asking me on a date, Miles?"

His laugh is a low rumble that makes my stomach flip. "Not exactly."

Grin be gone. "Ah," I say as my eyes slam shut and I ponder the physics of melting into oblivion.

"I mean. Not that I wouldn't love to take you out," Miles says in a rush. "I just f-figured . . . given everything going on in the press, you w-wouldn't be down for something so public right now?"

"Yes. That's right," I say, going along with his very sound, rational, *sane* train of thought. "There's a lot I have to work through right now, and it's all pretty complicated. So you're right, it wouldn't be a good time."

By now I've slid from the bed to the floor, where I lay prostrate with the phone propped against my head. I just basically asked myself out and turned myself down, and still, I have no idea why he's reached out to me.

There's a long stretch of awkward silence until Miles clears his throat. "Well, I'm hoping things aren't so complicated you wouldn't consider performing at this benefit I'm hosting next Saturday night at the Rainbow Room?" he asks in a rush. "It's for my foundation. I-if you'll be in N-New York still?"

I might be stunned speechless because Miles fills in the gap of my silence. "It's totally okay if you can't! I know you stay booked and busy. I just—"

"Miles," I cut in, smiling at how nervous he sounds. "I'll do it. Of course I will. I'm so far in your debt I could never tell you no."

"You can always tell me no, Ella," he says. "But I'm glad in this case you didn't. I can't wait to see you there."

It's quiet for a beat, and I can't tell if the conversation is over. If it *should* be over.

"So, where does one find a Blu-ray of *You've Got Mail* these days?" I end up asking, to test the waters and see if this has legs.

"Pfft! Amazon . . . duh," he says. We both laugh.

"And?" I add. "So what's the verdict? Did you fall under the spell of Tom Hanks's approachable wit and sarcasm? Or was it Meg Ryan's endearing sentimentality and charming cable knits that got you?"

"Honestly, it was Greg Kinnear that stole the show for me," he says. "Something about his complete lack of self-awareness really pulled at my heartstrings. And don't get me s-started on Parker Posey. She feisty!"

I'm not proud of the giggle that escapes me next. "I must say, Miles Westbrook. You are unexpected."

"Hopefully in a good way?" he asks.

"So far, I'd definitely say so," I admit.

We say our goodbyes, and after hanging up, it's a long while before I manage to pick myself up from the floor.

19

THE FIRST SONG I learned to sing was Whitney Houston's "I Wanna Dance with Somebody." I was three years old and hardly remember performing it at the 2000's Robinson family reunion. But ten years later, my mom signed up for Facebook and the amateur performance captured on video was one of her first uploads. It went viral among her Baldwin Hills circle of friends—in the same way video tours of the next-door neighbors' marble kitchen upgrades did.

With the memory so faint, that video serves as the only proof the performance ever happened. And I watch it still. Study it even. I was pitchy with the notes, and my articulation was muddy—what you'd expect from a toddler. But seconds into the grainy clip and it's clear to anyone watching that this little girl loves what she's doing. Like a sponge, she absorbs the limelight, channeling Whitney's every move from the flick of her tiny wrists to the arch of her shoulders, to the best of her little body's ability.

She's a performer.

So, when Angelo got a call from Miles's event coordinator

asking what number I was going to sing for the Evelyn Foundation benefit, the choice was obvious.

Deciding on a dress was a different story. The Glam Squad is back together again at my live-in hotel on the Upper West Side, and Rodney's currently holding up two contenders—both I'm on the fence about.

"The black one. Hands down," Sheryl says. "But only if you're really about that life and tryna get pregnant tonight." She sniggles while slicking my hair up into a high pony. "Otherwise, go with the red."

"Naaahhh," Jamie chimes in. "I say go with the red first. It'll remind him of the one you wore on the roof! Give 'im a little déjà vu." She winks and thrusts her hips suggestively.

The visual sends a subtle shudder through me, along with the memory of Miles's hips as they pressed mine against that brick wall. Although I'm tempted to want to jog *his* memory, I can tell by the way Rodney's mouth is twisted and his head's cocked to the side that he's not feeling either of these options.

Rodney rubs his neck and walks over to the rack of gowns, speaking as he goes, "Nice gowns. Beautiful gowns." He mumbles. "But I don't think we need you to sizzle tonight, boo." Pulling one off the rack, he turns back to face us. "I think we need you to sparkle."

The dress he's holding is a long sheath with thin straps and a high slit. The simple silhouette is cut from violet silk with elaborate beading that shimmers under the lights of my hotel room.

"Hmm," Jamie hums, twisting her mouth. "This one says Miss View Park 2023."

"Yeah," Sheryl adds. "For me, it's giving 'pop my cherry, it's prom night.'"

At this, Rodney cuts them a ferocious a look that says, *Damn it, I'll bite you.* I can't help but laugh, even though I think I'm kind of in love with this dress.

"Despite those very vivid descriptions, ladies, I think I disagree," I chime in. "This might be the one."

"Figures," Jamie and Sheryl both mumble in unison. Then they each stiffly return to their respective tasks. A quiet chill settles over the room and, with it, tension you could cut with safety scissors.

Rodney clears his throat. "Uhhh . . . y'all got a problem?"

A few seconds of tense silence pass before Jamie shrugs. "Not a *problem* like that . . . but we all know purple sparkles were *not* on the original mood board for tonight's look. But I'll just improvise the makeup, I guess," she mumbles.

"Mm-hmm," Sheryl adds, barely masking her irritation. "Typically *I* wouldn't pair an updo with that neckline either. But this pony is already snatched to high heaven, and let me tell you it's not budging." She makes a show of checking her watch. "A little late to switch gears now is all I'm saying."

I feel like a kid caught between the crosshairs of her parents' latest battle of wills. But even I know what's going on here is deeper than a dispute over a dress. For the first time in years, there is an elephant in the Glam Room.

"Okay, time-out," Rodney says, making a T with the blades of his palms. He straightens to his full height and adjusts the Fendi frames that balance elegantly on the bridge of his nose. "Last time I checked this was supposed to be the Dream Team, and I *never* had to worry about the three of us pulling a cohesive look together at the last minute. What's really going on?"

Jamie heaves a heavy sigh and makes direct eye contact with Sheryl, who drops her gaze to the floor before subtly giving her a nod of affirmation.

"Sheryl's quitting," Jamie says, voice slightly wobbly.

At this, the room seems to tilt, like I've been pushed off-balance. I look at Sheryl, and she's frozen like stone, still eyeing the floor. "You're not serious," I say, eyes scanning the room and locking with three very serious-looking faces. "What's happening?"

Sheryl clears her throat and finally meets my eyes. "I was going to come by next week and have a conversation with you," she says, her tone bleak.

"Wh-why?" I ask. "Are you unhappy? Is it the travel? The pay? Because whatever it is, you know I can make adjus—"

"Her husband is sick," Jamie says. And the words stop me in my tracks. Leaning back in my chair, I glance over at Rodney, who is shaking his head and mouthing the words *I didn't know*.

"We found out several weeks ago," Sheryl confesses. "And I just . . . I need to take some time. My family needs more from me than what I've been giving them while I'm here . . . with you."

Her words are a flashing yellow light, a signal to pause and really weigh the gravity of the moment. It's possible these past several weeks that I've been so caught up in the swirling storm of my own chaotic life I haven't stopped to really look at the state of things for the people surrounding me. "Sheryl, I'm so sorry. Why didn't you say anything?"

"Honey, I wish I'd known too," Rodney says, looking just about as deflated and bereft as I feel. Technically, as my glam coordinator, he's their boss. Having hired both of them on and being in charge with keeping the schedule and directing all the looks, he'd be the first to know of any personnel changes.

"Look," Jamie says, with her gaze directed at me. "And I'm telling you this as a real friend." Her tone is direct. But it lacks bite. Even so, I can tell I'm in for a read. "You're a *big* star and you've got *big* problems. But your problems aren't any bigger than ours. And lately it's started to feel that way. You and Rod have always been attached at the hip and in so deep with each other's lives, the dynamic can be a challenge. And with everything you've got going on with the divorce, I don't think Sheryl knew when the right time would be."

I sit with that. Let it really seep in. "I hear you. I get it," I say. Then I glance at Sheryl, whose eyes haven't left the floor. "Sheryl, can we please have that talk next week? And take all the time you need. *Anything* you need. It's yours, okay?"

She nods, then finally, she looks up at me with glassy eyes. "I know, girl. I know. And I was just playing before. The purple dress is fire."

"I'm still partial to the red," Jamie says. "But either way you're gonna be a knockout."

Rodney exhales loudly. "Woo, chile . . . y'all are gonna send me to an early grave, I swear."

Then he heads into the other room arm in arm with Sheryl with her head resting on his shoulder. The visual tugs at my chest. Jamie turns to follow them, and I gently touch her wrist.

"Hey," I say, to capture her attention. "I don't want to be that friend who just takes and takes in her relationships."

She stands there for a beat, regarding me with a deep emotion I can't quite name.

"You know, you don't only have Rodney in your corner, right?" she says. "I mean, I'm sure my time is coming when the rubber's gonna meet the road and I'm gonna need some reinforcements. And when that time comes, I'll be turning to y'all. I've been there before, and it *always* comes back around. But right now, I'm good. So what I'm saying is, you don't just have Rodney. You've got me too."

And for someone who feels lonely most days, even in crowded rooms, it's exactly what I need to hear.

COMING TO 30 ROCK HAS NEVER *NOT* MADE ME FEEL LIKE A total imposter. By now we've arrived, crowded together in the elevator, and are on our way up to the sixty-fifth floor for the Rainbow Room. This time feels just like the first time. Same old rain-slicked Forty-Ninth Street entrance. Same old butterflies wreaking havoc on my insides. It was almost seven years ago now that Elliot invited me to watch my first taping of *Saturday Night Live*. He was DJing a number for that week's featured musical guest, and he brought me along to watch from the wings.

The night has stuck with me as a first look behind a gilded curtain. Getting into the infamous and exclusive after-party with the cast was something Rodney and I had only dreamed of on late nights out in Boston, during our first weeks of freshman year. But that night, I got to live out those dreams and more—doing pickleback shots with Kenan Thompson and RuPaul, dancing on a table with Cara Delevingne, and somehow finding myself roped into an hour-long conversation on Italian neorealism with Alden Ehrenreich. Occupying even the smallest space on this ultra exclusive tapestry felt like reaching the summit of New York's celebrity culture.

But in hindsight, and with another half dozen *SNL* cast parties now under my belt, it was really just a slightly more sophisticated version of a frat party. The biggest distinction being that instead of jocks and legacy recruits, the crowd was more like a mixed bag of up-and-comers, offbeat creatives, and comedic legends sprinkled with some bona fide stars. Then of course there are the ones just lucky enough to score an invite, along for the wild ride.

Then, two years ago, I was asked to be the featured musical guest on *Saturday Night Live* myself. This, of course, being a major milestone in any recording artist's career, was a near out-of-body experience for me. Also, of course, Elliot and I had already started to show our cracks by then. So on the big night, he was not there watching from the wings.

Tonight, however, the butterflies have emerged for a different reason—one having to do with a certain six-foot-three-inch LA Dodger. In the days since Miles and I spoke on the phone, the sounds of his soft but deep voice, even the subtle riffs of his stammer, have all gone triple platinum in my mind.

I know there's a strong possibility that I won't even see the man tonight, and that if I do, it would be from across a crowded room. Not to mention the very likely prospect of him bringing a date—someone he wouldn't hesitate to be seen in public with because she doesn't have *all that stuff going on in the press right now.* Someone without my baggage. But the slightest chance we will get a moment to reconnect has sent me spinning with anticipation.

Ping!

The elevator doors glide open on the sixty-fifth floor, and Sanders leads me and Jamie out while Angelo and Rodney bring up the rear. They're all dressed to the nines in black-tie attire, just like the invitation requested. Sheryl's got the rest of the night off. I granted her an indefinite hiatus from the glam team so she can spend more time with family and support her husband through his treatment. Besides, I think between me, Rodney, Jamie, and a jar of edge control, we can maintain a sleek ponytail for one night.

A few steps into the hallway, we're met by a sharply dressed woman with a golden halo of curls. "Hello, Miss Simone," she says, before nodding to greet the rest of my team. "I'm Shelea Smith, Mr. Westbrook's event coordinator."

Next to her stands a man in a blue velvet tux. He steps forward to shake my hand. "And I'm Edward Yap, the hospitality director here at the Rainbow Room. It's an honor to have you with us to-night. May we show you to your dressing room?"

"So nice to meet you both," I say, giving them my most gracious smile. "But first, I'd really love to get a quick sound check in with my band . . . if that's okay?"

Ennio, my musical director, sent me a text while we were en route to let me know he and the rest of our six-piece ensemble had arrived and had already set up. We were up until the wee hours of the morning working on a special jazz arrangement of "I Wanna Dance with Somebody" and tonight, we'll perform it for the first time.

"Of course, Miss Simone. Right this way," Edward says.

He leads us into the ballroom, and when I step through the double doors and catch sight of my band members onstage, the nerves from before morph into excitement. This is the feeling I'm constantly chasing—like fairy dust dancing around me. The feeling that only takes hold when I'm onstage in front of a crowd whose applause makes me feel like I could fly if I wanted to.

Jamie takes my phone and clutch to head to the dressing room while Sanders goes to touch base with event security. Rodney and Angelo stay on to watch the sound check and take photos for my socials.

Once I've greeted everyone onstage and we're all situated, I give Ennio the customary nod, and he signals the band to begin. His opening chords on the piano give way to a seductively melodic acoustic guitar sound that wraps around the percussion section. I open my mouth to sing . . . and then we're off to the races.

"YOU'RE GONNA KNOCK 'EM OFF THEIR FEET," ANGELO SAYS, leaning close and looping my arm through his. We've just completed sound check, and after thanking the band, I hopped down from the stage to meet my boys.

Rodney joins me on the other side, and we snake through the tables, heading for the ballroom exit. "I think even Whitney felt that one," he says, and it gives me the best kind of satisfaction.

I want this performance to be special. Not just because an unspoken rule of show business is that you've got *no business* covering Whitney if you don't have the literal *and* figurative range, but because of what tonight means to Miles.

The Evelyn Foundation exists to carry out his grandmother's legacy. And as far as I can tell, Evelyn Garcia-Westbrook is the woman who made him the man he is today. She's the woman who showed Miles how to cut fabric on the bias and properly thread a sewing machine. And reading between the lines tells me she's the woman who's responsible for his kind, gentle presence.

He's never mentioned his own mom to me, and it hasn't felt right to look up what others have to say about her online. Heaven knows I duck and dodge any journalist looking to dig into *my* family background. But I get the feeling that the Evelyn Foundation's mission to support teen moms may have something to do with her.

"Sooo . . ." Rodney hums, drawing me out of my deep thoughts. "Has the man of the hour reached out at all since that late-night booty call?"

"For the fifty-leventh time, that's *not* what it was," I snap.

"Well, not with that attitude!" he replies, rearing his head back. "All depends on how you look at it, love."

"Oh, the plight . . ." Angelo deadpans, while scanning his emails.

I won't lie, the adrenaline rush from being onstage totally eclipsed any stress over not hearing from Miles, at least until Rodney mentioned him just now. With those familiar, tiny electric sparks coursing through my veins and my heart racing at the rhythm of the congas, I was squarely in my Ella-fierce zone.

But now, I'm replaying the too few times Miles and I were alone—out on the baseball diamond, backstage at the Grammys—and I'm wondering if we'll ever get the chance to be like that again.

"Ella." I hear my name in a dulcet baritone, and it makes me stop short. Rodney and Angelo follow suit, both dropping my arms when I turn in the direction of the sound.

What I find standing there leaves me speechless . . . it's Miles in a tux. And the view is decadent bordering on sinful. Like a cherry dipped in dark chocolate and dusted with gold flakes.

Sensing a sudden hot flash, I flap a palm in front of my face and clear my throat. "Oh hey, you!" I say, a bit too loud and a little wobbly. "Didn't think you'd be here so early."

Miles jabs a thumb over his shoulder. "I, uh . . . caught the end of your rehearsal and couldn't look away," he says. He swallows, and when his jaw clenches, I get a vivid flashback of that five-o'clock shadow gently scraping against my face and neck as he breathed against my skin under the rain.

Miles's eyes quickly scan me from head to toe—a cursory look, unlike those languid, thirsty glances on set that made me feel exposed but also desired. In only leggings and a zip up, I suppose my ensemble isn't quite *giving* what it needs to give at the moment.

"Oh, don't worry, I got the dress code memo," I say, barely masking how self-conscious I feel. "There's an actual gown I'm going to change into before . . . the *thing*. It's nicer than, well . . . this." I gesture toward my getup.

"And trust," Rodney chimes in, startling me because I'd honestly forgotten he was standing there, "it's a good one. *Very* expensive too. And on loan so . . ." Rodney points at Miles and mouths,

I'm watching you, and I wish I had something tiny and sharp to stab him with.

Miles laughs, rubbing his hands together and flashing his bright, sense-stealing smile. "Consider me properly warned. I'll be sure to keep my distance." At what must read like disappointment on my face, he rushes in with a save: "Or who knows . . . maybe we can behave ourselves long enough for one dance?"

"I think I'd like that," I say, shamelessly hoping he intends to follow through.

And I might be imagining this, but Rodney and Angelo seem to have disappeared, like they slowly backed away unnoticed to give us a moment of privacy.

"But for real though. I can't thank you enough for doing this," Miles says. "The band sounds amazing. And you . . . you're gonna make people fall in love tonight."

I thank him for the compliment. And when I turn to head for my dressing room, I can't help but wonder if maybe I already have.

20

TWO WHITE-GLOVED BUTLERS PART the main ballroom's double doors, revealing a view even more stunning than the one before. The space had been beautifully dressed when we arrived, but now that the sun has set, romantic uplighting casts a sapphire glow across the room. Lush ivory florals adorn every table as candles reflect off art deco windowpanes, which expose the glittering skyline. The entire ballroom has been transformed into a jewel box suspended high above the city.

It's finally showtime, which means the moment has come for my grand entrance. "Ladies and gentlemen, join me in welcoming the sensational, chart-topping, Grammy Award–winning recording star Ella Simone."

At the emcee's introduction, three hundred pairs of eyes shift their attention my way with a burst of applause. When the spotlight falls on me, Ennio takes his cue to play the lively opening chords on the piano. The crowd parts, marking my path toward the stage. I take a deep breath, raise my microphone, and sing the opening words . . . *Clock strikes upon the hour and the sun begins to fade . . .*

Despite the lyrics, I couldn't have possibly understood at three years old that beneath her electric smile, Whitney was singing about bone-deep longing. That the song was composed in major chords has always masked its subtle undertones of melancholy. But as those same melodies cascade from my lips, pictures flood my mind—memories from the last ten years intermixed with flashes of the past two weeks.

Images of all the nights I slept alone in the back of a crammed tour bus because Elliot chose last minute to fly private when I didn't want to break rapport with my band. Or weeks I'd spend roaming empty hallways in any number of his cavernous homes, or holed up in hotel rooms with service trays long gone cold— waiting for scraps of time we could spend together because when we did, it so often felt like magic. Like in our studio sessions where we'd spend hours on end refining a lyric or layering parts. But now I realize that even then, we were on opposite sides of the glass.

Suddenly, I've reached the center of the room as well as the pre-chorus. Scanning the crowd, I find Jamie swaying to the music while wrapped up in her date's arms. In the next moment, I make eye contact with Miles and am briefly held in place by the gravity of his stare.

It's possible I've never felt a song more intensely than the way I'm feeling this one now. *I want to dance with somebody. I want to feel the heat with somebody.* The words are simple and true, and they conjure images of the last time I danced with him and all the ways I want to do it again. Even if my baggage is too much of an obstacle for Miles to overcome in order to consider something as simple as taking me out on a date—right now, I don't even need that much.

Just a dance—a way to feel a little less lonely in all of this madness.

Because logically speaking, he's got spring training in just under two weeks. And I'm plotting a whole career rescue mission. So when it comes to a real relationship, I get it—ain't *nobody* got time for that.

But we have time for a dance.

We don't need to belong to each other, or make proclamations for the world to obsess over or rip apart. I've been there and done all of that. Seen it from every angle. And I'd rate the whole experience a whopping zero out of ten—would not recommend.

I ascend the stairs to join my band on the stage, and now it's time to *really* have some fun and let go. After attaching my mic on its stand, I spread my arms wide to support my diaphragm as I belt out the *big* note. *And when the night falls, my lonely heart calls . . .*

When my voice soars, the crowd cheers and my background singers come in strong with immaculate three-part harmony. I glance around to see each member of my band sitting squarely in the pocket, at the height of their game. It simply doesn't get better than moments like this—when that fairy dust kicks in, and suddenly, I'm flying again.

"THAT WAS ABSOLUTELY *SPECTACULAR!*" SHELEA SAYS, AFTER meeting me at the side of the stage. "I've never heard that rendition before—oh my god!" Her eyes widen with excitement. "Will there be a studio version on streaming?"

"First off, thank you!" I say, smiling politely while trying to catch my breath. "But this was just a special treat for everyone here tonight." I gesture toward the room, still buzzing from the performance.

"Well aren't we the lucky ones," she replies as she leads me through the main floor and guest tables, many of them still clapping and beaming. Some even filming me as we pass by.

Now that the performance is done, I am free to enjoy the night

with Jamie, her date, and the boys. For a ten-thousand-dollar do-
nation, I was able to secure us a small table that's been discreetly
situated by the windows with a breathtaking view of the Manhattan skyline.

"And here you are," Shelea says, once we arrive at the surprisingly empty table. "If you need anything at all, please don't hesitate
to have Angelo come find me. I hope you enjoy the night!"

"Oh!" I say, grabbing her attention before she leaves. "I'm sorry,
it's just . . . have you seen Angelo by the way? Or Rodney? Or Jamie, for that matter?" I ask, trying to mask my anxiety.

She smiles and points over her left shoulder toward the dance
floor. "I think they all got bitten by the love bug during your performance."

I crane my neck to find my friends wrapped in each other's arms,
mid spin in the center of the ballroom. The sight of it makes my
chest ache in a good way. All I've ever wanted for Rodney was for
him to find someone who recognized how much of a gem he truly
is. And that he's found it with Angelo, the best kind of person this
business has to offer, makes it even sweeter. As for Jamie, she's been
out playing the field for as long as I've known her—dodging fuck-
boys left and right. Marco, the guy she brought with her tonight,
seems like he *could* be another one. But, for her sake, I'll hold out
hope that he's a surprise. Only time will tell. And it always does.

Not wanting to interrupt my friends and their intimate moments on the dance floor, I opt to have a seat and nurse the glass
of bubbly that's just been poured for me by one of the white-gloved
waitstaff. People watching is a tried-and-true pastime of mine. So
it seems like an adequate way to busy myself until my friends return. That is, until one by one, I'm visited by guests who are intent
on telling me about my "inspired" performance and requesting
selfies or autographs in return.

After about the twentieth selfie, and my second glass of champagne, I decide to excuse myself from the table and go on a treasure hunt . . . for Miles Westbrook and that dance he promised me.

Rising from the table, I head toward the dance floor and begin to press through the bustling mix of bodies. The house band has taken the stage for the night and opted to play big band renditions of Top 40 hits, which have turned out to be real crowd-pleasers for a room that is full of millennial socialites and high-powered philanthropists. Overall, the vibe in here is far more freewheeling and fun than I'd expected for a two-thousand-dollar-a-plate celebrity fete for New York's upper crust.

The band makes a seamless transition out of Dua Lipa's "Dance the Night" into a cover of the Cure's "Lovesong," prompting everyone on the dance floor to grab someone and pull them close. As I am now even more keenly aware of my solo status, the search for Miles takes on renewed purpose. Then, suddenly, a sharp burst of laughter catches my attention from behind. When I turn to look, I spot his broad back and shoulders swaying to the music. And when a sultry flare of the saxophone floats across the room, with a slight turn and dip, Miles reveals his lucky dance partner. Her arms are draped around his neck as his hands rest at the middle of her back. She looks to be in her midforties, wearing a low-cut crimson gown that flatters her curves and shimmers under the lights. She also looks to be completely enamored and under his spell.

A well-adjusted person might take this opportunity to head to the bar for something dark and neat. Or she might steal off to a powder room where she'll take some deep breaths in, breathe the chaotic energy out, and return to the party to dance the night away with her friends. But I've never been credibly accused of being well-adjusted. So instead, I head for the exit.

SOMETHING ABOUT THE RAIN MAKES AN EMPTY HOTEL ROOM feel even lonelier. I'm standing at the window of my suite tracking the flowing streams on the glass, mulling over all the ways I played myself tonight. Half an hour ago I was in the middle of a very loud and crowded ballroom getting overly emotional over a pop song I might have taken a bit too seriously.

I cringe, thinking back on my performance. How it must have been dripping with such desperate innuendo—which clearly didn't land in the way I'd intended. If it had, maybe Miles would be spinning *me* around. Dipping *me* under the blue lights. And sure, I'm going through a public divorce. And there were a million eyeballs in there with just as many camera phones. And the man clearly doesn't want any drama—but, damn.

All I wanted was a dance.

I'm still in the dress. For some reason I haven't found it in me to take the thing off. Maybe it's because I feel like it's the kind of gown that deserved *more* out of tonight. Or maybe it's because I still haven't let go of the visions I'd played and replayed in my head of stumbling back to this very hotel with Miles, then watching as he slowly stripped it off me.

I shake the images away, walking over to the nightstand in search of the late-night room service menu. I'm willing to bet my current problems ain't nothin' a gourmet burger and a basket of waffle fries can't fix. I'm reaching for the room phone when my private cell starts to vibrate inside my clutch on the bed. Expecting a message from Angelo or Rodney wondering where I've scampered off to—even though this time I did text them and Sanders my exact plans and whereabouts—I quickly move to check it.

But when I swipe open the notification, a potent jolt of awareness zaps me upright, because it's a message from Miles instead.

MR. CURVEBALL: Are you still here?

I'm more than a little ashamed to admit the reasons why I left without saying goodbye—that I let my hopes get so out of pocket, I decided to pull another disappearing act the minute they were unexpectedly dashed. But I can't very well pretend I *didn't* flee the coop. So I opt for an honest, but short reply.

ME: No.

MR. CURVEBALL: Where'd you go?

MR. CURVEBALL: Can I come see you?

There's a flutter in my chest when I read his words, and my heart starts to race. *Giddy yet petrified* is the only way I can think to describe the feeling. It's been so long since I've done this, whatever *this* is. Given our track record, at this point he could be trying to chase me down with a paycheck for my performance— something I already assured Shelea was unnecessary.

ME: I'm in a suite at the Mandarin hotel.

ME: Ask for Lena Horne at the front desk. I'll let the concierge know to expect you.

MR. CURVEBALL: See you in twenty.

The minutes crawl like hours. I check the clock, and with five to spare, I consider changing out of the dress. But then I remember the two dozen or so tiny hooks up the back that made Rodney and Jamie curse the gods as they caged me in it, and I abandon the thought. Next thing I know the doorbell is ringing and I'm nearly leaping out of my skin.

When I open the latch and pull back the door, Miles is standing at the threshold with one arm braced on the frame. A smattering of raindrops dust his forehead and shoulders, and he's eyeing me with an intensity that makes my breath catch.

"Hey," he says, straightening to his full height and nearly filling the doorway. I notice his tux jacket neatly folded over one arm.

"Hey," I reply, while leaning on the door for much-needed support.

"Can I come in?" he asks.

Wordlessly, I nod and step back to let him enter the suite. Following Miles inside, I note the strong shape of his traps and deltoids as they move beneath the cream-colored cotton of his dress shirt. Somehow, even with a visitor, the room feels quieter in the stilted gaps of our conversation.

"So . . . can I get you a drink?" I ask, breaking the awkward silence. We've entered the sitting area, which seems to have shrunk down to the size of a matchbox.

Miles nods. "I'd love a water, thanks."

Get the man a water. *This* I can do. With measured steps I head over to the minibar, open the fridge, and grab a Voss bottle. All the while I am keenly aware of Miles's attention on my back, can practically feel the heat from his unbroken gaze. But when I turn around, he about-faces and starts to pace back and forth like a mass of pent-up energy. And I begin to wonder if he's as nervous as I am.

"Here you go," I say as I approach to hand over the bottle. When he takes it, our fingers brush just slightly, creating a tiny spark of electricity with the contact. Neither of us reacts.

With strong hands, hands marked by vein patterns I've basically memorized at this point, he unscrews the cap and takes a moderate sip.

Growing impatient and thoroughly confused, I cross my arms over my chest. "Can I ask you a question?" I say.

He swallows, and the moving contours of his neck nearly steal my focus. "Of course," he replies.

"Why did you come here?"

At this, he laughs but it's without humor—just a short, sharp fluttering exhale through smirking lips. "I think we both know the answer to that," he says, pinning me with his eyes.

Caught off guard by his directness, I straighten. "I think we both certainly do *not*."

Miles shrugs. "That's on me, then, for not making it clear." He sets the water down on a side table and steps closer to me as the tension blooms between us. "I'm here because I think you *want* me here . . . just as much as I want to be here."

Now it's my turn to laugh—more out of disbelief than anything else. "You're right. This is news to me, Miles. Because last I checked I had 'too much baggage' for you."

Miles shakes his head. "Since the day I met you," he says, stalking forward, "I have wanted to be alone with you." With his thumb and forefinger, he reaches up to loosen his bow tie. "When I said I think about you, I meant I do it all the time." The fabric unravels, falling loosely on either side of his neck.

My breathing is heavy as I back up toward the wall. At this moment, I can't think of anything I've wanted more than his answer to my next question. "What do you think about?" I ask, swallowing thickly and staring up into his dark eyes. "When you think about me?"

"I think about being with you like this," he says, gesturing between us. "Somewhere behind closed doors. With no one watching us. I wonder how you'd act around me, react *to* me, if you could really let go . . . if I could *help* you let go."

I swallow again. And this time I'm pretty sure he hears the gulp. Because for the first time since entering my suite, he smiles that broad smile that gets me weak in the knees. Miles is close enough to me now that my back is pressed against the wall, the same way it was that night on the roof. The night of our video shoot.

In tandem, our bodies expand and contract with the rhythm of our heavy breathing. "I think about that too," I say, almost panting.

"Yeah?" he asks, taking both hands and sliding them up my arms, leaving chills in their tracks.

"I want to know what it's like to let go with you," I confess on a shuddering breath.

Then the words "You never need to tell me twice" fall from his lips before they crash against mine.

21

OUR KISS IS INCENDIARY—A match struck in a room filled with kerosene. And I feel like I could stay this way forever, engulfed in this simmering desire and still somehow never be consumed. It may not be the first time we've touched and tasted and explored each other. But this time, it's not a performance. There are no cameras or onlookers. This time, it's only us and none of it's for show.

Miles interlaces our fingers and, raising our clasped hands above my head, he presses us hard against the wall. "Tell me if you want to stop." He breathes the command against my skin while pressing his thigh between my legs. As the movement presses me into him and braces me against the wall, I wonder how I could want anything in this moment but *more*.

Shaking my head, I am momentarily lost for words. Then finally a broken plea of "Please. Don't. Stop." cascades from my lips. I'd be embarrassed if I could find the will to care about anything outside of the press and pull of his full lips and the warm slide of his tongue.

We play like this for minutes, or hours, I really wouldn't know. Then just when my hands start to tingle from the loss of blood flow, Miles releases them, bringing his to either side of my face. I lean into his warm, rough touch and let my eyes flutter closed. Gripping his strong forearms, I savor this closeness—a feeling I haven't had in so long, if ever. I want to bask in this, let it seep into every pore. But I won't. Because if I allowed myself to dwell on this feeling for any longer, I'm certain I'd ruin the night by doing something absurd like crying.

"Hey," Miles says softly, which prompts me to open my eyes. When I do, I'm met with a look so fierce but tender it overwhelms me, like being pulled into the deep end. "Tonight, it's just us," he says. "Anything you want. Everything I've got, it's yours."

I might have just whimpered. I can't be sure, though, because every synapse in my brain, every nerve in my body, is firing at once. Still, by some stretch of magic, I manage to nod and say, "I'll hold you to that," in response, which solicits a rumbling chuckle from deep in his chest.

With one hand Miles traces a line from my clavicle to my breast, down my side and to my hip. As he ventures lower, the rough calluses of his palm scrape the exposed skin of my outer thigh until the top of the slit of my dress stops him. Not deterred, he dips farther beneath the fabric to grip my ass, pulling me tighter against him.

He throws his head back and groans, "You feel perfect in my hands," sending shivers down my back. I arch closer and get confirmation of just how good that feels for him.

Emboldened by his response, I grip his chin and draw him into another searing kiss. If all we did tonight was make out against this wall, I would not complain. An hour ago, the prospect of being here with him like this felt like nothing more than a fantasy.

But after having a taste of this, I don't just want more. I want the *everything* he promised.

Almost like he's read my mind, Miles firmly braces his hands on my hips and drops to the floor. I nearly black out with anticipation when he sweeps away the fabric of my dress. Then he traces his fingers downward from the tops of my thighs, setting me aflame as he goes. And when he reaches my ankles, he toys with a golden bracelet dangling over my left foot.

"I like this," Miles says, glancing up at me with sparkling eyes. "What's it for?"

"A sparrow," I tell him. "My first album."

"*Songbird*," he says.

Then he lifts my foot to his mouth, dropping a soft, warm kiss on the instep before repeating that kiss on the inside of my ankle and my calf, all the way up my shin. And since it's sensory overload, watching and feeling him at the same time, my head falls back against the wall, and my eyes slam shut.

He cups my knee and slides my leg over his right shoulder, and instinctively I drop my hands to his head for balance. Then he uses his teeth to tease away the thin layer of lace that covers the center of my arousal. I am bared to him, and he doesn't waste one second before giving me absolutely everything I want and more.

I'VE PRACTICALLY GNAWED OFF MY FIRST KNUCKLE TO AVOID getting us a noise violation from hotel security. So when Miles finally rises up from his knees, I'm equally relieved *and* bereft. But before I can even get my bearings, he spins me around to face the wall.

"Think I can get you naked the right way this time?" His question ghosts across the nape of my neck, making me shiver.

With my limp arms splayed against the wall and my legs like Jell-O from the residual pulses of pleasure Miles just wrung from me with his mouth, I'm absolutely no help.

"It's a lot of hooks. Just rip it," I sputter out.

"No, ma'am. Not this time," he says, with a smile I can hear even if I can't see it. "I'm already on Rodney's bad side."

I laugh and lean against his chest. I think back on that first night we met backstage as Miles peppers kisses from my cheek, down my neck, to my shoulder—he's driving me up the very wall I'm facing. And he hasn't stopped toiling with the tiny hooks.

After several hits and misses, he gets in the swing of things and deftly unlatches me one by one.

"Okay, if you lean forward just a bit, I think I'll have it," he says, with his voice steeped in concentration.

Smiling to myself, I do as he says, shimmying my ass a little as I go.

"Woman, I'm trying to focus," he playfully scolds me, and now we're both laughing. I love this—how we can flit from moments of breathless heat to breezy fun. "Oops. Got it!" he exclaims and I could cheer.

Still facing the wall, I flick off the shoulder straps, and the dress falls, pooling around my feet. I hear a sharp intake of breath from Miles and look over my shoulder, where I find his brow furrowed and his lower lip caught between his teeth as he takes in the view.

"Tell Rodney I loved the dress on you, but I liked it even more on the floor," he says.

I turn around, and under his intense stare, my breasts ache for his touch. But as much as I want him all over me again, the next time he touches me, I want us skin to skin. I step out of the circle of fabric at my feet and kick it to the side, then lean back against the wall and meet his eyes. He moves forward like he's ready to pounce, but I lift a finger and shake my head.

"Not so fast. Now it's your turn," I say. "Only fair."

A sly smirk curves the corner of his mouth, and I have to hold myself back from launching forward and tasting it. He slowly tugs his dress shirt from the top of his pants and unbuttons it from the bottom to the collar. Then, with one hand, he pulls his cotton undershirt over his head and my mouth goes slack. Clearly, not an ounce of energy was spared in crafting the muscular perfection of Miles Westbrook's shirtless form. I could skip pennies off his stomach, nickels off his pecs, and quarters off his arms. But when he steps out of his shoes and socks and undoes his belt buckle, I'm not thinking about loose change anymore. Because in one fell swoop, he rids himself of his briefs and pants and, no matter how many times I imagined this moment, I was not prepared for what he has going on under there.

"I'm dying over here," he says. "We good now?"

All I can do is nod, and in a flash, he is flush against me. Lifting me. Wrapping my legs around his waist. With only his hands under my ass, Miles supports my full weight while walking us toward the bedroom. When we reach the king-size bed, he lowers himself to the edge, bringing me down to straddle him. I reach up to loosen my ponytail—thanking the universe that I already took down the extra hairpieces Sheryl clipped in before he arrived. Then, with strong, purposeful movements, Miles reaches up to help free my hair from its constraints by massaging my scalp.

"I thought I'd memorized every angle of you by now," he says. "But this . . . this one is new. And I think it might be my favorite." Playfully, he nips at my neck and then covers the spot with a kiss. Smiling, I lean backward into his touch, an action he takes as an open invitation to taste the tips of my breasts.

There is a phenomenon in vocal performance called a poly-
phonic overtone. Achievable by only the most skilled of vocalists,
it's when you manipulate your vocal cords to produce the sound
of singing separate notes all at once. Lalah Hathaway comes to
mind when I think of it. I've never achieved such a feat, but if
there's anything that could make me come close, it might be the
sparks of pleasure spurred by Miles's touch. "God, that feels so
good," I manage to say. And in response, his erection jumps between us, which seems to momentarily ground us both.

"I didn't bring anything," Miles groans across my collarbone
before looking up at me with concern in his eyes. He threads his
fingers through the hair at the base of my neck. "That is . . . a-
assuming you want to keep going . . . and it's p-perfectly fine if you
don't." His words are now cautious and slow, eyes locked on mine.
"But if you do, do you have—"

"I've got condoms in the top drawer," I tell him, smiling down
from my perch on his lap. I tilt my head toward the nightstand.

With one strong arm wrapped around my waist, he scoots us
down the bed toward the headboard and leans me back so he can
reach for the drawer. After he retrieves the condom and takes care
of putting it on, I smooth my fingers over the scruff of his jaw in
my attempt to massage away the tension I just noticed take hold
there.

A line forms between his brows and he exhales heavily. "Con-
trary to what it might look like in the headlines, this"—he motions
between our chests with his index finger—"sharing this part of
myself with someone else has never been a small thing for me. I
get what you've been through. I wouldn't let myself be here with
you like this if I didn't. So I want you to know that I got my pre-
season physical last week and all my tests were clear."

With his disclosure, some unknown tension deep inside me

releases, causing me to sink further into him. "I've been tested since Elliot," I offer him in return. "And there hasn't been anyone since."

He kisses me again. First soft, then demanding. Then, slowly, we begin to grind our hips with rhythmic contrast, like a perfect duet. The feeling obliterates any thought of what might exist beyond his body and mine. Once we've rocked ourselves right to the edge of climax, Miles tilts us backward and gently lays me down on the bed.

With his hips settled between my thighs, he rests his forehead on mine. "Ella?" He breathes my name with almost reverent desperation, like the opening to a prayer.

"Yeah?" I reply, feeling half dazed, half crazy.

Miles smiles before he speaks, his dimples sinking deep into the hollows of his cheeks. "Can I have this dance?" he asks.

I nod. And now I'm grinning, too, like a fool. "I thought you'd never as—"

But I don't finish the sentence because with one purposeful thrust, he's inside me and slowly moving to music only we can hear. And as far as I'm concerned, the world stops for us. Maybe the universe too. In this moment there is only his body and mine, and the sounds of the breath between us. His groans and my gasps, and all the blissed-out proclamations you make to a person when it's never felt this good before.

22

MUST HAVE DONE SOMETHING sensational in a past life—
something that altered the course of history. Like, being The
First in the bloodline that spawned Beyoncé. Whatever it was, it's
paid me back in spades. Because I've just woken up to the view of
a sleeping Miles Westbrook, laying gloriously naked on his back,
with only a scrap of a white sheet strewn across his torso.

Begrudgingly, I tear my eyes away to glance at the nightstand
clock where I learn it is now nine in the morning. There was never
a question we'd both sleep in after all the energy we poured into
each other last night. When Miles said he'd give me *everything*, he
wasn't overpromising. The man put in *work*—didn't leave one angle, one position, or one inch of me unexplored.

But even after all that open discovery, I can't shake knowing
that there are still so many unknowns lingering between us—and
the one currently pressing through to the front of my mind is . . .
What changed for him? Between politely swerving me on the
phone to showing up at my hotel for a surprise session of mind-
and back-blowing sex, what changed? And if last night was truly

just about Miles helping me learn how to "let go" behind closed doors—his words not mine—now that his job is done, am I good with the simplicity of that? Or the potential *finality* of it?

It's a shame I was too emotionally and physically spent last night to think of drawing the curtains before Miles and I finally dozed off to sleep. Because the bright light of day has a way of making hasty decisions made under siege of heightened emotions feel like *big* mistakes. More than a year has passed since Elliot and I last slept together, and even longer still since he's felt like someone I could be completely vulnerable with.

After missing that closeness and connection for so long, last night was like a megadose. But any moment now Miles is going to wake up. And when he does, if he gets dressed and skips out the door, maybe never to be heard from again—I could be in for a serious case of withdrawal.

He stirs next to me now, grumbling in a groggy, almost-but-not-quite-roused-out-of-sleep way that is so utterly satisfying I want to commit the sound to my memory bank. On instinct, I move closer and he curls himself into me, laying his head across my chest and wrapping two strong arms around my waist. Then our legs lace together in a perfect knot, and I can't stop myself from lazily stroking his smooth, deep brown skin.

"Mmmm, what a way to wake up," he hums, in the kind of low rumble that *would* be soothing if I wasn't already preoccupied with running troubling scenarios through my mind. Like finding out he never actually got divorced and has a secret baby on the way, or maybe he has *nine* secret babies. I circle back to just how little I know about Miles Westbrook, apart from all the carnal things I learned last night.

Several seconds pass in silence as I brood, when Miles pops his head up to look at me. His brow is furrowed and his eyes search mine, as if checking to see if I'm still here. "Good morning," he says, and it's adorable the way his sleepy eyes are barely open.

I reach up with my thumbs to smooth away the tension in his forehead. But I'm afraid that if I open my mouth, something absurd will come out like *Have you ever thought about being a dad* or *What did last night mean for you?* So I simply wave at him—with my actual hand, then cover my face with that same hand because I have the awful feeling that I might start to stress cry for a second time this week.

"Uh-oh," he says, eyeing me warily and pushing up on his forearms until he's hovering above me. Our legs disentangle, and he notches himself between my open thighs. "What's going on inside that pretty head, baby girl?" he asks, gently pulling my hand away from my face.

I turn over to my stomach beneath him, and bury my face in the pillow. However, I should have thought that through. Because now I'm having vivid flashbacks of the last time we were in this exact position. Only we were sweat slicked and he was inside me, and now waves of residual pleasure begin to shoot to my core. I flip back over, closing my eyes to avoid being sidetracked by his face and chest and arms in the morning light.

With a grimace, I confess, "I'm thinking maybe we should talk about last night?" Then, one by one, I peel each eye open to gauge his reaction.

Miles simply flops back down on his side, propping his head up on his hand. The bulge of his bicep makes me want to bite it, but I swat away the intrusive thought. "We could do that. Or . . ." he says, reaching for my waist and pulling me into him, "we could talk about other things."

This makes me instantly tense. "Things like what?" I ask.

"Things like . . . how do you like your coffee?" While he talks, he's lazily tracing shapes on the surface of my back. And the farther down he goes, the more my muscles relax. "And other things like . . . what are we going to get for breakfast? And what are you doing for the rest of today? Or the rest of the week?" When he's done speaking, he squeezes my ass and gives it a little smack.

"Huh," I say, mostly to myself because I am utterly charmed but also still deeply confused.

"Hey, what's up?" he asks, taking his own turn at smoothing the worry lines out of my forehead. But when I don't quickly respond, he drops his hand. "Sorry, did you need me to head out?"

At this I straighten and grasp his hand again. "No! No. I don't want you to leave. I just . . ." An exhale. "A week ago, when you got my number and reached out, I thought you were asking me on a date, but you mentioned the bad press I've been getting and—"

I trail off, noticing the exact moment it dawns on him, the reason why I'm so out of sorts at his sudden changeup. I wait for a beat to gauge his response. His head tips back, and he pinches the bridge of his nose.

When he looks at me again, his eyes are clear and sincere. "Would you believe me if I told you I *did* get a little spooked by the headlines about you and Elliot? As you know, I've been dragged over the coals in the media this past year, and it's affected my team, my game," he admits. "So, when you asked me that question, I guess I sort of panicked and fumbled you in the worst possible way?"

I'm flooded with a sense of relief at his bare honesty. It's something I never had with Elliot, even when I was naive enough to believe that I did. In the early days, before I knew the magnitude of all his little evasions, I could somehow always sense his absence of truth, even when I had no proof of the lies. It was intuition. But hearing the truth from someone I'm only starting to know feels really good after so much time spent living with those lies.

"Of course I understand all of that," I tell Miles. "I mean, you said as much on the phone. And I get it, especially after what happened with your ex." And now I take a deep breath, because the *big* question is next. "I don't blame you *at all* for being anxious about my drama. But if that's the case, then what was last night?"

He sighs and nods his head. "Last night was me going about this all the way backward," he admits, pulling me closer. "And if it's not already obvious, I'm *really* into you. I don't know what that means or what it even looks like with the season starting and with everything you're going through. But if I can, I *do* want to get to know you more. I just hope you're not regretting what we did though? Even if we rushed it a little. Because I'm not."

I shake my head. "No, not at all."

"Good," he says. "Because I was thinking maybe we could . . . do it again?"

WE STUMBLE OUT OF THE SHOWER AND TAKE TURNS TYING each other into the Mandarin's branded bathrobes. When I cinch Miles's belt, he looks back at himself in the mirror and clears his throat. "Think this one's a little short on me," he says. "Gonna have my goodies on full display."

Laughing, I reach around and give him a squeeze. "That was kind of my plan." He grabs me and starts nipping at my neck, when a knock at the door to my suite interrupts us.

"Probably room service," I say, before heading to check. Leaving Miles in the bathroom, I toe on my slippers and pad toward the door, stretching my arms as I go. It's been a long time since I've had a purely lazy morning with nothing on my schedule. With a twenty-one-city tour kicking off in late summer, my last under contract with Onyx Records, I'll be starting rehearsals in a few weeks. So I need to savor every idle moment I have left while I possibly can.

THE PANCAKES WE ORDERED ARRIVE IN A GLORIOUS STACK, topped with berries and dusted with powdered sugar. I'm just about to pour the full contents of one of the little mason jars of maple syrup over the top of them when my phone begins to buzz across the room.

Immediately recognizing the haptic pattern, I deflate. "It's work," I tell Miles with a pout.

He quickly rises from his seat. "Do you need me to—"

I smile and gesture for him to sit by raising a hand. Then, rounding our table, I stop and bend down to kiss him on the lips. He cups the back of my knee with his warm palm, and it's these kinds of casual, intimate touches a girl could become addicted to. I'm tempted to ignore the constant buzzing, but reluctantly I pull myself away and head over to my nightstand. When I answer the phone, it's Angelo.

"Hey, Lo, everything all right?" I ask.

"How soon can you get to Steps?" As usual, he sounds like he's briskly making his way to a *very* important engagement.

I glance over at Miles, who's got his back to me now, having just answered a call of his own. "Uh . . . in theory I could be there in half an hour. But I'm *actually* a bit tied up this morning."

"Well, is there any way you can *un*tie up yourself? It's kind of pressing," he adds. "Listen. I just got word that the label's moving the tour up by adding fifteen new dates starting in June."

"That's almost two months ahead of schedule!" I nearly shout. Then, looking over at Miles, I see I've drawn his attention—and by the creases in his forehead, his concern too. He's still on his call, so I give him a thumbs-up to signal all is well. Speaking lower, I tell Angelo, "I guess it wouldn't be Onyx Records if I wasn't getting blindsided left and right."

"Well, naturally, there's more," he says. "Fatima's holding dance auditions today, and she's very firmly *requesting* your presence. Something about needing to get a vibe check from you."

At this, I grimace. Fatima's worked with me since my very first tour. And as one of the industry's most dynamic and sought-after choreographers, she is *not* to be played with. So as much as I'd like to blow off this "request" and veg out in my robe with Miles all day, or to concoct ways of disguising ourselves so we can traipse around the city for real this time, I'm an artist first, before anything else.

I end the call with Angelo around the same time Miles wraps up his.

"Let me guess, you also need to go?" he asks, looking about as dejected as I feel.

I nod, before catching the nuance of what he's just said. I stop short. "Same for you?"

"Too good to be true, huh?" He shrugs as he walks over to wrap strong hands around my waist and press his forehead against mine.

23

THE HALLS OF STEPS on Broadway are alive with the sound of music. I am slinking down one of them toward Fatima's auditions in studio three, as Tchaikovsky, Gershwin, and Timbaland each take their turn enveloping me with their signature vibrant cadences. This glorious sound bath is almost transportive enough to help me forget I've just said goodbye to Miles without knowing when I'll see him again.

I have spent most of the hour that's passed since we parted ways at the hotel replaying moments of our stolen night together. And I can still feel the fiery imprints of every touch, like phantom pangs of longing I can't quite shake. Like a song on loop in my mind, I repeat the sounding pleasure and release. I feel it all, just as clearly as the heavy bass that rocks the walls of the dance studio.

A buzz at my hip jolts me out of this waking dream, and glancing at my phone, I find a text from Jamie: Pinch hitting for Rod today. Be there in five. I smile at her text but roll my eyes too.

Since my mini meltdown before the video shoot and last night's four-way heart-to-heart ahead of the gala, Rod and Jamie seem convinced I'm in need of near-constant emotional support. And while they're not wrong, I don't want them to feel like they have to babysit me. Even if it's cute seeing them tag team like this.

Rodney called fifteen minutes ago to tell me he got tied up and wouldn't be able to make it to the auditions. Apparently, he'd received a last-minute invitation to Kleinfeld's for Angelo's sister's bridal appointment and saw it as a perfect opportunity to put his skills to use in order to win over his new love's family. I could only agree that it would be a *much* better use of his time. I stop in my tracks, though, when I realize the sudden switch just made today a bit more complex. Rodney may be my best and oldest friend, but where he might need a thing or two spelled out for him, *nothing* gets past Jamie. Now, I'll have to find a way to keep what Miles and I did last night under wraps from my *very* nosy and *very* observant girlfriend. And, frankly, I may not be cut out for this.

As I get closer to studio three, Fatima's voice calls out the steps to the audition routine, and the energy of the moment sends my heartbeats into overdrive. It sinks in that this may be my last tour as an artist signed with Onyx Records. And if Janet can't find a way to get me out of the predatory noncompete terms in my current contract, this could very well be the last album I tour with for a long time—possibly ever. The very notion is sharp and unrelenting, and all the more reason for me to savor every moment of today's audition.

"And one, and two, and three, and four. Five, six, seven, eight." I hear Fatima count out the choreography, along with the swishes and swoops of bodies moving through the air and heels turning on marley flooring. "And boom and crack, and shake, shake, shake.

Drop it low. Knees to the floor. And swoop. And swish. And crawl, crawl, crawl. Now toss the hair, toss the hair. Then roll it to the top. And pump it once. Pump it twice. Now move it to the center and melt . . ."

I reach the window to the studio for the final eight-count of Fatima's combination, just in time to notice the *interesting*, for lack of a better word, direction she seems to have taken with the choreography. She's selected a deep cut from my sophomore album called "Just One More Night" as the audition piece—it's an upbeat track with instrumentation that screams of Elliot's heavy disco influence. The lyrics are pure desperation, like soul cries from one lover to another who went away too soon. But the dancing seems to communicate something else entirely. Something that, dare I say, you might find in a TikTok challenge?

"Yes! Dancers! I need you to bring it just like that when Ella Simone comes in. Now one more time from the top, let's go!" Fatima's voice filters out into the hall to where I'm standing, or hiding, more precisely. I like to get my first look at the dancers from the shadows, before they know I'm watching. My presence almost always alters the vibe at an audition. Sometimes for better, but usually for worse. Some dancers thrive under the pressure of seeing the artist in the room, while others stiffen or wilt under the raised stakes. But in those few moments before I enter, after the muscle memory sets in and the true artistry starts to take flight—those are the moments I feast on.

But this time, something here feels very off.

"Fancy meeting you here." The words, spoken from behind, make me jump and flail and nearly bang my head against the studio door. "Gosh, I know you're happy it's me and not Rod, but no need to damage property," Jamie says flatly but with a twinkle in her eye that gives away what an unserious person she is.

Rolling my own eyes, I pull her into a hug. "Nice of you to finally show up," I tease.

"Given that I learned of this less than an hour ago, I'd say my response time is on point," she volleys back.

"Touché," I concede. "Shall we?" I reach for the door handle, and we enter just as Fatima's given everyone a five-minute water break.

When my choreographer spots us, she bounds our way. And Fatima is a sight to behold, practically floating across the studio in billowing sarouel pants and a loose-fitting halter top. As she draws closer, I notice her familiar mahogany skin glowing with the slightest sheen of sweat and am once again struck by her sage green eyes, which match the charm that dangles from her gold septum piercing. We greet with a tight hug.

"You made it!" she exclaims. Then in a hushed tone as her eyes dart around us, she says, "I'm so glad, you have no idea."

I glance at Jamie to see if she's catching the same *off* vibes that are pinging my radar. "Of course, I wouldn't miss it for anything," I lie, because I can think of one thing I'd miss this for, and he's on his way to the airport right about now. "How's everything going?" I ask.

As if searching for a hidden camera, Fatima's eyes scan the studio before landing back on mine, and my suspicions from a moment ago double in intensity. "So, listen, I've received some . . . 'direction' we'll call it, from marketing at the label that's . . ." She pauses, and I can sense emotion welling behind her eyes. "Look, if I thought for a second that this was your call, I wouldn't be bringing this up to you at all. But when I saw the email, it didn't sit well with my spirit. That's all I can say," she eventually gets out.

"Can you . . . can you show us this email?" Jamie asks. And thank goodness for her, because I've apparently lost the ability to speak due to the steam spewing from my ears.

Fatima brandishes a phone from her pants pocket and swipes open the email in question. Jamie and I crowd in on either side of her so we can all read it together.

From: lydia.caplin@onyxrecords.com
To: fatima4lyfe@gmail.com

Subject: Ella Simone—Tour 2024

Fatima—we're so excited to learn you've signed on as dance director for another tour with Ms. Simone. I know you're working with the promoters on all the logistics, but as you prep for auditions, I wanted to pass on some of the feedback that marketing has for Ella ahead of this tour. Full disclosure, the dept is concerned the music this time around may need a boost from the visuals. That's where we think you'll be clutch! We're really hoping for a punchy new look/vibe for these shows, which as you know, go hand in hand with album sales.

To put it plainly, we'd love to see viral dance challenges come out of this tour. We're talking kids in the audience recording the show and posting clips in real time. We're talking kids in their high school hallways shouting "hit that," then Ella's song comes on. Can you imagine how major that could be? The worry is, we won't get there if we don't change things up—sexify things a bit. Bring a little shock to the system. Think of Miley's Bangerz era. I think this is clear but feel free to give me a ring if you need some clarification.

Lydia Caplin
Marketing, Talent & Publicity
Onyx Records

"Gah! Could that have been any longer? Talk about saying a lot and nothing at the same time." Jamie scoffs. "At least this explains the 'pump it once, pump it twice' I heard out in the hallway."

Fatima looks at me with tears streaking her cheeks, and this is when I realize how deeply troubled she is by this. And damn, I was not prepared to walk into such an emotionally charged environment today.

"I'm just trying to give them what they want," she says, voice wobbly, "but, girl, my heart isn't in it. I can't create like this." She whispers the last part as her shoulders begin to shake.

"Oh, honey, no!" I tell her, placing a hand on one of her quivering shoulders as I glance over at Jamie, panicked. My emotionally stunted, "no help" friend simply shrugs and turns her face to the ceiling.

"I'm sorry, it's just, I didn't want to have to show you that email. But how else could I unburden myself of this load?" she asks, and Jamie's eyes lock with mine and go wide. If I could shush her facial expressions, I would. Fatima presses on. "I just, felt so in tune with this album. I mean, I pressed play and I instantly saw the movement and the timing in my head. Then they throw this curveball . . . I repeat, I cannot create like this, my love."

After drawing in one slow, deep breath and exhaling steadily, I say, "So, here's what we do . . . absolutely nothing."

Both Fatima and Jamie stare at me like I've sprouted antlers. Undeterred, I continue, "We stick to your original plan for the choreography and we say fuck 'em!"

"Okay, great!" she says, without skipping a beat. "But there's one issue with that . . . I don't want to get fired." Understandably, her voice drops to a more serious tone.

"Well, technically, Onyx Records didn't hire you," I tell her. "The tour promoters did. So, if the label has an issue with this, they can talk to me."

At the sudden reassurance of her job, and the reinstitution of her creative license, Fatima perks up real quick. After blowing me a kiss, she turns back to the room.

"All right, dancers! Shoes off. Let's feel the floor under our feet. We're going to change things up a bit after I introduce you all to some special folks who've just joined us!"

And now, it's time to have some fun.

ALL IN ALL, WE SPENT TWO HOURS AT THE AUDITION. BY THE end, four women and two men were selected to join us on tour later this summer. Apart from how things started, it was a productive day. So after we left Steps, Jamie and I decided to indulge in a little retail therapy.

"Hello, ladies, welcome to Gucci," the salesman greets us upon entry at the flagship Fifth Avenue store.

"You had a birthday last week," I say, with the intention of offering to purchase her anything her heart desires. But I'm stalled from making the offer when Jamie cuts her eyes at me as if I've just accused her of high crimes.

"Shhh!!" Her eyes dart around the store. "That's nobody's business," she hisses at me.

I roll mine. "Jamie, you're thirty-five, not a hundred."

At my mention of her age, Jamie's face goes blank. Then she turns and stalks toward the exit. I skip to catch up with her and gently tug her sleeve, all the while clocking the salesperson whose eyes haven't left our spot. "Hey," I say softly. "I'm sorry, I didn't . . . mean to strike a nerve."

Jamie slowly turns with her face in an exaggerated pout. She shrugs me off. "It's fine," she says unconvincingly, "nothing that a Marmont mini in white can't fix." Her eyes cut to the left, where a stack of chevron leather cross-body bags with golden-chained straps strike a bold presence.

Sighing I say, "I was going to say," then I drop my voice to a whisper. "Because you had a birthday, today's haul is on me."

"Well, when you put it that way." At this, she perks up, and I look forward to finally enjoying some shopping.

"This green would look better on you," I tell Jamie through the shared wall of our changing room. I open the curtain slightly to ask the salesperson to pass the garment over to my friend. A few moments later, we both emerge from our stalls looking somewhat ridiculous in items from Gucci's spring ready-to-wear line.

"My legs are too short for pants like these," Jamie laments.

"And I don't have the shoulders to pull off this neckline," I surmise by scrutinizing myself in the mirror. When my eyes flit about two feet over, I find Jamie *also* scrutinizing my reflection. "What's up? Something in my teeth?"

"Oh no," she says. "Nothing like that. I'm just . . . wondering how you're doing. Divorce is hard, you know?"

And this is the part where I remember that of all the people close to me, Jamie's the one who's experienced what I'm going through. Only she did it with a kid—something I can't imagine. Her question makes me jumpy all of a sudden, like answering it will expose me to the elements. I mean sure, I had sex last night and it completely rocked my world. But I also nearly fell apart this morning out of fear of abandonment, which is far too much responsibility to rest on Miles's shoulders at this point. So, these conflicting emotions are clearly the explosive residue of the battle that was my failed marriage.

"It's fine," I say, shocked to find myself on the brink of tears. "It's just . . . here I am dealing with all these broken pieces, of me, of my life. All these questions I'll never get the answers to. And

the one thing I want, that I never got and probably never will . . .
is just an apology. How can a marriage end and no one say sorry?
If it's going to hurt this bad, then *someone* ought to be sorry." I'm
full-on crying now. By the looks of it, the salesperson is silently
wishing they could kick us out. But I think they may recognize
me, and therefore they've decided better of it.

Jamie doesn't hug me, and that's okay. It's not her thing. But she
does step closer, her arm within a few inches of mine—and still,
we're seeing each other in the mirror. "You can't wait for sorry,
girl," she says, her voice soft and low. "If he was sorry, he would
have changed."

At this, a full sob breaks free. And then she does put her arm
around me, albeit awkwardly. "I know it sounds like I'm being
harsh, but I'm only speaking from experience," she says. "I spent
years accepting 'sorries' from Milo's dad only for him to turn right
back around and make a fool out of me over and over again. Eventually, I realized that when someone is truly remorseful about the
way they've treated you, their *actions* change. Saying 'sorry' is like
putting a Band-Aid on a bullet wound and expecting it to heal
without any other interventions."

The imagery of what she's just said quells the tears. I'm about
to thank Jamie for her sage, if harsh, wisdom when—

"Excuse me, ladies," the salesperson interrupts our overly emotional shopping experience. "Could I interest you both in a glass
of champagne? Seems like it might . . . help."

"I'M SORRY, MISS SIMONE, YOUR ACCOUNT AT THE STORE HAS
been closed as of two weeks ago. We can't process these purchases
without a credit card," the sales associate at the register, whose

name is Kevin, according to the gold plate that's fixed to his lapel, chirps at a volume too loud for my liking.

"I'm sorry, there must be some mistake," I say, trying to keep my voice low and my tone neutral. "Can you check again?"

Kevin hesitates, opening his mouth, possibly to object when—

"At least help us out and tell her who authorized the closure," Jamie cuts in, with enough sass to send Kevin's dubious eyeballs back to his computer screen.

His mounting unease with our situation is evident. But, ever the professional, Kevin proceeds to dutifully tap on his keyboard in search of the answer. After a few seconds, his eyes flit up to mine with an emotion that resembles nothing short of pity—and I want to evaporate. He clears his throat, eyes darting about the store, before speaking in a low whisper. "It appears that the request was made on behalf of Mr. Elliot Majors, ma'am."

Next to me, there's a barely audible gasp. It's Jamie. I turn to see her mouth wide open.

"That petty little bitch," Jamie hisses. "Honestly, I'm impressed. Pissed. But impressed, no less."

It's a good thing my friend can talk, because I am internally seething—alarm bells sounding in my mind. If ditching me at the Grammys was a declaration of war, then this? This is the launching of a thousand ships. You don't leave a woman stranded at a cash register with a rack of clothes and no way to pay. This is Gucci, not Burlington. There is no layaway.

"So, um." Kevin proceeds with caution, likely out of deference to our waning dignity. "As mentioned, we will need a credit card to complete your purchase today." He clears his throat.

I stand motionless. Speechless too. Likely with steam emanating from my ears. All I have is cash, and not nearly enough to cover our total. At my rescue, Jamie leaps into action, digging in her purse to retrieve her credit card.

"Here," she says, handing the plastic rectangle over to Kevin. "No, wait." She abruptly snatches it back from him before digging in her wallet to brandish another one. "Better if we use this one." She offers him a tight grin before turning to me with a shrug. I could implode.

And just before Kevin is about to swipe . . . "Wait!" Jamie exclaims. And the poor man looks like he's about to cry. "My bad, it's just . . . I get better rewards through Chase," she explains. "Here you go." She hands him her third and final card. He holds it in the air with his eyebrows raised as if to say, *You sure this time?*

"Swipe it, dude," Jamie sharply demands, and Kevin almost jumps.

WE BURST THROUGH GUCCI'S DOUBLE DOOR EXIT ONTO THE pavement of Fifth Avenue, where a strong gust of wind nearly blows our bags away. Scrambling to collect ourselves and our things, Jamie and I end up standing face-to-face and eye to eye. With anyone else, I might cry right now—out of humiliation, disgust, or just pure incandescent anger. But with Jamie, it seems the only right response to this moment is laughter. I crack first when a chuckle bubbles up from my chest, splitting my lips apart until my cheeks hurt from the stretch. She follows almost instantly, and then we're both doubled over on the sidewalk, probably giving passersby cause for alarm.

"Bitch! Did you see his face when you asked him to check again?" Jamie guffaws. "He was *this* close to waving over security," she sputters, attempting to catch her breath. "Elliot almost got us bounced out of Gucci!"

"*We* almost got us bounced out of Gucci before Elliot did," I say, "Remind me we can't shop together. We're a liability."

"And to think, you're even on a Gucci billboard!" Jamie shouts.

She's right. I'd forgotten about that. In fact, it's probably why Elliot did this in the first place. He always resented being upstaged. When we regain our composure, we straighten our bags and link arms as we saunter down Fifth Avenue into the sunset.

"Happy belated birthday, by the way," I tell Jamie. "I'll pay you back as soon as I get to my hotel."

"Oh, no rush," she replies. "I know you're good for it. And if not, I know where you live."

At that, I chuckle. "So about those credit cards . . . How many do you have, exactly?"

"Enough to make it work," she says. And then after a beat, she repeats, "Enough to make it work."

24

We can't plan life. All we can do is be available for it.

Lauryn Hill

Two weeks later

Mr. Curveball: Voice Notes Sent:
March 14, 2024 8:15 p.m.

"Hey, Ella . . . I've been dying to get you on the phone but with our s-schedules so out of sync since New York, I thought I'd just record myself talking and send it your way. I considered writing you, but then I remembered how much I hate emails. Like, d-despise them. My inbox is always overflowing with travel schedules or deal memos and things like that. I'm s-sure I wouldn't hate getting an email from you . . . but I would rather hear your voice. Anyway, I was just over here wondering about your day and how it went. I was also thinking about how much I wish we could have stayed in that hotel room a little longer.

"I recorded that message probably ten times

before I hit send. S-so, I hope this take was the best."

Me: Voice Notes Sent:
March 15, 2024 12:01 p.m.

"First of all, I'll offer my apologies in advance if this comes out like complete word salad—I am running on three hours of sleep. But I did watch your game today, and you won! I'll admit that I have never been more drawn to a little patch of raised dirt in my life. I couldn't take my eyes off you. Apart from that, I was completely lost for about eighty percent of the game.

"But after it was over, I did find this Baseball 101 YouTube channel that's run by a former pro turned minor league coach, and I subscribed. I've already seen enough to know that this might be the most complicated sport ever dreamed up. I'm gonna have to take notes if I want any of it to stick.

"Also, I guess I'll tell you now that after we met at the stadium that night, I ordered a biography of Jackie Robinson and last week, I started reading a little of it each night before bed. Soooo yeah . . . that's how my day was, apart from several hours of grueling rehearsals. I did catch a second wind, though, when I saw your voice messages. So, please keep these coming? I always want to hear from you, even if we can't find time to talk on the phone . . .

"By the way, how's your arm feeling? It looked like you strained something in the last inning?

"Okay. Last one, I swear! I just wanted to say that I think I'd sleep better with you in my bed. Can we run that back sometime?"

Mr. Curveball: Voice Notes Sent:
March 20, 2024 9:00 a.m.

"I will gladly come to your bed. Anytime. Anyplace. If I can get to you, I'm there. Only I can't promise you more sleep.

"I'm interested in that little n-notebook of yours, Dream Girl. I want to know what baseball facts s-strike you as worthy of writing down. By the way, you know you can ask me anything you want to know, right? I could be like your little baseball encyclopedia. I would love that, actually.

"You mentioned rehearsals . . . how are they going for you guys? Rodney sent me a s-short clip of you in a dance studio, and I'm embarrassed to admit how many times I've watched it at this point—could probably do some of the moves myself by now. And please don't get mad at him for sending it because then he'd probably stop . . . and that would make me sad. You wouldn't want that, right? Besides, I can't help that I love the way you move, and the way you sound. And . . . n-now this voice note is taking a turn. Which means it's probably a good thing I have to go get ready to meet the team. After we close out this series, we have one day off and then we're on the road for another five. We don't play in New York until June. But let me know when you're back in LA. I'd love to run it all back, s-sooner than later.

"To answer your question, the arm is fine. I over-rotated on the last pitch, but it's nothing an ice bath and a TENS machine can't fix."

Me: Voice Notes Sent:
March 20, 2024 11:00 p.m.

"One of the stats I wrote down is from last year. Apparently Black players only made up six point one percent of the Major League in 2023. I was shocked but also not at all by this. I imagine the number's even lower when it comes to starting pitchers, like you. Does that ever make you feel invisible?

"Rehearsals are exhausting, but I love this part of the work. Everything's a mess before it starts to come together. But it's a beautiful mess, like an artist's studio, all the elements of a masterpiece are flung all over the place, they just haven't come together yet—if that makes sense at all.

"My tour dates start in June and we open in LA. So, you and I will be like two ships passing in the night. But . . . and right now that's a big but . . . there's a slight possibility that I could get back to Cali for a few days in the middle of April when Google tells me you'll have a short stretch of home games?"

Mr. Curveball: Voice Notes Sent:
March 21, 2024 10:00 a.m.

"I wouldn't say those numbers make me feel
invisible, no. I know you said you're reading
about Jackie Robinson. You ever seen that movie,
42? I've probably watched it a hundred times by
now. W-well, in case you haven't, there's this
scene where they're at a game. It's after Jackie
makes the Brooklyn Dodgers, coming out of the
Negro Leagues. The team's manager, this guy named
Ben Chapman, he was racist and loud and proud
with it too. So, anyway, at this game Chapman
decides to taunt Jackie, starts calling him the n-
word over and over while he's out on the f-field—
just trying to humiliate him and get a rise. And
for a while, Jackie just absorbs it. You can see
the rage just bubbling up inside him until
eventually, he explodes. He goes to the dugout and
busts his bat on the back wall.

   "Anyway, I know it's not the fifties anymore,
but some times more than others, I get glimpses
of that kind of unspoken rule that Chapman was
trying to get across—baseball belongs to 'them.'
And I'm just allowed to be here. Now th-that can
make you feel like the opposite of invisible.
Makes you feel like you're s-sticking out like a
sore thumb.

   "Well, I did not mean to go that deep on you
like that. It's not something I've really talked
about with anyone before. Outside of my

grandparents at least. In lighter news, I love to
hear that about your tour rehearsals. Maybe one
day I can come and watch you. Also, you are
correct! I have a stretch of home games starting
in two weeks. So if you can make it work with
your schedule, I would love nothing more than to
fly you out here. Most game days I'm free until
the afternoon when I have to get to the stadium
for warm-ups. And then after the games, I'd be
yours. So, think about it and let me know.

"One more thing. I watched our music video for
the first time the other day. I couldn't bring
myself to watch it before. I really liked dancing
in the rain with you."

Me: Voice Notes Sent:
March 22, 2024 12:01 a.m.

"Miles, I hope you feel like you can talk to me
about anything. I don't exactly know what we're
doing, sending these messages back and forth, but
I feel like whatever this is, I need it. And maybe
you do too?

"I said all that to say that I get what you mean
about feeling hyper-visible. Or like you're just a
visitor in someone else's space. It's scary how
many times I've felt the same way. This one time
I was on set for one of those "Next in Music"
ensemble magazine covers. And I get how shallow
this may sound in the grand scheme of things, but
this shoot was for Rolling Stone, so it was huge

for me at the time. But I was the only talent on the shoot with "textured hair" and a "medium/dark skin tone." That's how they put it at least. Naturally, the entire hair and makeup crew was terrified of touching me and prepared to do only the bare minimum. I'd tried to get permission to bring Jamie and Sheryl with me, but this was a fully sponsored shoot, so everyone on set worked for the brand.

"I feel like I'm in the weeds here, and it can all feel so vapid and unimportant compared to Jackie Robinson's experience, and even yours. But so much of my career has been walking into rooms filled with people who are fully empowered, but either completely uninterested or totally underprepared to do what it takes to support me. You can probably guess how the final cover image turned out. I was rightfully dragged by Black Twitter for having a 'hard wig,' and that part I can laugh at. But when I was accused of skin bleaching because the photographer's lighting was overexposed and the makeup was off by a solid two shades, I'm embarrassed thinking back on how long I cried about it. None of the shot callers behind the shoot took ownership of how they fell short. And the fans were relentless at making me the butt of the joke. Granted, at the time I was twenty-two. An adult, but just barely. I really believed back then that it was enough that I could write and sing and that somehow the rest would just fall into place. But I learned fast that this *business runs on excess—good and bad. 'Enough' doesn't exist.*

"And now I've bared my soul, haven't I? Well, I have some really good news. I asked Angelo to help me negotiate for a short rehearsal break in April and he did it! So, it looks like I'll be seeing you in two weeks. If that still sounds good?

"And now it's time I admit that the song I sang at your benefit gala, 'I Wanna Dance With Somebody,' was definitely a deliberate choice. But I didn't want to just dance with 'somebody,' I wanted you."

Mr. Curveball: Voice Notes Sent:
March 22, 2024 11:52 p.m.

"I am angry for you about that whole photo shoot s-situation. And I can only imagine it's just the tip of the iceberg too. I don't take for granted the fact that as a male athlete, my looks don't really impact my success. But for what it's worth, and I'm not trying to minimize anything you just said—but I have n-never seen a bad photo of you. And this is still my take even after googling that Rolling Stone shoot. Haters will say I'm biased, because I've had a thing for you for a while and all. But, objectively speaking, even with a hard wig and bad lighting, I still get chills lookin' at you. B-but to be serious, I'm amazed at how you bear the weight of all the public scrutiny. It doesn't stop. If nobody's told you since I last said

it, I'll say it again—Ella, you're strong. I wish you didn't have to be as strong as you are. I wish I could make things softer for you, somehow.

"On another note, does Angelo need a kidney? Or does he know anybody, a cousin m-maybe, who needs a kidney? If you ask and he s-says yes, tell him I have one up for grabs. And your timing couldn't be better with the good news, because the team took an L today. It's not just that we lost that's getting to me either. We play more than a hundred and fifty games a year, so losing is bound to happen. But losing to the Rangers is another level. They're the team that snagged the World Series from us last year after the "locker-room brawl" heard around the w-world.

"I don't know how much you do or don't know about what went down with that. I have a feeling you know at least a little bit, given what you were saying when I walked back in at the end of the m-meeting at Janet's. But I've never been in a lower place than before and after that series. It's like one minute you're on the highest of all highs, at the top of your game and leading your team to greatness. Then suddenly a rug gets pulled out from under you and everything and everyone you put so much trust in just s-slips through your hands. Of course, the fight was on camera, so everyone saw me throw the first punch. No one but me heard what Morales said to provoke it though— and I know that's never an excuse. But in this case it was a reason.

"Anyway, I paid my fine and took my suspension and the team took our L at the end of what had been a phenomenal season. Then Morales got traded, and I swear, with everything in me, I wished it had been me. I wanted out of the contract and out of this city so bad. It felt like there were cameras hiding behind every corner in LA ready to get pics of my shame. And everything about this city s-screamed out the life Monica and I had built here together. All the places we went together, I started to picture her there with him. Felt like I was losing it. So I numbed it for a while, got defiant. I figured, if our marriage didn't stop her from stepping out, then why should the divorce push me in and isolate me? So, I forced myself to be less of a homebody—went out on a lot of dates. And whatever got printed, I pretended not to c-care.

"Then that day in Janet's office, after hearing the things you said about me, it was the first time I stopped to think about the way my image no longer reflected who I was, or at least who I was before. At first I thought you were just an asshole, if I'm honest. But the more I sat with it, the less I could blame you. I put myself in your shoes and realized I'd think the same things about me. But I couldn't figure out why I was so mad. And it was Gabe who gave me that light bulb m-moment. I was so heated over it because since everything went down, you were the first person I'd met whose opinion really got under my skin, *before I even knew you. And that surprised me, big time. It pissed me off too.*

"Then tonight, when we lost to the Rangers, on the way back to the locker room some heckler shouted some cheap shots from the stands and I just wanted to blink and be home. And I wanted you to be there. So I get here, and I open your message to find out you will be here in two weeks. And now I can't stop smiling. I don't know what's going on with us, either, but you're right, I need it too."

Me: Voice Notes Sent:
March 23, 2024 8:25 a.m.

"Miles, I know I said it once but it will never be enough. I'm sorry for judging you. I knew better, even then. After five minutes with you backstage I could tell I was in some big trouble because you weren't going to be someone I could easily write off. It had less to do with how attracted to you I was and everything to do with . . . just the way I felt standing there alone with you in the wings. Maybe you can't tell, but I'm an anxious person— kidding, how could you not tell? But being with you backstage for that short time was like this still, quiet calm in the wildest storm. It rattled me. And everything that happened afterward threw me for such a loop I couldn't even process the 'you' I'd met with the 'you' I was being linked to in the blogs. So, I hope you can understand that the things I said about you were just me projecting my

own frustrations. And I hate that you felt you had to wear any of them, even for a moment.

"I'm not judging you, either, about what happened in that locker room. Obviously, I'll say the obligatory 'I don't condone violence' bit—but I don't condone fuckery either. And it sounds like Morales and Monica were up to nothing but that, which I'd say is an emotional violence given their relationship to you. And then of course there's the whole, 'you do the crime, you do the time' thing. It sounds like you're still reckoning with the aftermath. As someone who's been cheated on more times than I'll ever be able to count, I know what it does to a person to have that trust broken. There were times I wanted to act out too. Times I wanted to test out other facets of me I felt like I'd denied before. Especially since I'd married Elliot before I even knew what I wanted from myself, let alone a partner. And when it was all said and done, I didn't trust myself anymore at all. If I'm honest, sometimes I still don't.

"But the one thing I am proud of is knowing when I'd had my fill and that it was time to leave—that staying would be the easier route, sure. But then, how could I respect myself? Even though it's been really fucking hard. And even though my own mother takes his side. Anyway, again—that's a topic for a day that ends in 'never.' I'm sorry for what you and I have been through. And I'm even more sorry that anything I said or did could have added to the pain of it for you. And *for what it's worth, I don't think your image needs rehabilitating. I look at images of you often—and you get no complaints from me."*

Mr. Curveball: Voice Notes Sent:
March 28, 2024 11:52 p.m.

"I'm sorry it's been a few days since I've gotten back to you. We've been on the road with some tough losses and the schedule's been really hectic. But for whatever it's worth, I wanted to tell you that I'm proud of you. For getting out of that situation with Elliot. And I hope you're not blaming yourself for any of the things you put up with either. I mean, that's what love looks like, right? Endurance. But loving yourself can also look like walking away.

"I'm also really sorry to hear that about your mom. Because of my own mom, I always try to give people's parents the benefit of the doubt. I figure everybody's just doing the best they can with what they've got—and we're not all working with the same tools. But some parents aren't worthy of the title. I hope she does right by you in the long run, Dream Girl. You deserve nothing less."

Me: Voice Notes Sent:
April 1, 2024 8:20 p.m.

"Miles, can I ask you a personal question?"

Mr. Curveball: Voice Note Sent:
April 2, 2024 12:52 a.m.

"Of course. You can ask me anything. Everything."

Me: Voice Note Sent:
April 3, 2024 9:27 a.m.

"Will you tell me about your mom?"

Mr. Curveball: Voice Notes Sent:
April 4, 2024 12:05 a.m.

"My mom's n-n-ame is Maria Evelyn. And she works at a restaurant here in Cali as general manager. I don't talk about her in interviews, but that's by her request. If it was up to me, I'd shout her from the rooftops because I'm so damn proud of that woman.

"She turned s-sixteen on the day I was born, and it was a really rough go for her for a long time after that. To this day, I don't know who my biological father is. I don't think she would tell me if I asked either. But I do know my grandparents tried everything to keep us together at the beginning. But having a baby that young was too much to handle for her. And I love my grandparents, don't get me wrong. I'm h-happy to be here too. But I also know them and their ways, and I can't imagine my mom felt like she could ask them to help her find another option, outside

of having me and raising me . . . if you know what I mean.

"S-sometimes I lose sleep thinking about how trapped she probably felt in that situation. She ended up moving out before I turned one. And my grandparents had a hard time tracking her down for a long time after that. But sometimes I got birthday cards, and when the phone would ring and they'd pick up but no one was talking on the other end, I always felt like it was her. I was sixteen when I m-met her for the first time. She had been clean for a year at that point, had gotten a job at a restaurant and was living in a group home in the Bronx. I tried my best to keep in touch with her as much as I could. I found out she stuttered like me, and we kind of bonded over it a little. She's the one who taught me about tapping my leg, go figure.

"But after I made the pros, I heard she relapsed and was living on the streets. It took us weeks to find her but when Pop and I finally did, she agreed to go back to rehab and she's been s-sober now for six years.

"You might be wondering why the mom of an athlete who makes the kind of m-money I do works at a restaurant. And trust me, I had to eventually force myself to s-stop asking her the same question. But now I get it, why she wants things this way. I don't know if this crazy life I have would mess up the stability she's got going for

herself these days. She says what she's doing
works for her, and I respect that.

"S-so . . . that's my mom in a nutshell. I'll
text a picture of us from when I was in high
school. Couldn't tell me nothin' about that haircut
back then.

"Now it's your turn. Tell me about the woman
that birthed the Elladee Robinson, aka Ella
Simone . . ."

When the photograph of Miles and his mother comes through, I instantly have to catch my breath. He's right, his Caesar fade with shiny waves probably *did* drive the girls wild—with a smile and dimples like that to boot, I probably would have risked it all for his attention back then myself.

In the photo, Miles and his mom are at what looks like his high school graduation. Their matching almond-shaped eyes and twin dimples etched deep in their cheeks instantly give away the family connection. Her head stops just below his shoulder as he proudly drapes his arm around her. And she stands there beaming at the camera in a bright yellow sundress, face aglow with an emotion I can only describe as deep satisfaction. It strikes me that I can't tell who was proudest in this moment, Maria Evelyn for her son's accomplishment, or Miles for all the obstacles his mom had to overcome to make it there that day.

My heart tugs for this younger version of Miles, whose compassion shines through, even in this years-old photo, in the exact same ways I've had the privilege of seeing for myself face-to-face. And I realize just how skittish I've been during this back-and-forth we've kept up these past few weeks. Especially now that I find myself leaning further into all the ways I want this man—physically, emotionally, intellectually—even despite the weathered, frightened parts of me that scream for me to pull back.

But the Miles I see in this picture has ignited a tiny spark of relief, flickering with possibility that maybe this time I have met a man who is just as he portrays himself to be. That maybe the beautiful parts of him that I'm getting to know are not just a performance. Maybe they are true and constant—because they are who he's always been.

Me: Voice Notes Sent:
April 4, 2024 9:27 a.m.

"Wow, Miles. I think now I understand why you have such a soothing presence. You learned early how to be your own calm in a storm. Your mom and grandmother seem like phenomenal women in their own ways, and it's no wonder you started the foundation to honor them. And looking at this picture, it's clear to me why you're so beautiful . . . you come by it honest.

"Soooo . . . you want to know about my mother? Miss Black America 1990? She is . . . perfection personified. Never a hair or a sofa cushion out of place. Or else, I'd get this pursed-lip look of disapproval that never failed to make me feel antsy, like my skin was zipped on too tight. That's how I felt most of the time growing up in our house, if I'm telling you the truth. Like, if only I could let down my hair or open a window or go one size up on the dresses she always picked for me to

wear to Sunday service, then maybe I could
actually breathe.

"At first, she loved that I could sing. I think
because it was a cute party trick she could pull
out to show off to her friends. And my dad was so
stoic and removed. He was the kind of husband and
father who prided himself in providing material
stability but not much more. So my singing was
inoffensive enough to them until it became clear
that I was going to try to turn it into something
more than a hobby. And that was so far out of the
question that when I defied them and accepted my
admission to Berklee for songwriting instead of
UCLA for premed, they cut off contact with me
entirely. It was that drastic too. You'd think I
was going off to join a sex cult by the way they
basically disappeared on me. We went from the
picture-perfect family at every social function to
Baldwin Hills' main subject of gossip the summer
of 2013. It got back to me that our neighbors were
under the impression I'd gone to rehab instead of
college that fall.

"Anyway, my mother miraculously started to
come around after Elliot and I announced our
marriage and got the Grammy nomination. I
always suspected she'd gotten too many questions
from friends at that point and had grown tired of
having to pretend like we'd been in touch. It took
me years and a few therapists to fully see that
our entire relationship for her has hinged on
appearances. And I've played along, because I know

what it is to be a motherless child. And I guess
this is better than none at all . . .
    "But enough about Beverly Robinson. I will
see you in one week. I hope you're ready.
I know I am."

From: beverlyr@gmail.com
To: ellaelladee@gmail.com

Date: April 4, 2024

Subject: Lunch?
    Elladee, I regret that our last phone call ended on such
a sour note. I accept responsibility for the part I played
and want to apologize to you. The next time you're back
home in Los Angeles, I was wondering if you'd let me take
you to lunch? There are some things I'd like to discuss with
you that it won't do to say over the phone or by email.
Otherwise, I hope you are doing all right.
    Your mother

You've got to learn to leave the table when love's no longer being served.

Nina Simone

Two years ago

IMAGINE YOU'RE PUSHING THROUGH A BUSTLING UPSCALE bar. Except this one is open air with a bloodred carpet that seems to shimmer under broad daylight. You are surrounded by hundreds of people, and each one has an agenda—to either be seen, adored, or envied. Or to get a scoop, a money shot, a win, or maybe their next big break. Even *you* want some of these things, and you're still figuring out what that says about you.

You are dressed in bespoke clothing and near-priceless jewels. Jewels that are insured, on your dime, and that will be removed from your person by a brand executive at the end of the night. The dress, you'll get to keep though—if only because it's been cut to your exact measurements. And these are measurements an executive at your label just recently told you you have begun to "fill out." Naturally, this was said in a tone that made it clear it wasn't a compliment.

And when you tell your husband about the off-color remark, he simply shrugs it off before suggesting that maybe you should look into hiring a nutritionist or consider taking up Pilates. You store these little digs away in the secret place where you collect the things that have pricked and jabbed you over the years, even if the tiny slices and bruises they've left behind remain etched into your skin.

Most things about this part of "the game" are the things you've come to accept in the name of going along to get along. But you'd almost always rather just be somewhere on a stage with a mic in hand, a three-part harmony backing vocal, and a six-piece band accompaniment. Or in the studio on a quiet night with the man you fell in love with because he told you you were a star, made you believe it, and then made it true. And you're holding the hand of that man now, except you suspect he's lying to you . . . again.

But the cameras are flashing now. And if you think too deeply about any of this, you'll forget to smile.

"Joining us now are one of the most undeniable talents behind so many hits and his stunning songbird of a wife—Elliot Majors and Ella Simone!" Sherelle Fox introduces us to E!'s cameras as we ascend the stairs hand in hand. When we join her on the platform, she blows air kisses as Elliot snakes an arm, possessively, around my waist.

"Would you look at this stunning couple!" Sherelle says, cheating toward the camera. Then, beaming back at us, she asks, "So tell us, who dressed you both tonight, and who are you wearing?"

Elliot flaunts a dazzling smile, surely blinding the audience with his brand-new diamond grill. "Oh, you know me," he says. "We had to come correct in Gucci, head to toe."

I affectionately pat his chest, making sure the camera sees my borrowed Lorraine Schwartz diamond cuff, before proudly answering the first part of Sherelle's question. "Our stylist, Rodney Jenkins, put these beautiful looks together."

"Her best friend from college! Can you believe that?" Elliot adds, and I don't miss the faint hint of condescension in his tone.

Sherelle quirks an eyebrow. "Oh? How cute!" she chirps, before quickly moving on. "Well, Elliot, I have to ask after that provocative profile of yours in *Rolling Stone* where you spoke so candidly about your . . . we'll just call them reservations with the Recording Academy . . . how are you feeling going into the awards tonight?"

Elliot's grip on my waist tightens to the point that I can feel the press of each finger through the thick fabric of my gown, and I brace with anticipation of how he'll choose to handle this question about the (now infamous) *Rolling Stone* interview wherein he likened the music industry to a slave plantation. He could play the diplomat and keep things clean and simple, tell her he's excited for the nominees and happy to be out on a night celebrating the best in music. Or he could keep it all the way real by going in on the exploitative, artificial machine we're all a part of. Whichever way this goes, I know my role is to stand here and maintain my smile for the cameras.

"Listen," he begins. "I've been in this game a long time . . . long enough to see a lot of folks like me come and go. And long enough to learn that the *only* thing with any staying power is the music. The awards and accolades and the hype . . . nobody remembers any of it at the end of the day."

He pauses, and this is the moment of truth. The moment before my husband decides to either "keep it cute" or say *fuck it* and unleash a barrage of frustrations about this very awards show and the industry it props up. With that same fixed smile, I glance from an enthralled Sherelle Fox to my husband, who appears to be weighing his next words carefully.

"So," he says, before looking at me and flashing a mischievous grin, "I'm happy to be here with this beautiful, talented woman at my side. And when it comes to the rest"—he gestures at the hustle and bustle surrounding us—"it is what it is. I'll let what I said in *Rolling Stone* speak for itself."

The breath I was holding seeps out of me in one slow exhale. Sherelle thanks us for our time and we exit the podium to dive back into the cluttered stream of glitz and glamour.

Back on the carpet, Elliot's manager, Coco, greets us with her eyes sparkling. "That was *fantastic*," she says. "Just spot on! And the two of you look sensational! Four more to go, then we'll get you to your seats."

THE SHOW IS OVER AND SANDERS IS LEADING US THROUGH A throng of after-party hopefuls and flash photographers toward our waiting car at the curb. As we go, a clamor of voices yelling out both of our names makes for an almost deafening distraction. At one point, I lose grip of Elliot's hand. Then turning, I find him snapping a selfie with a group of young women who appear to be the age I was when I married him.

When we get to the car, Sanders gives me a boost up into the back seat with Elliot sliding in close behind me.

"Majors, man! You comin' in?" someone calls from the direction of the nightclub. And for a split second, I envision Elliot shutting the door to the Escalade. Somehow, in my mind, by doing so he'd be shutting down all the rumors spinning about his late-night escapades when I'm not around. But instead, he looks at me with those brown puppy dog eyes. Like denying him another chance to be the life of the party would be akin to me denying him the air.

"I'll only be a minute, babe," he says. Then with a pout, "Promise."

Sucking it up, I manage to smile. "It's fine, I'll just come with." It's the last thing I want to do after the overstimulation of the last several hours. But I am intent on ending this night like we started it—together. I begin to scoot forward to exit the car when Elliot holds up his hand.

"No! No, stay here. I'll be right out, I swear," he says. "I'm just going in for a shot with the guys." He winks and then disappears into the crowd.

An hour goes by . . .

Bzzz!

Elliot's phone leaps back to life in the car seat that has long gone cold. It's the third notification in as many minutes, and I glare at the little rectangular device with the most dangerous curiosity—they say it killed the cat, but I wonder how many marriages it's brought to their untimely demise. Peering out the window, I notice Sanders outside having a smoke and chatting up the bouncer. With tinted windows, there's no one around to witness what I'm *thinking* about doing. I could take a tiny peek, and no one would know. No one but me of course.

With my luck, Elliot has changed his password and this will be a nonstarter. Or worse, he could have a secret phone—one that's reserved exclusively for hidden paramours. I shake my head, laughing without humor at how ridiculous this all feels—how foolish it feels to be reduced to snooping in my husband's phone. But in this moment, suspicion has met opportunity. And I don't know when I'll have this chance again. As for Elliot, perhaps it's the price you pay for making a woman wait.

I snatch up the phone and tap in the first six digits that come to mind—our wedding day. Then, my mouth falls open in disbelief when the home screen comes into view. With full access to Elliot's secret world, it's as if I've lost control of my body—like a marionette with some other scorned woman operating my strings. I tap on the messaging app, and when it opens, my mind scrambles to make sense of all the unread texts. There are scores of them, all names I hardly recognize or numbers he hasn't even added to his contacts. It's no wonder he's got so many people on the payroll to make sense of his life. Elliot Majors does not deal in minutiae.

Overwhelmed and feeling sillier by the minute, I give up on his texts. I'm about to give up on the whole mission, too, when something intangible, intuitive even, tells me to check his Instagram DMs. I'm not sure if it's the devil on my left shoulder or the angel on my right, but it's irrelevant now, because I already crossed the line when I unlocked his phone. And now I'm staring at a lengthy conversation between my husband and his artist, Miss Thing. And it has nothing to do with music.

Now

PALM DESERT IN JULY HAS NOTHING ON THE HELLSCAPE THAT is the conference room of Spradlin, Waldorf, and Associates. The tension within these four walls grows thicker with each passing minute.

To avoid a drawn-out court battle, Janet succeeded, only barely, in convincing me to accept Elliot's request for a single attempt at negotiating a settlement over the terms of our divorce.

And while I haven't uttered a word since we walked into this holding cell of a conference room, I must be giving off *why am I here and when can I leave?* vibes, because Janet takes the opportunity to explain herself once more.

"Again, we're only here to see *what* they're putting on the table," she argues. "Think of it as us peeking at the deck before we have to draw our hand. Whatever we discuss today won't be binding. So, there's nothing to lose."

"Oh, nothing except for my pride, dignity, and about a gallon of water weight," I reply dryly. "Seriously, what's with you lawyers and your vendetta against air-conditioning?"

Janet smirks while raising an eyebrow. "Don't you know? Reptiles are cold-blooded—comes with the occupation," she deadpans.

I chuckle at this, relieved for a moment of levity before Elliot and his attorney are due to waltz in here, most likely sporting smug grins and expensive cologne—the kind that reeks of mansplaining and condescension.

Now that the prenup has been dissolved, we are essentially starting with a blank slate. All those exploitative clauses that strapped my future earnings to Elliot have been done away with—but so have the ones that mutually excluded us from ever being accountable for each other's financial stability. In short, because California is a no-fault state, now *I* could end up having to pay my philandering ex in monthly spousal support. It's solely dependent on how the earnings numbers balance out in the end.

The mere thought of things falling in his favor has me praying my anxiety hasn't made itself known in the form of massive sweat stains on my pale silk blouse. Taking what I hope to be a discreet glance down at my top, I confirm that I am in the clear—but only for now. When a sharp click sounds at the door, my spine shoots up straight. I turn toward the sound, where Elliot and his attorney have just entered the stuffy room. As expected, they wear matching smiles, each dripping with self-satisfaction—like our showing up today means they've already won. I could hurl on the table.

Larry Spradlin, Elliot's toupeed, square-jawed, and nearsighted attorney slides into the chair directly across from me while Elliot squares off with Janet. And my no-good, very bad ex sits there, cool as an organic cucumber, with his perfectly manicured hands clasped atop the expansive cherry oak–stained table.

He's been in the room all of thirty seconds, and Elliot has yet to make eye contact with me. I know it's a scare tactic—something he used to do during our marriage when we were privately on the outs but in the presence of others. We could be at the studio, a party, a meeting, and he'd pretend I didn't exist. He'd have me seeking out the smallest acknowledgment, a nod, a head tilt, even a glance, for reassurance that we were okay, that we'd *be* okay. Invariably, by the end of the night, I'd give in first and walk back my part of whatever disagreement caused the tension. But this time he's sorely mistaken, because he doesn't realize that his games aren't ones I'm willing to play anymore.

"Thank you, Ms. Simone, for joining us today," Larry blithers across the conference room table. "Or should I say Ms. Robinson? We have yet to establish the future status of your professional name, as I believe Mr. Majors holds the copyright."

I hope the side-eye I'm leveling Larry's way isn't as apparent on the outside as it feels on the inside, because I'm on the verge of a migraine. I used to love Larry. Or, at the very least, I appreciated the service he provided Elliot. But this man clearly harbors an unnatural allegiance to losers, my ex-husband being captain of the ship.

"Ms. Robinson will do just fine," Janet chimes in. "And my client wishes to release the professional moniker of Ella Simone upon conclusion of her upcoming tour. As they say, 'Out with the old.'"

At this, Elliot shifts in his seat. Bet he didn't see this coming. He and Larry likely planned to catch us off guard out of the gate with that one. But Janet and I came ready to play ball—on our terms. Besides, shedding my old persona, the one crafted and carefully curated by my ex, has been a dream of mine since the moment I realized I'd outgrown both her and him. Elliot may be under the impression that I'll be rudderless without him. But that's simply because in all the years he spent sizing me up, molding me into something he could tote and sell, he never truly paid attention.

Those lyrics didn't cowrite themselves. I never used Auto-Tune in a booth. And every night I found myself on a stage, my mic was on. Every time someone catcalled, ridiculed, objectified, slandered, and yes, even groped "Ella Simone," it was Elladee Robinson who picked up the pieces and kept it pushing . . . not Elliot Majors. So yes, I'm more than prepared to "release the professional moniker." As prepared as I am to close this chapter of my life completely.

Larry clears his throat. "Noted, I'll have the team draft that into the agreement," he says, before directing his gaze back at me. "I trust Ms. Waterman has provided you with a list of the terms Mr. Majors and I hope to discuss today?"

At the mention of my ex, my eyes slide about two feet to the left where the culprit himself is seated, looking equal parts bored and annoyed. For a moment, our history passes before my eyes— the unvarnished joy on his face when I said *I do* at the chapel. The way he lit up when I told him I was finally open to the discussion of us starting a family together. The placid expression he maintained throughout every lie he told.

I made every part of me available to this man—my future, my talent, my mind, heart, and body—but most of all my trust. And he took them all, giving me only a façade in return. I used to wonder what more I could have done, who else I could have been to have had things work out differently for us. But looking at this man through weathered, wiser eyes—eyes that have seen him wreak havoc both on those deserving and not—I see now that I could have been *everything* and still, he'd have cheated because of who he is and what he lacks, not because of me.

"Please direct your queries to me, Mr. Spradlin," Janet requests, and she's so straightforward it snaps me back to the moment. "Yes, my client is aware of the terms. How would you like to proceed?"

Larry clears his throat and wipes his brow, uncharacteristically rattled—perhaps by having a woman challenge his energy. "My client is amenable to splitting the value of all community property by a ratio of sixty-forty," he states. "We believe this to be more than fair given the relative value, and lack thereof, of each party's assets upon entering this union."

Janet doesn't respond, she merely jots down a few notes, then returns Larry's searching stare when she's done. "Next?" she asks.

Larry, seemingly taken aback once again, this time by Janet's minimalist approach, shuffles his pages before scanning for the next term up for discussion. "As for spousal support . . . upon a full accounting of all income streams for each party, my client wishes to receive a monthly twenty-five percent royalty derived from ticket and merchandising sales from Ms. Simone . . . ahem . . . Ms. Robinson's cut of upcoming tour sales."

Unable to stop it, my neck swivels like a bobblehead on steroids. And if I'm not mistaken, a squeak of objection just burst from my lips. Then Elliot has the nerve to . . . *laugh*.

"This is funny to you?" I demand, my voice cracking from the onslaught of shock and disgust.

Never mind the fact I've gone completely rogue now by speaking out of turn. The plan was for me not to utter a word once they entered the room. Let Janet do the talking. Hit this and quit this, before the gas lamp explodes. But this man . . . ooooh, he gets under my skin. You don't lie, cheat, and steal the most precious parts of someone—their time and energy—and then turn around and request *more*. Even if, by some stretch of imagination, a case could be made for Elliot earning a portion of proceeds from my tour, has the man not already taken enough?

Janet has placed a firm palm on my right forearm, which is currently vibrating with cellular rage atop the conference table. She's about to say something, but Elliot beats her to the punch.

"Nah," he says, finally meeting my eyes. And the disdain I'm met with makes my stomach turn. "Not funny. Just seeking what I'm owed, baby doll."

"Majors," Larry emits in admonishment. And for a second, I think I notice a spark of shame flit across his face.

Elliot waves him off, the same way he dismisses all his minions. "I'm paying for this room, so I think I'll get a few things off my chest before she goes off again with her little baseball player boyfriend," he says. And his mention of Miles sends a chill down my spine.

"You wouldn't have a career without me," Elliot declares flatly, as if it were a matter of science. Like I'm the plant and he's the sun. And it's not the first time he's said the words. So the fresh bite he intends to inflict lands more like a dull gnawing at old wounds.

"Everybody knows. You tried on your own and you got nowhere. And you know why too. YouTube. Reality shows. Demo tapes. Everything failed," he states. "Because you were derivative. No one at Onyx wanted to sign you until I made you something special . . . something marketable. They didn't believe in you, sweetheart. They believed in *me*. And that's what got your foot in the door. So yes, a cut of the tour isn't just what I have earned. It's what I *deserve*."

"On that note, gentlemen," Janet interjects as she rises from the table and collects her things. "This meeting is over. My client and I will see you both in court."

Momentarily frozen, I take a second to realize that Janet is standing by to assist me with getting up from the table. When our eyes meet, a look of contrition in hers communicates to me without words that she's sorry for putting me through this. For playing directly into their hand. As it is now evident as ever that Elliot's goal here was not to negotiate in good faith, but to debase me in living color.

But Janet need not apologize, because this was not a total waste of time. Something happens when faced with a bully who no longer has a hold on you. Eventually, you get the spark to fight back.

26.

EXCUSE ME. MISS SIMONE?" Our flight attendant's words break me out of my retrospective haze. Looking up from the window, I see his smile is polite but a bit strained. "This is embarrassing," he says, "but your friend here is disturbing the cabin. Would you mind . . . waking her up?"

He's not wrong. Jamie's been snoring so loud for the last twenty minutes, her honks and purrs have rendered my noise-canceling headphones useless. I could blame our five a.m. pickup time for a ride to the airport, but that wouldn't cover it. Because after witnessing the speed with which she downed her third mimosa, I could tell she wasn't long for this world.

Despite my many protests, Miles insisted on covering my flight out to see him in LA. But we still compromised on splitting the difference by having me purchase Jamie's ticket so she could tag along. It's true the point of this trip is to get in quality time with Miles—and after Elliot's emotional ambush disguised as a settlement discussion, it couldn't come at a better time. But I also know Miles is a professional athlete with a grueling game schedule, and

I refuse to sit around twiddling my thumbs in his empty mansion—been there, done that. So, Jamie and I booked a Malibu rental and I've scheduled enough meetings this week to occupy the gaps and ensure the trip isn't a total loss in case things fizzle out with Miles.

Rodney's off visiting Angelo's family in Miami, and given this special occasion, I promised I'd only contact them in the case of a "life- and/or career-ending emergency." Sheryl's updates have become few and far between, which I've taken to mean she's really in the thick of it with her husband's treatment. Still, the Glam Squad has kept up with sending our weekly care packages to her house in Westchester. And she always sends us three emoji hearts to confirm when they arrive.

After returning my lie-flat seat to an upright position, I gently nudge Jamie. But that just draws out a snort and a gargle, followed by what sounds like a possible aspiration event. Afraid for her safety, I start vigorously jostling her shoulder.

"Gah! What? What'd I miss?" Like a bull in a china shop, it's possible she's more of a disturbance when awake than asleep. With lines from the armrest etched into her skin, she wipes a little drool from her chin and looks at me with bleary eyes. "Did we land?"

"Two hours to go," I tell her, part amused and mostly relieved her airway seems to be intact. "Getting some beauty rest there?"

"Well . . . I *was*," she says, cutting me some major side-eye. "Before you basically assaulted me awake."

I shrug, and with a straight face say, "The flight crew said your snores were interfering with air traffic control signals."

Jamie's eyes narrow. "You know, lying looks good on you," she says. "You should do 'bad girl' stuff more often."

At this, a small tingling sensation starts to creep in. I've been itching all morning to let her in on my close-kept secret, internally debating when to tell her, knowing it would need to be before we touched down in LA. Apart from Rodney, I have told absolutely *no one* about my night with Miles after the charity benefit, or the countless voice notes we've exchanged baring our souls to each other in its aftermath.

For all Jamie knows, this LA trip is about getting a break from New York—taking a meeting with Janet, doing a talk show here, podcast there. And maybe fitting in a couple of recording sessions with an up-and-coming artist I've been dying to collaborate with. And sure, all of that is true. But she has no idea the real reason this trip is happening is a certain someone I haven't been able to stop thinking about. Everything else, I could have handled just as well from the East Coast.

"I have a confession to make," I tell her.

"Let me guess. You been bangin' the pitcher?"

My jaw drops, and my body falls slack against my seat. "How do you know?" I whisper shout. "Also, it was only one time!"

"Hello!" she says. "Because I actually *observe* my surroundings."

"Replace 'observe' with 'disturb' and you might be onto something," I shoot back.

Totally unbothered, she presses on. "Anyway, it was obvious to me the night you stormed out of the gala that you had caught feelings. And, girl, please . . . we all picked up what you were putting down with that song choice. 'I Wanna Dance with Somebody'? Subtle, my ass!"

I open my mouth, but nothing comes out. I am gagged.

"We should get another drink, huh?" she asks, eyes scanning the aisle for a flight attendant, totally unmoved by what we've just openly acknowledged.

I simply nod in agreement and press the call button.

"I COULD GET USED TO THIS," JAMIE SAYS, BEFORE KICKING OFF her slides and sinking her feet into the sun-warmed sand.

"Well, for a week it is yours," I say, in my best James Earl Jones impersonation. "Everything the light touches!"

We're on the back deck of our two-story Malibu rental, which opens up directly onto a private stretch of beach. After landing at LAX, our driver took us to In-N-Out for some much-needed fortification for the one-and-a-half-hour trek up the 405 and Pacific Coast Highway.

Now that the late afternoon sun's golden rays are falling across our faces, and our bellies are full of milkshakes, double-doubles, and animal fries, I can scarcely recall the last time I've felt this content, apart from when I was wrapped in Miles's arms.

My back pocket vibrates with a call from the man himself, as if conjured by the thought of him. Swiping across the screen, I feel my face stretch into a wide smile. "You actually called me this time," I practically purr at the phone. "How did I get so lucky?"

"Well, for starters you flew across the country to see me," he says. "It's really the least I could do."

I close my eyes and luxuriate in the deep velvety sound of his voice. We've spoken on the phone a handful of times since our night after the gala, but our crazy hectic schedules and the three-hour time difference have made syncing up an arduous task.

"Ella, you still there?" Miles asks, when I've apparently forgotten that holding a conversation means you take turns replying to each other, usually without long, weighted gaps of silence.

Clearing my throat I say, "Mm-hmm, yeah, I'm here. It's just, throwing me for a little bit of a loop how good it feels to actually be talking to you on the phone right now instead of recording a voice note to send to you."

"Dream Girl, you have no idea," he says, and hearing that nickname again makes my chest flutter and my face heat. "So, I know you and Jamie probably want to take tonight to hang out and get settled in. But our manager gave us a 'show 'n go' schedule for tomorrow's game, and I don't have to be at the stadium until about three. So, I was thinking maybe I could come by and make you both breakfast?"

"Oh, so he's a world-class pitcher who's easy on the eyes, loves his family, gives good voice note, *and* he cooks too?"

"I can give more than 'good voice note,' and if you don't recall, I'd be happy to jog your memory," Miles says, and right about now I'm glad Jamie's already strolled off toward the shoreline. "Also, and feel free to object if you think it's a bad idea, but I was planning to maybe bring Gabe?"

This makes me laugh and sigh. Somewhere along the way, Miles got the brilliant notion that Gabriel Pearson and Jamie needed to meet. And while his sports agent made quite the first impression on me, albeit under very tense circumstances, it's Jamie I'm more concerned about in this scenario. She can be a real ballbuster. The woman tends to run off anyone who so much as hints the tiniest bit at being a "nice guy."

"I won't object, so long as you warn your best guy that Jamie's packing sharp teeth and maybe even talons too," I tell him. "Also, can we make it brunch for tomorrow? I have an early meeting with Janet that should only be an hour."

Miles clears his throat. And I have to remind myself that it must be awkward for him when I make mention of anything having to do with my divorce attorney. After all, I may be legally separated.

And even though my relationship with Elliot ended what feels like ages ago, our divorce won't be final for another three and a half months in the best-case scenario.

"Oh, no worries," he finally says after a few moments of stilted silence. "I never want to get in the way of that. Brunch it is." His voice trails off just slightly at the end, and I worry I may have irrevocably killed the vibe.

THE WOMAN IN THE OVERSIZED SUNHAT AND LINEN MAXI dress couldn't possibly be my divorce attorney. But then again, when I left my sleeping housemate behind at eight in the morning to come meet Janet for "breakfast," I was expecting coffee, not pressed juices at the Brentwood Country Mart. Not to be fooled a second time, I even stopped for a couple of egg bites on the way. Now, after valeting my rental and meandering through the mart's labyrinth of matching shops, cafés, and boutiques, I'm dubious of the lone woman outside our designated meeting spot.

"Janet? Is that you?" I ask as I approach. The hat bobs and swivels, before revealing her stark but elegant features and piercing blue eyes. Today, my typically stoic yet chic attorney looks California casual, like the product of an expensive wellness retreat.

When she spots me, she smiles broadly—another new thing for her. "There you are!" she says, leaning in for a double-cheeked kiss. "You look well."

"So . . . do you," I say, a little bewildered by this new zen vibe wafting off her.

"Here you are." She hands over a bottle filled with beet-colored liquid. "It's the best one they've got. Great for the skin."

Given her flawless complexion, I accept mine without argument, then fall in step with her as she beckons me along. We end up sitting at a sunny table in the Country Mart's upper courtyard, surrounded by a blend of families with young kids and older couples out and about for early breakfasts.

"How are you? How's New York been?" Her knitted brow suggests she's not just probing me superficially, but that perhaps she's been worried about me since the meeting with Elliot crashed and burned.

Maybe it's the potent drink, the bright sun, or the intense blue of her eyes. But suddenly, my knack for pretense melts away. "I'm good. Great most days, actually. I'm busy . . . and happy getting ready for the tour. It's doing what I love," I tell her, and all of that's true. "But . . . at the same time," I add. "I can't shake this feeling that the other shoe is about to drop any day now. The meeting with Larry and Elliot couldn't have been less productive, and with their team stonewalling us at every turn now, I can't even anticipate what his next move's going to be."

Pressing her lips together, she nods. "Well, anticipating moves is *my* job, not yours. But this is normal for someone in your shoes," she says. "When it comes to the divorce proceedings, we're just going to have to maximize our leverage. As for Onyx Records, well . . . we've talked about how difficult creative contracts are to dissolve or amend. And yours is no exception. It's actually why I wanted to meet you in person today." She pauses, and her eyes dart around us as if checking for eavesdroppers. "There have been some rumblings I was just made privy to. But all of it's still very confidential."

I set down my juice and lean in. "Rumblings . . . about Elliot?" I ask.

Her head bobs from side to side. "More broad, but they are concerning top brass at Onyx Records," she explains, and her voice drops lower. "The company is on the brink of a reckoning of sorts." At this, my ears perk up. Janet continues. "Misconduct, misappropriation, misdemeanors . . . you name it—and all from the very top. I'm being told the Onyx board and its creditors are in the middle of enacting a leadership change."

Janet might as well have dropped a bomb on the table with the way my ears are ringing at this news. "So . . . what would all this mean for the artists?"

Her mouth curves into a subtle grin. "It means very soon there's going to be a lot of upheaval and uncertainty," she says. "And anyone who's got an attorney worth their fees is doing exactly what we are up to right this second. Because with a strategy in place, you'll have an incredible opportunity here, Ella."

"An opportunity to get out of my contract and start fresh? No more Ella Simone? I can finally rebrand as just . . . Elladee?" I ask. After all, it's what I've wanted from the beginning.

"Or . . ." Janet says, slowing my roll, "depending on who the incoming leadership is, it could be an opportunity for us to draw up a new contract and chart a new path as Elladee *with* Onyx," she explains. And when I don't respond immediately, she continues, "Either way, you don't have to decide that right now."

I let this new information marinate for a moment. The prospect of Onyx Records operating under an entirely new guard is a curveball to say the least. In recent weeks, I'd started to imagine what my life and career could look like if I did manage to get out of this contract. Would I go indie? Invest in my team and myself with my own significant, albeit still limited, capital? Could I cut back on touring altogether, and try my hand at something I've been itching to do for years—writing and producing for other artists?

Essentially what this all means is . . . my options are open. And for the first time in a long time, I get to decide what the next steps look like.

27

DING!

"That should be the boys," I tell Jamie at the sound of the doorbell. She's just come in from her late-morning yoga session on the beach, and by the mean mug she's aiming my way, I'm guessing I just wrecked her state of calm.

"Remind me to shank you later for setting me up on a blind date in the middle of what's supposed to be *my* vacation," she tells me. "I haven't waxed in weeks, and Aunt Flo is in town. A sister coulda used a heads-up is all I'm sayin'."

"Sorry, boo, wasn't my idea," I offer as a futile defense. Even so, I don't miss the slight sparkle in her eyes or the grin on her face as she practically skips up the stairs.

I'd bet that the first second she had to herself after I gave her Gabriel's full name, she pulled up Google and started salivating over the Images tab. He's about an inch shorter than Miles and only slightly less filled out. On the day we all met at Janet's home office, he wore an olive green suit that was clearly tailor-made to his long, lean frame. And with that charming crooked smile, those

light brown eyes, and his deep black curls—the man is as beautiful
to behold as the athletes he represents. So, while I can certainly
understand Jamie not being keen on the element of surprise here,
there's a strong chance she could end up thanking me later.

On my way to the door, I check myself in the foyer mirror.
Since Sheryl's been out, I have felt wholly uninspired to find a
temp replacement. Instead, I've been trying my hand at natural
and protective hairstyles—something I never would have had the
guts to do while I was with Elliot. Last night, for example, after
co-washing my hair I used a moisturizing serum and twisted it up
using flexi rods. The result this morning after taking it all down
didn't quite match the tutorial I'd followed, but a few hours later,
the twists have fallen to my shoulders with a flirty curl pattern
that's starting to grow on me.

In the two seconds I take to look at my reflection, I make the
choice to love this version of me—the one without a full face on.
Just tinted sunscreen, well-shaped brows, and a little bit of lip oil,
all wrapped up in a plain blue sundress with a brand name I didn't
care to check. It's been a while, but I recognize this girl. She's a
mess, but she's trying. And right now, there's a fine-as-hell man on
the other side of the door who came to see her.

When I open that door, Miles is standing there holding two
shopping bags in one hand and a bouquet of sunflowers in the
other. His smile stretches wide as his eyes sweep me from head to
toe, drinking in the view. Mine do the same. We stand there for
several seconds. No words. Just casually eye-fucking—as you do,
when you've had sex just once but spent the following weeks com-
municating with words what you'd rather be saying with your
bodies.

Speaking of bodies, his is even more striking than I remember.

That brown skin has been kissed deeply by the California sun, and I am tempted to take off his clothes and see for myself just where the borders of his tan lines lie.

"Hi," he says, his rich voice breaking me out of a semi-trance.

"Hi," I reply, absently reaching up to finger a curl at my shoulder.

His eyes dance around the edges of my face, and for a moment I wonder if he's not into the new look. Then, setting down the grocery bags, he steps forward and with his free hand plucks a curl between his fingers. "This you?" he asks. I nod. "It's beautiful. You're beautiful."

At this I reach up, placing both hands on either side of his face. Our eyes meet for a second of acknowledgment before his lips firmly claim mine in an open-mouthed kiss that makes my knees go week. He drops the flowers, wrapping one hand behind my back to brace me, and with the other he cups the back of my head. Then he's kissing me—my mouth, my nose, my cheeks and forehead.

"You're better than I remember, Mr. Westbrook," I manage to say, when we pull apart and I've had the chance to catch my breath. And then I gasp, because in a swirl of lust and longing, I totally forgot he hasn't come alone. "Miles, please tell me Gabriel is not sitting in your car watching us make out right now."

His laugh floats up from the well inside his chest, and I feel tethered to the sound, from the way it tugs at the center of mine. "Nah. I gave myself a little bit of a head start," he says. "My guy won't be here for another five minutes."

"Well, in that case, let's get all this inside," I say, before drawing in a deep breath in an attempt to regain some composure. "Jamie should be down any minute." I bend to pick up the flowers as Miles grabs the bags.

Leading him through the foyer, I try to mask my big sigh of relief. Last night, I devoted about two hours of lost sleep to the potential that this reunion could crash and burn. I got married so young I never really had the chance to dip my toes in the pool of dating in the wild. But I've seen enough episodes of *Catfish* to know that strong romantic connections built long distance over phones are liable to either fall apart or descend into chaos under the pressure of face-to-face interaction. We may have had a scorching chemistry, even before we finally acted on it, but there has still been this nagging worry that my flying out here in the midst of his season could somehow alter the magic.

"Nice digs, Dream Girl." Miles whistles in appreciation while following me through the great room of the beach house. When we arrive in the ultramodern kitchen, we set the groceries and flowers down on the massive island. And, searching for words, I find myself absently running my fingers along the dark gray veining in the marble. When Miles's warm, calloused hand smooths up the exposed skin between my shoulder blades to cup the nape of my neck, chills run down my arms, and I turn to look at him.

"You seem nervous. What can I do?" he asks.

"You can reveal your intentions with my friend, slugger!" We both turn to discover that Jamie has entered the room. "Kidding," she deadpans, looking fresh and with a full beat while leaning against the entryway as Miles crosses to give her a hug.

"For starters, I intend to cook you and your friend brunch. How's that sound?" he says, voice as bright as the smile on his face.

"Sounds . . . woefully unoriginal, sir," she teases. "And what's this I hear about this sports agent of yours?"

Ding!

"Speak of the devil," I say.

THE HYPNOTIZING AROMA OF BUTTERMILK PANCAKES, APPLE-wood bacon, sliced avocado, fried eggs, and smashed plantains—or mofongo, as Miles says it's called in Puerto Rico—seasons the air of our patio dining setup. The midmorning weather is crisp and bright, and after working up a bit of a sweat at the stove, our chef is now down to a plain white T-shirt and basketball shorts, something I am *not* complaining about.

Our sous chef Gabriel, on the other hand, arrived at ten thirty on the dot packing mimosas and two carafes of coffee, and was dressed to the nines in a cashmere sweater and slacks with a fresh lineup.

"Look at *this* guy," Miles said as I led his agent into the kitchen after greeting him at the door. "Always gotta make me look bad."

"Nah, my brotha," Gabriel replied as they clapped hands and patted each other on the back. "A face like yours doesn't need these bells and whistles."

Peering over the two of them, I watched Jamie size Gabriel up. And when his gaze panned the room and latched on to hers, I think I saw the moment it mentally knocked her off-balance. She recovered quickly, though, sauntering around the island and sticking out a hand for him to shake.

"Jamie Marshall, makeup artist to the stars," she said, very matter of fact. "I'm told this is some sort of setup."

His laugh sputtered out of him, and he took her hand in both of his. "Pleasure to meet you, Jamie. I'm—"

"Gabriel. I'm aware," she cut him off. "Now what is it you sports agents actually do?"

And just like that, the sports agent and the makeup artist

waltzed out of the kitchen in rapt conversation. Now the four of us have sat down to feast on all of Miles's hard labor, and I'm finding it hard not to pinch myself at how well things are going. I'm on my second mimosa. Miles is having coffee since he doesn't drink before games. And Gabriel and Jamie are going back and forth on MJ versus LeBron—an argument Miles and I backed out of almost as soon as it began.

"So, you ready for the game tonight, big guy? How's that arm?" Gabriel asks Miles, after laying down his sword, likely out of pure exhaustion. In a debate, Jamie has the stamina of a rabbit in heat.

I don't miss the subtle grimace on Miles's face. He's seated across from me, and though our feet are entwined beneath the table, he's been a little quiet throughout the morning since his agent showed up, mostly attending to his dishes. "I'm good, man. Had an intense rehab session with Mario last night, but woke up feeling brand-new."

I run my foot up Miles's calf under the table, a wordless play for his attention. And when it works, I say, "What's that about?"

His face falls just slightly before he explains. "An old injury in my pitching arm that's just giving me some problems lately. G-man and my trainers have been trying to convince me to have another surgery."

I balk at the sound of the word *surgery*, then I see a mental picture of that long, raised scar running up the inside of his right arm along his elbow. "The Tommy John operation?" I ask.

Miles's eyes go wide, and then, taking me by surprise, his mouth curves into a smile. "You still watching that baseball YouTube channel, huh?"

As much as I'd like to bask in the idea that I've impressed him, there's a pit in my stomach. "So you're in pain when you pitch?" I ask.

At this, Gabriel chimes in. "It's a really typical injury for his level of play," he explains, eyeing his client and then looking to me. "Nothing to be alarmed about."

"Well, now I feel bad," Jamie says. "If y'all had told me the man's arm was busted I might have offered to hold a spatula or something."

This makes everyone laugh. But mine is only half-hearted. Instead, I'm watching Miles while he watches me come to the stark realization that I am in *deep* for this man. Deeper than I might be ready for.

"SO, LADIES." GABRIEL THROWS THE WORDS OVER HIS SHOULder on his way out the door, with Jamie following close behind him. "Can I interest you both in a suite for tonight's game? 'Cause . . . I might know a guy."

At his car in the driveway, he stops and turns to see Jamie roll her eyes. But deep down somewhere in that cold, cobwebby heart of hers, I know she's beside herself with anticipation. I can tell by the way she looks over at me, eyes pleading—like an eight-year-old who *swears* her friend's mom said it was okay for her to sleep over on a school night.

"You go!" I tell her. "Have a Dodger Dog for me. And some of those nachos with the fake cheese." At this I wink at Miles, whose eyes haven't stopped sweeping me up and down all morning.

"You sure you can't come?" she asks. "We can get you a wig. Put you in a romper or something."

I glance over at Gabriel and then back at Miles, who both appear to understand my hesitation without me having to voice it. The last thing I need right now is paps catching me cheering on my rumored boyfriend at a game—especially after what Elliot said at the meeting with our attorneys. And not before we've even had the chance to figure out what we are to each other.

"I think I'll hang back," I say, meeting Miles's eyes where I don't miss an inkling of disappointment. "Maybe meet back at your place after?"

"That works for me," Miles says, with a nod and slow-creeping smile that suggests having me at the game would have been great, but coming home to me *after* is the real prize.

"Okay, so it's settled." Jamie claps her hands, bouncing a little on her heels and beaming at Gabriel. "You're taking me out to a ball game."

"Pick you up at four?" Gabriel says, before slipping into his sleek black Mercedes.

28

TMZ:
Industry Insider: Onyx Records' exploitative and
predatory practices led to toxic company culture

BUSINESS INSIDER:
Activist group calls for music mogul's ouster amid
internal investigation

FORBES:
President of Onyx Records, Anthony Monzano, said to be OUT
after board casts no-faith vote

THE HOLLYWOOD REPORTER:
With Monzano out, culling of top brass may be next at Onyx
Records

PEOPLE:
What the shakeup at Onyx Records means for top artists like
Elliot Majors, Blake, Violet Olivera, Werewolf Holiday, Malik
North, and Ella Simone

I SAW THE NEWS ON X FIRST. AT THE BOTTOM OF THE FIRST IN-
ning, the Dodgers were at bat and with Miles in the dugout, I took
the opportunity to do some scrolling. It's one thing to have an insider tip for when a giant is about to fall, and another to get to watch
it come to pass. The first headline made my stomach drop. And by
the last, I started to feel the all-too-familiar signs of an anxiety attack coming on. But when texts started to flood in from the Glam
Squad (sans Sheryl), I began to feel a weight lift from my chest.

RODNEY: Ella girl, you must have an Angel
watching over you. Cuz this is some bible era
retribution if I ever seen any 🙏

JAMIE: Service sucks in this suite but I caught
the gist

JAMIE: Manzano out. Great. Now do Majors next!

ME: Crazy right? Wonder what Miss Thing's up
to now

RODNEY: Probably somewhere punching the air

RODNEY: Or fighting for her life in the comments

ME: Jamie, how's your date?

RODNEY: WAYMENT!!!

RODNEY: I go to Miami ONE TIME and Jamie
falls off the fuckboy wagon???

ME: I don't think that's how falling off the wagon
works.

RODNEY: Bitch. You know what I meant

JAMIE: The jury is still out on Gabriel. I will let you
heffas know my thoughts tomorrow 😘

ME: JAMIE!

JAMIE: Glass houses! Bc I know where ur
spending the night and it ain't in Malibu

RODNEY: Not both of you out there boo'd up!
It's too much! Don't make me get on a plane.
What would Sheryl say?

JAMIE: Speaking of . . . we need to check on her.
All of us.

ME: Agreed. When we're back in New York, let's
do a drive by.

RODNEY: You got it.

JAMIE: Consider it booked. Now back to the game.
G's about to show me what a "strike zone" is

RODNEY: Oh I bet tf he is 💦

ME: Rodney. Ew.

RODNEY: Don't hate! Participate!

After I opted out of going to the game, Miles called to give me the code to his security gate and told me I was more than welcome to watch from the comfort of his house—in fact that he'd prefer it. While I did experience sharper pangs of FOMO than I'd expected when Jamie sent me selfie pics of her and Gabriel in the game suite, I couldn't pass up the chance to explore Miles's living quarters unchaperoned—or to be there waiting for him when he returned home like he described in one of his voice notes.

When I pull up to his lot, I'm struck by the sheer size of the house. Thanks to Angelo, I was made aware of the number of zeros in Miles's contract before I even met him. Still, I always pictured him as the type to live in a sleek high-rise in DTLA or maybe even Century City. But I've just arrived at an ultramodern home situated on a tranquil street that's populated by what appear to be family estates on either side—not at all what I'd expect for a single athlete living in Los Angeles in his prime.

After punching in the security code and parking out front, I let myself into the house, where a retractable skylight frames Santa Monica's radiant sunset. Oranges, pinks, purples, and blues cast kaleidoscopic beams of light across the creamy white walls and sleek black fixtures of the home.

Walking through the center of the great room, I pass two massive dueling sofas, each draped in Hermès throws with matching sculptural end tables. At this point I make a mental note to grill Miles on his interior designer's contact and whereabouts. I may be living in a series of bi-coastal hotels at the moment, but like my grandmother always said, *Trouble don't last always*. Eventually, I plan to put down roots of my own and set up a place that feels like me . . . like home.

Just past the kitchen stands an expansive wall of sliding windows that let out to a glittering zero-edge pool that is surrounded on all sides by different parts of the home. It's clear Miles's architect had the place built with optimal privacy in mind. And that presents the perfect opportunity for me to coax him into a skinny-dipping session later on. I make *another* mental note and continue on with my self-guided tour.

Once outside, I'm tempted to dip my toes into the pool to see if it's heated, but I also don't want to miss another minute of the game. So, I venture downstairs to Miles's plush movie theater room, where he sent me detailed instructions for how to operate the projector and controls, inclusive of a tutorial on how to work the built in nacho machine. After successfully turning on the game—where the Dodgers are currently up by two—I head to the back of the dimly lit theater armed with my trusty nacho-making tips. When I approach the machine, I find a sticky note attached to the front of it.

> *Only the best for my Dream Girl.*
> *#fakecheese*
> *—M*

Within five minutes, I'm deadweight, sinking into the velvet cushions of an oversized reclining lounger, cradling a plastic tray of tortilla chips and steaming orange goo. For the second time in as many days I'm basking in my own contentment. It could be the high-quality seating or the low-quality carbs, but more than likely it's the fact that, this time, he called me *his* "dream girl." And it felt so damn good.

I WAKE UP TO THE FEELING OF STRONG ARMS SNAKING AROUND my waist from behind. Groggy and disoriented, I stretch out my stiff limbs on unfamiliar, but very soft cushions, and pry my eyes open to a room that's completely dark save the dancing icon that's projected on the screen. Turning over, I find Miles laying there, cradling me. He's crisp and fresh from his post-game shower. And somehow, waking up to him next to me isn't jarring at all, even after being used to sleeping alone for so long. Something about it feels right, familiar even. Maybe it's because lately, I've been dreaming of exactly this on a near constant basis.

"I'm sorry I kept you waiting so long," he says. "Had to do some press interviews after the game."

At this I realize I fell asleep before the final score. "Oh my god, did you win?" I ask.

His chuckle is a deep rumble, and I love it. "Yeah, we did," he says. "Score was nine to seven in the end."

"Ugh," I groan, covering my face with my hands. "I'm the worst."

"Not at all," he replies, smoothing back my hair with his warm hands. "You've been working hard. Want me to take you to bed?"

I sit up straight, suddenly wide awake and wiggling my eyebrows. "Actually, I was thinking we could try the pool first. If it's heated, of course," I tell him, shrugging a shoulder.

His eyebrows notch upward. "Oh, it's heated," he confirms. "You bring a suit?"

Biting my lip, I very slowly shake my head and mouth the word *no*. And he responds by lifting me over his shoulder and taking the steps to the exit at a fast clip.

EARLY APRIL IN SOUTHERN CALIFORNIA MAKES FOR COOL
nights that hardly rise above sixty degrees. But watching Miles
Westbrook strip off his clothes on a private pool deck more than
makes up for the drop in temperature. He's just flung his long-
sleeved workout tee over his shoulder and hooked his thumbs in
the waistband of his joggers.

"Let me," I say, stepping closer. "I didn't get to do this last
time—undress you. It's only fair."

At this, his smile stretches across his face as he raises both
hands in surrender. I lift up on my tiptoes to get closer to him,
pressing soft kisses to the center of his chest while slowly eas-
ing down his pants. He groans in pleasure, and the sound spurs
me on to take his growing length in my hand with one long, firm
stroke. His head tips back and *fuck yes* falls from his lips. Then he's
burying his hands in my hair and pressing his open mouth to
mine.

And this kiss is different than all the ones before. This one is
primal. Needful. It's desperate. Unlike words and music—there's
no thinking or craft to it. Only feeling and desire. And unlike
baseball, no one's keeping score. It's just the two of us, together,
both letting go and grabbing hold of the things we've lost and yet
somehow still found.

"Let's get you naked," he says as his hands skate down my sides,
gathering the fabric of my dress before wrenching it up and over
my head. Since I'm not wearing a bra, only my lace thong is left to
discard. He kneels down to remove it with his teeth. Then he begins peppering warm, wet kisses from my stomach down to the
apex of my thighs, and I *almost* let him keep going. But then this
would be over far too soon.

"Not yet," I tell him, clasping his hands that are splayed on my thighs. He looks up at me and I nod toward the pool.

Catching my hint, he stands and takes my hand to lead me to the water's edge. We descend the steps together, and when we submerge in the warm water up to my breasts and his waist, he lifts me and I cling to him. With his arms around me and my legs around him, I arch backward, throwing my head back and spreading my arms wide to skim the surface of the water, like making snow angels. Keeping his hold on me, Miles frees one hand to run a flat palm from my stomach up to the center of my chest.

"Hey, Dream Girl," he calls out.

"Mm-hmm," I hum, before sitting back up in his arms. "You got something to tell me, Curveball?"

"Is that what you call me?" he asks.

Nodding, I explain. "Because you're entirely unexpected, Mr. Westbrook."

His hands squeeze my ass, and I wrap my arms around his neck, pressing our foreheads together. "Well . . . you know back in the hotel room when I said I wanted to see you let go?" he asks. "This is what I was talking about—I love every second of it. Just wanted you to know that."

I let his words sink in, and a knot forms in my throat. "Thank you," I tell him, my voice thick with emotion.

"For what?" he asks, and a line forms between his brows.

"For seeing me," I tell him. Then we just embrace, clinging to each other, with my chin resting on his shoulder. We breathe each other in as the water swirls around us.

Everything about tonight feels surreal. The blue light dancing off the ripples of the pool. The glittering stars in the all-black sky. The neo soul playing on his sound system. It's all so beautiful, so perfect, I'm afraid I might start crying for real if he's not inside of me soon.

Thankfully, I don't have to find out because he carries me over to the steps, where he's laid two towels. We get out and dry off before he leads me over to a cabana that's equipped with a heat lamp. He lies down on his back and I climb on top of him, kissing my way up his torso, making a pit stop as I go.

Then I take him in my mouth, like I've wanted to for ages. Now, I get to relish the sounds he makes when *he's* the one to lie back and let go. And they're glorious. I've performed in arenas filled with screaming fans, thousands singing the words to songs that I have written. I've ridden those waves and felt those highs. I chase them in every studio session and anytime I step onto a stage. But the feel of Miles Westbrook coming undone from the pleasure I'm wringing from his body—this could be the high I chase forever.

Then Miles interlaces his strong fingers with mine and gently tugs me upward until I'm now straddling his lap. "I'm never getting over this," he tells me.

"Good. Because I don't want you to," I say back.

He firmly plants his hands on my hips and lifts me up to sink down on his rigid length. The stretch as I go is the most brutal bliss imaginable. I cry out with the first few strokes of my hips, collapsing so that now we're chest to chest. Now, he starts to drive into me from below—slowly stoking the flames of an impending wildfire.

"Tell me if it's too much, I want to see you," he pants through ragged breathing.

At this, I rise again as he brings his hands to my breasts. "That's it, Dream Girl. *Fuck*, you're gorgeous."

His words spur me on to ride him in earnest. And the rocking motion of our bodies is a giving and taking in return. It's a continuous pouring into each other. It's radical and real, like something I've never felt before. And when looking into Miles's soul-baring eyes becomes too overwhelming, I tilt my head back to peer up at a sky that's blanketed with stars and allow myself to get lost in a sea of possibilities.

29

*The love of my life . . . I'm much too young
to answer that question.*

Aretha Franklin

N "DAY DREAMING," ARETHA Franklin sings about the kind of
guy you'd give your everything to—your trust, your heart. She
says that with him, you'd share all your love until death do you
part. I always wondered if I'd find the kind of guy Aretha day-
dreamed about. One who'd say, as the song goes, *Hey, baby, let's
get away, let's go somewhere far, Baby, can we?*

He'd be my escape and I'd be his, and as long as we were together, it wouldn't matter where we were going.

Growing up, on the nights when my parents stayed out late
attending galas hosted by the local chapter of my dad's Boulé fra-
ternity, I'd walk down the hill of our View Park neighborhood to
my grandparents' house. Mimi would be in the kitchen, sneak sipping her dirty martinis. And Grandy, he'd be out on the back patio
with a crumpled detective novel and his tobacco pipe. Then I'd
invariably end up alone, in the front room with vinyl spinning on
the record player—probably waving a hairbrush like a microphone
in front of their grand mirror, singing for an audience of potted
plants.

When I look back, that old soulful music probably sparked the fantasies that ripened me for a guy like Elliot Majors. For an only child who was content with being alone more often than not, music was my way of imagining the people and spaces I'd hope to one day belong to. So it made perfect sense that this "daydream guy" would be one who spoke my same language. But after the night I just spent with Miles, I might have discovered a new way of speaking.

I'm awake now, blissfully tangled in his sheets and arms, with the rhythmic rise and fall of his chest pressed against my back lulling me into a calm, quiet comfort I could stay in for hours. But today is Sunday, and he won't play again until tomorrow. So I have plans to sneak out of bed and make him the only breakfast that's in my culinary repertoire.

Gently, I lift his arm away from my stomach, and he's so knocked out, he barely stirs. I slide to the edge of the bed, turn to look back at him and nearly lose my breath at the view of his beautifully naked cinnamon brown body laid across the white sheets like the most gorgeous stretch of rock-hard mountains peeking above a bed of fluffy white clouds.

Last night he told me if I got cold, I could help myself to any of his clothes. So, after taking a quick shower, I pad into his walk-in closet for a fresh pair of boxers and a crisp, clean white T-shirt. Then I zip downstairs to the kitchen in search of all the provisions I'll need to make my specialty . . . jelly pies. Essentially, they are grilled cheese sandwiches made with strawberry jam in lieu of cheese.

Miles's pantry puts the aisles of Erewhon to shame. With everything neatly jarred, canned, color coded, and labeled, it's not long before I've successfully procured the butter, sourdough, and preserves for my jelly pies—along with the Nutella, eggs, and cured meats I want for my sides.

Once back in the kitchen, I sync my phone to his surround sound system and turn on my meticulously curated *Sunday Kind of Love* playlist. Then, in the warm glow of the morning light, I start to prepare Miles's feast to the soul-stirring rasp of Otis Redding's treatise on loving someone too long to stop now.

MILES JOINED ME IN THE KITCHEN AT AROUND THE TIME ROberta Flack's "Feel Like Makin' Love" entered its second chorus. I'm almost positive he stood there, watching me dance while I toiled at the stove, for far longer than I was aware of. But it wasn't until I set off his fire alarm by charring the salami that he made his presence known.

After dumping the crisped-up meat and disabling the alarm, we brought the edible remnants of my efforts out to the cabanas by his pool. I've just popped a cube of cantaloupe into my mouth and am chewing slowly, anxiously awaiting his reaction to my jelly pies.

He sinks his teeth into the buttery grilled toast, and his eyes flutter closed. When he hums and does a little shimmy, my stomach swoops, and you'd think I'd topped the charts. "You don't hate it?" I ask, in search of his verbal affirmation.

Still chewing, he smiles with his eyes and gives my ankle an affectionate squeeze. "Mmm . . . it's perfect," he says. "Tastes like being a kid again."

My heart gallops hearing this, and the swell of emotion catches me off guard. Growing up, I was never taught to cook or clean or do any of the "traditional" gendered domestic things. Still, when I got married, that never stopped my mom from nitpicking all the ways I'd fallen short as a wife. And as far as Elliot was concerned, there were "people for all of that," so he never expected or even wanted it from me. As long as I looked the part on camera, kept the records and tours on schedule, and didn't make too many demands of him, we were good in his eyes. The chances of me making him a breakfast this basic and him even *pretending* to enjoy it were laughable. But watching Miles take pleasure in the smallest things affects me in ways I didn't expect. It's possible that this relationship, whatever we are, is changing me—like sensing a shift in the tectonic plates of my inner world in real time.

"What's churning in that head of yours?" His question draws me back to the moment.

And instead of telling him that what's been happening between us these past two months has only magnified what I was missing for a decade, that each micro-instance of intimacy and affection—like him watching a Blu-ray of *You've Got Mail* simply because I mentioned it once in passing, or trusting me enough to tell me about his mom's recovery, or devouring my silly jelly pies in minutes, or lending me the literal shirt off his back, or showing me what it feels like to make love, because after what we did last night in this very cabana, everything else could only ever be just sex—has only made me love him, helplessly. Instead of telling him all of that, I choose this moment to, as Jamie would call it, *freak the fuck out.*

I should be basking in this revelation—rolling around and rejoicing in the overwhelming joy of it. Instead, I feel myself clinging to the ledge, terrified of the fall. But I spare him all of this with my response, by reducing it down to its simplest form. "Just thinking about us," I tell him. And even though it's the truth, it is so watered down that it feels like a lie.

"Mmm, same over here," Miles says. And he's smiling a smile that tells me he's blissfully unaware of the chaos churning in my head.

I swallow hard as my chest continues to thump violently. "Oh yeah? What about?" I ask. And my breathing kicks up as I try to mask my growing panic.

"I . . . w-was just thinking about a question I want to ask you . . ." Then he shakes his head, like he's mustering the courage to say it. He looks at me with gentle eyes and an expression so open and hopeful, I want to preemptively say *yes* to whatever it is. "Come . . . to my game tomorrow?"

Chances are, whatever reaction he was looking for from me is not the one I just gave him. Because in a flash, all the vulnerability that was evident in his open, raw expression visibly crumbles.

"I'm s-sorry," he rushes to say. "It's too soon. I shouldn't have done th-that."

I've made him anxious, and it's the last thing I wanted. "No, no. It's okay," I tell him, although nothing about this is. We're a race car seconds from spinning out. "I just . . . I don't know if we're ready for that?" I try to mask how rattled I am by keeping my voice calm and steady.

And again, I've clearly said or done the wrong thing, because his look of confusion has now shifted to one of hurt. "Just s-so I understand you, what is it *we're* not ready for?" he asks. And his voice has taken on a weightier tone.

Any of this. All of it, I want to say. I want to tell him that if it's possible to want things you're not sure you can or should have, that's the spot I'm currently occupying. But it all sounds wrong and insufficient. "Miles, I'm not sure this is fair."

"I'm sorry," he repeats. "You're probably right." When he speaks, his words are flat, lacking their usual full, rich texture, which strikes a discordant tone that rings harsh to my ears. "But I think that's my answer either way."

"Please, Miles, no," I beg, without knowing what I'm even asking for. "We said we didn't know what this was, right?"

At this, he moves to stand. "Right," he says, gathering the plates and flatware. "And that's how you feel now? After last night?"

"Damn it, Miles. I don't have all the answers," I practically shout as I scramble to get up from my seat and follow after him as he heads back into the house.

He stops and turns back to me. "Ella, I don't need you to have *all* the answers," he says, his eyes pleading. "I just need you to have one. What do you want?"

I take one long deep breath in, hoping, *reaching* for some level of divine clarity. Then a rush of memories floods in. One particular night, I was maybe eleven years old, my parents were off at my father's Boulé chapter's holiday party—I remember thinking as I watched them leave, *How can two people fight so ugly but look so beautiful together?* Those nights at my grandparents' house, after Grandy went off to bed and Mimi had had her second or third martini, she often got loose-lipped about things. This time I asked her how they'd made it work, why she'd stayed. And I remember her linen apron, how it was covered in burnt-yellow peonies. The curving smoke from her Marlboro Light as it wafted out of the kitchen sink window, the aged mahogany of her elegant hand as it clasped her martini glass, and the sparkling diamond that adorned her left ring finger. She snuffed out the cigarette and set down her drink, then looked me square in the eye. "I was young and dumb," she said.

Then she turned out the lights and went to bed.

The moment of clarity comes when I release a slow and steady exhale. "I don't want to belong to anybody," I tell Miles, and my voice breaks apart on the words.

Miles's face softens, and he sets the breakfast tray down on the island. "And, baby, that's okay. I'm good with that. After what you've been through, I *understand* it," he says. "But what if I want to belong to you?"

His confession puts a crack in my shield. It amplifies the thoughts I've been trying to silence since realizing I'd ventured far beyond letting go and acting on my desires, to a place of uncharted territory—a point of no return. What if *he's* different? What if *we* could be different together?

Female artists . . . you're all the same, Elliot told me once, when I asked to bring in a new producer on my latest album. *You just want to be different in all the same ways.*

The dissonance is too much, and I need some space to breathe. I trust Miles. I love this man. I am *in love* with him. But I have been this way before. I have been completely overcome by a feeling—by a man. So, this time around, it's *me* that I don't know if I can trust. I want to be ready to lean into what I have right now with Miles, but to do that in front of the world? That would be like taking a trust fall right after just barely surviving a crash landing.

Stepping forward, I take his hands in mine. "This." I gesture between the two of us. "It's so good sometimes it's scary. It scares me, Miles. I'm scared." The words are barely above a whisper, and my voice ripples when I say them.

"I know, Dream Girl, I know," he says, pulling me closer to him and wrapping me up in his arms.

Otis Redding is playing again now. This time it's "These Arms of Mine." And maybe it's without thinking, but Miles begins to rock us back and forth to the melody.

Then, beneath the music, I hear him softly whisper the words "I am too."

I'VE REALLY FUCKED UP THIS TIME. I COULD HAVE SHUT UP, gone to that game, worn a wig like Jamie suggested, cheered on my guy, sat there, and ate my food. Instead, I've plunged us into an existential crisis on the morning we should have been able to bask in the afterglow of the night things shifted for us. Irrevocably. *But what if I want to belong to you?* he'd asked. After what he's been through—the betrayal, the hurt and shame. Sure, he's had more time to heal. But his wounds from Monica are no less deep. His past no less painful. And still, he presented me with an open door to his heart while I stood frozen in place.

I guess post-traumatic stress really does a number on a person.

Miles and I left things unresolved. Like a scratch in a record, my alarm sounded in the middle of our slow, rocking embrace, and instantly, I remembered the recording session I'd booked in Studio City. If I hadn't been trying to coordinate with this artist for the past six months, I would have considered pushing it—but flaking on studio time is one of the industry's highest forms of disrespect.

I didn't lie to Miles, but I did withhold a truth in a moment when I think he needed it most. And I'm not sure, but that seems like the bigger transgression. I could have and probably should have told him that I'm in love with him right there in his kitchen. Instead, as I was leaving and he asked me what I needed from him, I took the safer route and simply told him I wasn't going any- where, that there was nothing to worry about—that I'd see him before and after his game tomorrow, but that for today, I just needed some space to clear my head.

I park in front of the studio, when a call comes in over the Bluetooth speaker. Checking the display, I see it's Janet. "Please tell me this is a good news call?" I ask as I answer, probably sounding like I haven't slept in days.

"Well, I am billing you on a Sunday. If it was bad news, I'd at least wait until tomorrow," she says with her custom brisk de- livery.

"Praises up for small blessings," I muse in jest. "So what have you got for me?"

"Mamie Houston is stepping in as chairperson and CEO of Onyx Records," Janet explains. "And she's requesting a meeting with you tomorrow."

"Uh. Wow. Okay. I . . . I hardly have words," I stammer. "Mamie is a legend. She's an artist, and a producer. She's an advocate for marginalized creators. She's . . . well, she's Black. My goodness. How did this happen?"

"That's *not* the kind of question I'm paid to know the answer to, Ella," Janet says flatly.

Touché. "Okay. Well . . . how about this one," I try again. "What should I expect from her on Monday?"

"Now *that* I can work with," she says. "I sent over some preliminary terms based on what you and I discussed regarding what you'd require in order to stay on with the label. The fact she's proactively asking for a meeting with you, I'd say, is a sign that she's willing to play ball."

"Janet, I don't know what I'd do without you," I say. "Actually, maybe I do. I'd be sliding down a wall staring blankly ahead into the unknown abyss of my future."

"This is what I do," she replies. "Work to keep the inevitable wall sliding and nihilism to a minimum for my clients when they are at their lowest point. Sometimes I get lucky, and the arc of the moral universe does its job . . . it bends toward justice," she says. "Now, if you don't have additional questions, I've got to roll some calls."

And with that, she's off my line.

I'm still twenty minutes early for the studio session, which is more than enough time to sit and dwell on the current status of my professional and personal lives, which both appear to be suspended in a state of flux. Mamie Houston taking over the reins at Onyx could be the catalyst for the career shift I've always wanted—one that surrounds me with a team that believes in the ways I'd like to evolve as an artist and not just the tried-and-tested image that Elliot Majors crafted for me when I was nineteen. The possibility that this could be within my grasp is a heady feeling.

So, when I catch a glimpse of myself in the rearview mirror, I nearly jump upon discovering that I'm smiling, probably for the first time today. But that smile doesn't quite reach my eyes. And that likely has to do with a certain someone on the other side of town whose future I can't quite picture my place in just yet.

30

M AMIE HOUSTON LIVES AT the top of Beachwood Canyon in the kind of Spanish bungalow I could see myself putting down roots in, whenever I finally get my act together and stop living in hotels. Lush topiaries frame the white stucco exterior, teal window trimmings, and a scalloped clay roof—forming a postcard-worthy meeting place to discuss what my future might look like if I stay on at Onyx Records.

She answers the door with a smile that is warm enough to curb the chill of the late morning. Around my mother's age, Mamie sports a floor-length duster made of vibrantly embroidered silk. Her platinum blond coils create a striking contrast to the deep complexion of her blemish-free face. It's almost hard to believe the woman in front of me made it big in the eighties as an emcee, with now-classic hits that were once deemed too transgressive for even MTV's airwaves. She is the epitome of Chaka Khan's "every woman"—the auntie *and* the DJ at your cookout, who happens to now be at the head of the table in the boardroom too.

"Ella, I'm glad you could make it," she says before waving me inside the foyer. Stepping forward, I thank her for the invite, then quickly lose my train of thought as I am instantly swaddled with dueling scents of jasmine and thyme. Her home is a delight for the senses, with every nook and corner providing an elaborate treat for the eyes.

"Your home is gorgeous, Ms. Houston," I tell her.

"Oh pfft!" she says. "Call me Mamie. But thank you. Everyone deserves a sanctuary to call their own." She levels me with a pointed glance, and the words feel loaded with meaning. I've been a vagabond for months. I wonder if she knows.

"I thought we'd have some coffee out on the terrace," she says, interrupting my thoughts. "But if you prefer tea . . . I've got that too."

"Coffee is great," I tell her. "I'm easy to please."

She chuckles at this, as if to say, *We'll see about that*, before leading us out to the terrace.

Mamie's garden is picturesque, with a sitting area she's meticulously designed for the warm, cozy kind of outdoor entertainment you'd expect from the party-planning matriarch of a large family—not a music mogul who's just benefited from a hostile takeover. Fuchsia and periwinkle bougainvillea climb a latticed pergola, with potted plants and string lights suspended overhead. An outdoor Moroccan rug lays at our feet, where I've just noticed a chocolate Lab is taking a rest. I startle when I see him.

"Oh, don't worry, he's friendly. That's Clarence Clemons," she tells me, warmly eyeing her dog. "He's an old boy. Doesn't have much energy anymore, but he's the best company in the world."

"He's beautiful." I kneel to scratch him behind the ears. "And what a tribute," I say, referencing her dog's namesake—the legendary saxophonist for Bruce Springsteen and the E Street Band.

Her smile stretches a mile wide. And the setting is so inviting,

I expect we'll ease into business talk with a getting-to-know-you chat. I open my mouth to ask if she's lived here long, when she beats me to the punch . . .

"So, I have to be honest with you," she starts, just as my butt hits the plush love seat across from hers. "A birdie told me you're seriously thinking of becoming an indie artist. So I've asked you here to convince you *not* to jump ship. Because there are things I want to do at Onyx Records that I'd really love for you to be a part of."

"Well, I'm not used to people showing their cards right out of the gate," I admit. "I have to say it's very refreshing."

"I learned a long time ago that holding back the things I'm really after doesn't usually serve me in the long run," she explains. "I may not have all the kinks figured out. The plan might need some tweaking. But voicing what you want, even if only to yourself, isn't just the best place to start. For me, in business and in life, it's the *only* place to start."

What she's just said flashes before me like a blinking sign. *Voicing what you want is the only place to start.*

"By the way, you've got a fireball of an attorney vouching for you. I *love* to see it," she says. "She's already sent over a list of terms you'd want negotiated in a potential contract extension. But I want to know what, say, your top three nonnegotiables are?"

She's right about Janet. I was well prepped before walking into this meeting and advised to come in with a handful of asks to put in front of Mamie. *Think "pie-in-the-sky, if this world were yours" kinds of things,* Janet told me roughly twenty minutes ago over another Bluetooth-car chat. *The worst she could say is no, and then we'd be right back where we started.*

"After I finish touring this album, I want to explore artistically . . . tap into genres outside of pop and R&B for once. I'm really inspired by neo soul, even jazz. And I'd love to experiment with a whole new kind of instrumentation," I say.

"Ah, jazz. Something like that Whitney rendition you performed at the charity gala in New York recently?" she asks, which takes me by surprise.

I perk up. "You were there?"

"I was not." She shrugs casually, taking a sip of her coffee. "But the internet is *everywhere*. I love what you and your band did with the arrangement. I'll admit I've always been excited to see more of what you're capable of . . . beyond covers and samples. Matter of fact, I might still be subscribed to your old YouTube channel. What else are you looking for in a partnership?"

For starters, I'd like for my relationship with the label to actually resemble a "partnership," I think but don't say. Instead, I go with, "So, with this kind of departure, I think it only makes sense for me to drop the 'Ella Simone' persona entirely and rebrand as just myself, 'Elladee.' "

Mamie appears to consider this with a bit of hesitation, and I inwardly cringe. "I'm not married to your original stage name, but out of curiosity . . . why change now and risk shedding the brand recognition?"

"Well, that's sort of the point," I confess. And when her eyebrows knit together, I go on to explain. " 'Ella Simone' was Elliot's creation, in every sense. Her hair. Her clothes. Every single off that first album. All him."

As I speak, she nods her head in recognition. "Got it. Anything else?" She says, simply. Like my reasoning here is not only adequate but convincing. I sit up a little straighter.

And now for the *big* ask. The words I've been terrified of saying out loud in stuffy rooms with starched suits and stern faces for years. The dream that Elliot entertained only in theory, like the marathon training you push off year after year because you know running that far isn't really for you. I've been so terrified, and still am, I practically say the words with one eye closed. "I want more time and resources, so I can produce and write for other artists too."

And to my surprise, when I've finished the scariest sentence I have ever uttered—apart from *Elliot, I'm leaving you*—a creeping smile spreads across Mamie's face. It's not a small, polite grin aimed at placating me only to dismiss me later. And it's not a teasing smirk that threatens to break apart with laughter at my grandiose plans. This smile is broad and genuine and accepting. It looks like affirmation—like real recognizing real. Like she's taking me and my plans seriously.

"Okay," she says, clapping her hands together. "I like it."

"So, that's it?" I ask. "Just . . . okay?"

"Well, of course there'll be some red tape. And you've got a long list of other concerns that legal will need to do its due diligence with, but if these are your main nonnegotiables, as president of the label, I'm in full support. And look, I can't promise you there won't be any pushback or roadblocks along the way. I may be chairperson and CEO but I've still got a board of directors to answer to. On top of that, come next week, I'm walking into murky waters, what with Monzano loyalists already calling for my head. So, I can't promise you easy, but I can promise you an ally." She pauses for another sip of coffee. "So, can I answer anything else for you before you consult with Janet and decide?"

"Yes," I say, peering at her intently. "Why me?" I ask. Partly because I'm an artist, and we *always* need the reassurance. And partly because I've had my fair share of too-good-to-be-true, and I need to understand her reasons.

"It's really as simple as this . . . I'm motivated by legacy," she says, placing her mug on the table between us. "I'm a fan of your talent. Not just your music, or your brand. But of what I've seen you do and what I think you have left in you to accomplish." She crosses her legs and leans back. "There are people who have made decent money and good music with you. I would like to see you make *great* music . . . albums that will play for the next sixty to one hundred years. It's what I want for all the artists I sign and work with at Onyx two point oh." She leans forward to take a final sip from her coffee. "I hope that answers your question?"

I BOUND OUT OF MAMIE'S BUNGALOW AS IF FLOATING ON A cloud. I've still got some things to consider—terms to discuss with Janet. Plus, it's always best to sleep on life's big decisions before we make or break them. And it might even be best for me to wait on signing the contract until the divorce is final.

But all of that aside, I've just had the best meeting of my life. The sheer freedom of giving voice to what I want in the presence of a person with the ability and desire to make it all happen is something I don't think I've ever experienced.

As I hop in my car and turn on the ignition, Mamie's words flash again across my mind's eye . . . *Voicing what you want is the only place to start.* So I might as well start there.

31

S HE'S KEPT ME WAITING so long, I've made up my mind to leave and then chickened out no less than three times. It's funny how we never really grow out of being our parents' children. Because sitting here frozen with indecision feels like being in time-out, and the second I turn my nose away from the corner, Beverly Robinson's going to jump out of the closet and add five more minutes to my punishment.

The server has topped off my sweet tea twice, and my leg is bouncing with so much vigor, I've nearly shaken the flatware off the table. I hadn't originally planned on taking my mother up on her request to meet for lunch. But when Miles asking me to simply *show up* at tonight's game sent me into an emotional tailspin, partly spurred on by my unprocessed childhood trauma, I figured facing things with The Source might do both of us some good.

But just when I've settled on dropping some cash so I can bounce, Beverly Robinson appears on the patio of South LA's Post & Beam. And like Lena Horne's Glinda the Good, she is the picture of beauty and grace in her crisp linen set and fresh silk press. It's not until she arrives at the table and takes her seat, however, that I see her delicately placed mask crumbling.

"I'm sorry I'm late, honey," she says, removing her Chanel shades. "It's um . . . well, let's say it's been . . . *a day*." Her eyes are red-rimmed and slightly puffy, with fine lines etching worrisome grooves around her mouth.

Unsure of whether or not to overlook her obvious distress or to call attention to it, I offer a handful of crumpled napkins. "Mom, are you okay?" I settle on asking.

"Perfectly so," she says, her words clipped and perky. Then she blows her nose in the most dainty, unobtrusive way. "Tell me about things. How are you? How is the . . ." She pauses, eyes glancing around the patio. When she looks back at me, she lowers her voice. "How are the divorce proceedings?"

I bristle at this because the last time we spoke, confirming I'd served Elliot, might as well have been the same as telling her I'd stormed the Capitol on January 6. In my stunned silence, I notice an errant tear escape the corner of her eye. She moves quickly to swipe it away.

Having had enough of the pretenses, I place my palms flat on the table. "Okay, Mom. You're clearly crying. Please. What's going on?" I ask.

She pushes out a gust of air, then gently folds her hands in her lap. "We're going to need something stronger than that sweet tea you've got there," she says, nodding toward my glass.

We order Bloody Marys and while we wait, my mother drops a mini bomb. "So, I saw your music video. The one with the baseball player. He's *very* attractive." She tells me this before sipping her water and waggling her eyebrows. It's a diversionary tactic, I'm sure. And while it won't knock me off course for getting to the bottom of her poorly masked trauma, it has succeeded in making me very uncomfortable.

I don't know how to calibrate my response. If she and I had a healthy mother-daughter relationship, we'd probably share a giggle or two about the hottie I got to make out with on a rainy rooftop in the name of show business. Then she'd probably take a nostalgic detour and recall the story of how I ran home crying in seventh grade because I'd had my first kiss with Sammy Larson on the bus and sparks didn't fly. But our relationship has never been healthy. And she wasn't even home the night after I'd kissed Sammy in the back of the school bus.

"I'm in love with him," I tell her. I hadn't intended to. But it sort of just flies out of me like a caged bird set free. "That 'very attractive' baseball player I was in the video with. His name is Miles Westbrook. And I think I want to try to make things work with him . . . for forever. If I can swing it."

That my cold, distant mother is the first person in the world I've confessed this to could probably hold its own in the second verse to Alanis's "Ironic." But here we are. And there it is—the truth.

At my confession, Beverly gurgles her water. Just about spits it up. I could laugh because Beverly Robinson is typically nothing if not composed. After taking a moment to get herself together, she says, "You—you're telling me the rumors they're printing have all been true? That you cheated on . . ." She pauses, adjusting her rising volume back down to a whisper. "That you cheated on Elliot?"

Of course this would be her response to my declaration of love. I close my eyes and exhale through my nose. *Shoop, shoop*, as Whitney Houston would say. "Nothing happened between me and Miles before Elliot and I legally separated," I tell her, resenting the fact I have to persuade even my own mother that I'm not the Jezebel the tabloids have painted me to be. Never mind the fact that Elliot's rampant, well-documented cheating seems to be a total nonissue for her, and seemingly everyone else too. "Hell, I never even met Miles until *after* we were legally separated."

She takes a moment to process what I've said. Adjusting her crisp collar and fiddling with an earring, she appears nervous to ask her next question. "Does he . . . are you happy with him? This Miles Westbrook person?"

To say I'm knocked off-balance by this would be an understatement. Suddenly, my eyes sting and I fear I might cry. Wordlessly, I nod yes.

Without looking at me, she asks, "Could you be happy without him?"

This question surprises me in a different way. Not only because it's one I have yet to consider, but because something about the way my mom asks it makes me think it's more for her than me. And now she's crying again.

"Mom, can we cut through the pretenses here? Will you just tell me what's going on with you?" I ask.

She sucks in a long, slow breath, then lets it out on a shaky exhale. "Your father has decided to file for a divorce," she says, her words measured but thick with emotion. "The writing has been on the wall, I suppose. But I was served the papers this morning . . . by his sister . . . the bitch always loathed me. Had the nerve to smile as she did it too."

Apart from knowing that my mother seldom ever curses, I feel queasy and defensive of her from the visual she describes. And yet the fact that I immediately default to empathy for a woman who has so often shown me the opposite makes me want to book an emergency session with my therapist.

"How did you know when Elliot was cheating?" she asks me next, and I'm thrown for another loop. I glance up in search of our server, or *any* server, in hopes our alcohol is on its way soon.

"Ah. Is that what's going on? Dad's been fooling around?" I ask, trying to contain my alarm.

She looks over her shoulder. "Would you keep your voice down?" she scolds.

Exasperated, I glance at the sky and pray for rain, a comet, anything to end this. "I'm sorry, Mom, I'm having a hard time understanding why you asked for this lunch. I don't know if you were expecting an emotional support daughter to show up today, but news flash, last I checked my life's in shambles too."

At long last, the Bloody Marys arrive. Our server sets them down, and I immediately ask for another shot for mine. It's a good thing I Uber'd here from Studio City, because at the rate we're going, I wouldn't be fit to drive back to the rental in Malibu anyway. "Ella, I'm sorry. Again, it's just that all your life you've seemed to skate by so unbothered and untouched by things. It all seemed to come so easily for you . . . even this divorce. I mean here you are mere months later already onto the next! I guess I was a bit hands off with you growing up . . . but some of us had to struggle for the things we have in life. I simply don't think you understand."

Oh, I'll be needing that extra shot all right. "You know what's not easy?" I ask her. "Growing up knowing the person you admire most, the person you most want to make proud, couldn't be bothered to give you even the smallest validation," I say, voice quivering. "So you get to a point where you discount it all and pretend it doesn't matter that to your mother, you'll never be enough. But deep down, it will *always* matter. And no, Mother . . . things have not been *easy* for me. It might look that way to someone who hasn't cared enough to pay attention. But that's beside the point, because you know what? Parents should want things to be easier for their children than they were for them . . . and not resent them because of it."

The server arrives with the extra shot, and before he sets it down on the table, I intercept it, thank him kindly, and take it down the hatch. Then I do what I should have done before Beverly Robinson arrived. I get up and leave.

ESPN:
LA Dodgers Star Pitcher Miles Westbrook & Mega Producer Elliot Majors Scuffle in Alleyway

A representative from Elliot Majors's communications team has signaled his intentions to file charges with the LASD against LA Dodgers starting pitcher Miles Westbrook. In recent months, Westbrook has been romantically linked to R&B singer Ella Simone. According to publicly available court documents, Simone filed for divorce from Majors in January.

Photographers snapped the above photos of an apparent scuffle between the two men which took place in the alleyway of West Hollywood fine dining establishment Sempre, Mia. In the photos, Majors is seen taking a tumble to the ground while partially entangled with a visibly upset Westbrook. In subsequent snaps, Majors is seen with cuts and bruises to his face. Bystanders also reported he departed the scene with a limp. Westbrook is pictured cradling his pitching arm.

These photos come as a shock and potential setback after what has become a critical year for Westbrook following a disastrous end to the Dodgers' 2023 World Series run.

Sports fans will remember last year's physical altercation between Westbrook and Dodgers right fielder Jorge Morales. Sources close to the situation reported at the time that the team was in warm-ups when news broke of an alleged monthslong affair between Morales and Westbrook's then wife and college sweetheart, Monica Westbrook.

Footage from the locker room that was obtained and disseminated by TMZ showed Westbrook throwing the first punch. This resulted in his immediate suspension and a $25,000 fine. Morales was traded to the Marlins. The Dodgers would go on to lose the championship to the Rangers.

While video footage of the alleged altercation between Westbrook and Majors has yet to surface, this development is sure to complicate what league experts have coined a much-needed "Road to Redemption" year for Miles Westbrook. Images of the ace pitcher cradling his pitching arm are sure to raise eyebrows with Dodgers coaching, management, and fans. If Majors were to press charges, Westbrook's status with the Dodgers could very well be in serious question.

I toggle over to select the silent ride option on the Uber app as I lean on the parking meter outside of the restaurant. I'm not a smoker, but if one walked by, I'd be tempted to bum a cigarette for the first time in my life. I don't know what I hoped to get out of a lunch with Beverly, but I did walk away with some unexpected clarity. Now I know that I don't want to become so jaded about my past that it stops me from experiencing the full spectrum of what the rest of my life has to offer.

Reaching in my tote for my phone to call Miles and tell him that yes, I will take him up on the offer to attend tonight's game—

cold feet be damned—I notice a barrage of missed calls and texts. Before I can swipe open to check them, I'm getting an incoming call from Jamie. I answer on the first ring.

"Hey," I say. "What the hell is going on?"

"Are you sitting down?" she asks, and for once there's no levity or sarcasm coming from her.

"Don't have that option at the moment," I say. "Is everyone all right? You're scaring me."

"It's Miles . . . and Elliot," she says, and instantly my heart plummets to my stomach. "It's being reported that they got into some sort of physical altercation last night?"

For a second, everything goes black, and if it weren't for the meter, I'd have surely fallen down. "Jamie, tell me no one's hurt," I demand, surprised I can even speak at the moment.

"Only cuts and bruises," she confirms. "And Miles's arm is fucked up. He's on the injured list for tonight."

At this I put Jamie on speaker so I can sift through my notifications, hoping to see something from Miles. Swiping with my thumb, I see a dozen texts from Rodney, calls from Janet and Angelo, even a message from Sheryl . . . but nothing from Miles.

"Jamie," I say, on the verge of tears. "Where is he? I have to get to him, okay?"

"I know, babe," she says. "Gabe's on his way to you, I sent him a pin of your location. You'll be with Miles soon."

32

CANCEL THE UBER JUST before Gabriel's Mercedes pulls up to the restaurant. He hops out of the car to open my door as I rush over to him on shaky legs. I glance at him and notice his unusually ruffled appearance. He's in sweats and clearly hasn't slept a wink.

"Ella," he says, voice raw from what can only be exhaustion. "You gotta know he didn't do what's in those reports. Elliot showed up—"

"How is he?" I cut in. I probably sound wild with desperation. And if I do, I can't bring myself to care. The last time I saw Miles, I had the chance to tell him I think the world of him, that I adore every part of him, and I didn't. Now *his* world is crashing down around him, and it's partly my fault.

Once I'm settled inside the car, there's a beat as Gabriel buckles his seat belt as he casts me a sidelong glance. In that moment of silence, I forget to exchange air. "He's fine. Physically," Gabriel finally confirms. "Apart from his arm. The team doctor's taking a look at that right now."

I breathe a sigh of relief, but it's only half-hearted. Because while I'm relieved to know that Miles is physically okay, I need eyes on him, and hands on him, before I truly believe it.

"Did you read what they're saying happened?" Gabe asks me, and I want to say that I don't care what whoever is saying about whatever. But I did get the chance to scan ESPN's article after I hung up with Jamie. And even if half of what's printed is true, I'll never be able to apologize enough for bringing this level of drama into Miles's life. That feeling I had at my breakfast with Janet, that sneaking suspicion that, just like my mom said, things were happening a little too easily for me. That at some point the other shoe would have to drop . . . it finally has.

I'm afraid that if I speak too much I'll cry, so I keep my answer to Gabe's question short. "Yeah, I did." I glance at him and find his mouth pressed into a hard line.

"Miles didn't swing at Elliot," he says. "I was there at dinner with him last night at Sempre, Mia."

This draws a gasp from me, and Gabriel looks over. "It's where his mom works. He's told you about her, I know."

I nod. "In our voice notes," I confirm. "He told me all about her."

"Well, I left early to meet up with Jamie," he continues, shaking his head. And I can almost feel the regret in his voice. "Miles always leaves out the back alleyway entrance . . . for security reasons and to help his mom keep her low profile."

"He doesn't want press to figure out she works there," I guess aloud. At this, Gabe nods.

"Anyway, Elliot must have been tracking us somehow, because according to Miles, the guy shows up in the alley, drunk off his ass and looking for a fight. He swings at Miles a few times and misses. But on the last swing, he loses his footing but latches on to Miles's arm on the way down. Elliot takes a tumble, bangs himself up. But he dislocates Miles's arm in the process."

I drop my head into my hands. Of all the potential outcomes of me divorcing Elliot Majors, I never saw this one coming. He and his team have ghosted me and Janet since the botched settlement discussion. So I've had no insight into what angle they'd be coming from next. But the recent headlines out of Onyx Records and whatever they might spell for his image and career must have rocked him to his core. Or maybe he got word of my meeting with Mamie Houston, saw that I was about to escape his clutches, and decided to set things aflame on his way out the door.

Or maybe, like my Mimi used to say, *chaos doesn't need a reason.*

BY THE TIME WE PULL INTO THE DRIVEWAY AT MILES'S HOUSE, his team has already gathered at the stadium for their warm-up. I turn to Gabriel. "Does he even *want* to see me?"

"You're the *only* person he wants to see right now," he tells me. And hearing this pierces through the guard I'd started to defensively erect around myself somewhere along the 10 freeway. "I texted to tell him you're on your way up."

After punching in the security code, I enter the house. It's an unnaturally overcast afternoon in Santa Monica, which replaces what was once warm and radiant with a dark and imposing interior. Padding up the stairs, I hear the sound of our version of "No Ordinary Love" coming from the direction of the primary suite. My heart slams against my chest, and I start taking the steps two at a time in a rush to get to him.

When I open the door, Miles is at the window, head bowed, in his oversized sitting chair. His arm is in a sling, and seeing that crushes me. I pad forward, and he must sense my movement, because his head lifts and he turns to face me. When his eyes latch on to mine, Miles doesn't speak. He simply leans back against the headrest, and as if in full surrender all the tension drains from his body.

I draw closer, and with his uninjured arm he reaches for me. Careful not to hurt him, I step between his legs and clamber up until I'm straddling his lap. I press him close against my chest and rest my cheek against the crown of his head. Even in the midst of such desolate circumstances, I take simple pleasure in holding the man I love—siphoning off his pain.

"I'm so sorry, Miles," I tell him, with my voice thick from unshed tears. "You'll never know how sorry I am that this happened."

"Baby . . ." He drags out the word, rocking back to look me in the eye. With a gentle hand he smooths back my hair. "Don't do that, okay. This was all *him*. Tell me you know that?"

I take his words and swallow them whole, knowing they are true but also that it'll take me a while to fully believe them. I nod anyway.

"And *you* know everything's gonna be okay, right?" I say. "Even if he's dumb enough to press charges. If it goes to trial, I'm more than willing to be a character witness against him."

Miles shakes his head. "I'd never put you through that. Besides, the people I need to convince most won't be a jury. They're in the front office."

At this, I grimace, and my worries start to compound again. Miles could lose his career all because my trifling ex-husband was trying to settle a score.

"But let's not talk about this anymore," he says. "We can't change any of it today anyway. Can we talk about yesterday, though . . . before you left?"

Swallowing hard, I say, "Now *that* I do need to apologize for." Then, reaching up, I smooth out the worry lines in his forehead. "There's so much I could have told you yesterday and I held it all back. I left you here without telling you how I feel, and I've never regretted anything more."

"You want to tell me now?" he asks, smiling at me with glassy eyes. "Think I could use some good news. Been kind of a bad day."

"Miles Rafael Westbrook, two and a half months ago I pretended to fall in love with you on a video shoot. But, turns out"—I shrug as a single tear falls from my eye—"it was for real."

And now I've said it. For the second time in my life, I have told a man I love him. And this time, like the last time, it feels like swimming out to sea. But instead of facing a vast, empty horizon, now I'm looking at a glittering island. And Miles is standing there waving back at me, beckoning me to join him on the shore.

"I'm in love with you, Miles. *You* are who I want. When we're alone behind closed doors and, I don't know exactly how, but I want you out in the open too."

Miles exhales and with the release of air, his body deflates beneath me—like all that pent-up doubt has finally released at once. "Well, Elladee Ashley Robinson . . . since we're using government names. That's a good thing. Because you've had me since the Grammys. Before I broke your dress. Before you put on my shirt. I knew I loved you the s-second you looked me in the eyes and challenged me to name three of your songs."

"Is that right?" I ask.

"Mm-hmm," he confirms. "I would have taken any opportunity to be in a room with you again. Even a music video across the country."

I sink farther into his lap, prepared to take off my clothes and show him just how much this confession has bound us together. But then Miles's phone rings. He reaches in his pocket to check the caller ID.

"It's Coach Carlin," he says. "He's at the gate."

This sudden reminder of the heaping shitstorm beyond these four walls makes the tiny hairs on the back of my neck stand at attention. I rise off Miles's lap and help him up from the low chair since he's only got use of one arm at the moment.

"Coach has to be at the . . . s-stadium in an hour, so I'm s-sure this will be quick," he says, and his words fall like bricks. Like he's bracing himself for a verbal onslaught. "Do you mind hanging back up here?"

The request stings, but I know I have no place participating in this conversation, or even listening on. So I simply nod and kiss him once before he heads downstairs to face the music.

33

One week later

THIS COULD TURN OUT to be a complete disaster. But at least if things go south, I've put on a pretty convincing disguise— auburn, curly, about chin length. Fortune favored me this time around, and Sheryl was able to help with the wig. She's still on her sabbatical. But given the circumstances, she jumped at the chance to walk me through each step over Zoom. God knows I can't afford a slipup that gets me spotted by another ridiculous man with a phone. The stakes are too high.

My Uber driver drops me off at the corner of Melrose and Robertson, right in front of the entrance to Sempre, Mia. Crawling vines cover its aged, rustic exterior, and warm candlelight sets the spot aglow through its many leaded-glass windows. It isn't hard to picture Miles and me coming here for a dinner date—our first out in the open. I imagine our feet tangled beneath the table with our fingers interlaced on top. With our free hands, we'd nurse twin glasses of wine while talking about throwback movies like *Boomerang* and *Who Framed Roger Rabbit*.

Realizing I have fallen head over feet in love with a man I have yet to share a public meal with is enough to make my stomach do a few flips. But with any luck tonight, a solution will present itself. And soon enough, the tides will turn in our favor, and we'll be out from under the cloud of doom and suspicion cast by the nefarious exploits of Elliot Majors.

The past seven days have been a dueling swirl of frenetic activity and monotonous waiting. Waiting for Miles to get out of surgery—his first rotator cuff repair and his second Tommy John operation on the ligament that stabilizes his elbow, both on his pitching arm. Waiting to hear from Coach Carlin and the Dodgers front office about their plans for disciplinary action—they're biding time, likely waiting to base their decision on Miles's recovery and any criminal charges against him. Then there's waiting to see if Elliot would actually follow through on his threat to press those charges—spoiler alert, as of this morning, he has. And finally, waiting on a miracle to put this runaway train back on its rightful tracks.

But waiting gets old. And truth is, I'm tired. So tonight, I'm a woman on a rescue mission. Tonight's wouldn't be the first I've considered either—after all, the Glam Squad group chat *has* been known to concoct some elaborate schemes. It was Rodney who started planting seeds in the chat about mid-week:

RODNEY: If only there was a way to find out what really went down in that alley . . .

RODNEY: Where the hell is TMZ when you need 'em?

RODNEY: How you gon' catch a family brawl in an elevator but when it comes to a back alley in WeHo you got nothing?

JAMIE: Mhmm. Starting to smell like tilapia

ANGELO: I'm sorry, I'm lost. We're cooking now?

JAMIE: Who let the prude in the chat?

RODNEY: AYE. Not too much on my man.

RODNEY: Also, prude? WHERE? 🫐

> ME: She's saying something's fishy, Lo. And she's
> right! How has there been no security footage
> leaked of Miles and Elliot's "brawl"?

RODNEY: Can't Miles's lawyer contact the
restaurant management to get them involved?

Rodney came swinging with the million-dollar idea. But he wouldn't know, couldn't possibly understand, that Miles would *never* be willing to involve his mother and risk potentially compromising her privacy—not even if it meant keeping him away from jail, more heavy fines, or saving his sports contract. That the altercation even happened at her place of work has already spooked him to the point of decision paralysis.

Even when I suggested he go on the offensive and consider filing charges against Elliot, given the fact he's the one who lunged at him, causing a potentially career-ending injury, he flat-out rejected the idea without offering an explanation as to why. Being the "new girlfriend" and all, and unsure of my place in all this, I called Gabe in hopes he'd talk some sense into his best friend and top client.

Instead, he hit me with a doozy. "Ella, I adore you. I do. But I'm going to speak plainly here. There is no way in hell Miles is filing charges. To him, that's equal to fanning the flames of another public scandal involving a fight over a woman . . . which nearly wrecked him last time. He'd sooner watch his career go down the drain for it all to blow over on the path of least resistance."

And if that wasn't enough to make my head spin, he sealed it off with a gut punch. "But you want to know what makes it even worse this time? I've never seen him *so* in love, but this broken."

If my need to fix this was raging before, those words made it grow tenfold. Hearing this level of resignation from Miles's best friend cut deeply, sure. But watching the fight dwindle from Miles more and more each day has made it a gaping wound. Because I know what it's like to watch the person I love give up on *me*. But it causes a special kind of anguish to see Miles give up on himself.

I guess it's a good thing, for him, that the love I confessed last week isn't the fair-weather kind. Because if he's lost the will to fight for now, I can muster enough for the both of us. Maybe this is what happens to a heart after it breaks—with time and healing, it becomes reinforced along the cracks. And when it's right to love again, that heart's a stronger muscle for having learned what it should take. What it can give.

"HELLO, I'M HERE FOR AN EIGHT O'CLOCK RESERVATION UNDER the name Roberta Clementine," I tell the host upon entering the restaurant. I keep my smile reserved, yet polite, so as not to draw too much attention to my face, which is only partially obscured by oversized sunglasses, indoors, at night.

When Maria Evelyn texted me her alias, I smiled inwardly at

the not-so-subtle homage to Miles's childhood hero, Roberto Clemente.

"She's waiting for you at the table," the host informs me, while motioning for me to follow. At a gliding pace, he takes us across the dining room floor toward the back corner of the restaurant, where a petite woman sits at a quiet booth. "Here you are, ma'am. Enjoy your meal," he says before swiftly departing. For a moment, I wonder if Maria Evelyn has let him in on what we're up to.

Before I can sit, she stands from the table and draws me into a tight embrace. It lasts only a few seconds before she seems to remember herself and pull back. "I'm so sorry," she exclaims. "I forget that some people don't like that. I hope that was okay?" She's flustered, and instantly, I want to put her at ease.

"Oh, thank you for asking. But yes! That was more than okay," I tell her. "With what Miles has told me about you, I've wanted to hug you for a long time."

We're both sitting now, and at my words, she brings a hand to her chest and her eyes melt with what looks like gratitude mixed with a bit of humility. It occurs to me that given her past struggles, it's possible she still battles bouts of shame. I only hope she can feel how honored I am to meet the woman who, with the help of her parents, made the man of my dreams.

"Well, I can say the same about you, Ms. Simone," she replies, and automatically I tell her to call me Ella. "So . . . Ella," she says, her voice sinking to a more serious tone. "We have good news and bad and in this order. My son is in love." She says these words with a warmth that almost makes me forget that bad news is coming next. "B-but he's in a lot of trouble."

"I know," I tell her. "And I want to help him. But I also love him too much to disrespect his wishes. I came here tonight because you reached out to me. And I would never turn down the opportunity to meet you and tell you how much he means to me. But I just came out of a marriage that was built on lies. So, I can't help you get the security footage to TMZ, or Glitter 'N Dirt, or any other tabloid. Because I know he'd never forgive me for participating in a plot that could end up exposing you."

At this, Maria Evelyn grunts and smacks the table, which makes me jump. "That boy is *so* stubborn," she says while smoothing a hand back and forth over her knuckles. "You know what started that locker-room fight?" she asks, and I shake my head. "That Morales kid called me a d-deadbeat and a j-junkie. Only way he could have known about my past would have been through pillow talk with Miles's ex Monica."

Hearing this makes my stomach turn. Miles had alluded to Morales saying something vile, which made him throw the first punch in that locker room. But learning that his own wife betrayed his confidence, and their vows, in such a callous way makes me ache for him—and stand even more firm in my decision not to go behind his back to get the tape out.

"The reason I'm saying this is because I know my son." Her voice breaks, and tears well in her eyes. "When it comes to the people he loves, he'll throw himself on the s-sword every single time. He's always last to defend himself." She's actively crying now, and I am too. "I know him," she says again, this time with more force. "He is the best kind of friend. The best teammate. The best partner. The best son—"

"Maria Evelyn, I see it too," I cut in, if only to stem the flow of her tears. "But right or wrong, we need to find another way. Because I won't betray him . . ."

At this she straightens, grabs a napkin, and dries her eyes. "I was prepared to be upset with you for refusing to help me," she says, her voice calmer now. "But I see now you'd never hurt him the way she did. I see why he loves you . . . apart from the obvious," she says with a smirk.

I start to laugh, but it's cut short when a deep voice pierces the quiet surrounding us.

"What are you doing here?"

I look up to find Miles at the edge of our booth. Maria Evelyn and I were so engrossed in our conversation, neither of us clocked his approach. I meet his eyes and the look of confusion and hurt I find there makes my stomach drop. I open my mouth to speak, when Maria Evelyn beats me to it.

"I asked her to meet me here," she says. "Practically begged. P-please . . . don't be upset with her, son."

At this, Miles's eyes flutter closed, and he pushes air through his nostrils. "Ma, you know how risky this is."

I sit, still as a statue—quietly contemplating the repercussions of my decision.

"Yes, and you standing there with that big cast on your arm is only going to cause a bigger scene," she says with some sass. "Now come. Let's move this to my office."

34

THREE OF US STANDING in Maria Evelyn's tiny, windowless office only heightens the tension that began to bloom at Miles's arrival. Following the two of them back here felt like walking toward a perp lineup. I know, technically, I was only responding to his mom's urgent request. But I wasn't transparent with Miles about my plans for the evening, and given the relationship traumas we've both endured, that's pretty much a cardinal sin. Which probably explains why he currently can't seem to look me in the eye.

"I'm going to say my p-piece, then I'm going to leave the two of you in here to sort through your . . . feelings," Maria Evelyn says. "You." She points at her son. "If you're mad at her for coming here tonight, stop it. I am your mother and I demand it of you. This woman refused to help me leak the tapes, even though I cried. She knew you'd f-feel betrayed, and she won't be the cause of that for you again. That is love. So don't waste a second more on anger."

"And you." Now she's pointing at me. "Talk some sense into my son, okay? Love should make you brave, not foolish. Plus . . . I am the mother here. I am the one who sacrifices." Her voice cracks there, just slightly. Then she turns to her son. "And *I* am the one who is responsible for m-my sobriety. If leaking the tape blows my cover or ruins my peace, I will survive. It's what I've been doing my whole life."

She holds her son's stare with fresh tears welling in her eyes. Then she takes his good hand in hers and squeezes. "I love you, baby boy. I am not your responsibility."

Tears coat Miles's eyes now too as the muscles of his jaw tighten with emotion, and I don't know how much more of this I can take. With her proverbial mic now on the floor, Maria Evelyn exits the room, leaving two formerly scorned lovers and their freshly open hearts to find a way forward.

"So," I say, stepping closer to Miles, gauging his reaction. When instead of retreating, he leans into me, snaking his good arm around my waist, I could almost cry from the relief. "You still mad?" I ask, voice thick from trying not to cry.

He blinks to rid his eyes of tears, then after shaking his head a smirk creeps along his lips. "Can't be. My ma says so," he teases, before dropping a kiss to the corner of my mouth. I turn my face to catch his lips directly on mine and we spark electricity with the contact. But instead of pulling back, we absorb the jolt, melting further into one another—a metaphor for the kind of love life I envision us making together. One that weathers every storm.

"I have another question," I tell him when I eventually do pull back. "You gonna let us leak the tape?"

Exhaling slowly, Miles drops his forehead to mine, seemingly weighing his options. "My mom always told me that a simple life is what she needed in order to stay sober," he says, his voice rough with emotion. "But somewhere along the way, I think I got so caught up with trying to protect that for her, I didn't consider that her power is in how she gets to grow and change and make these decisions for herself."

Smiling up at this beautiful man as he comes to his own realizations about life might be one of my new favorite pastimes, along with smoothing my hands up his chest to wrap them around the warm skin of his neck, where I can feel his strong heartbeat.

"So yes . . . I will agree to the two of you leaking the tape," Miles relents through gritted teeth.

"Attaboy!" I shout, before smacking him on the butt. "I've never been more proud."

"Yeah?" he asks, eyebrows raised as he flashes a broad smile. "This mean that after all of this you still love me, Dream Girl?"

At this I laugh, and tipping my head back, Miles takes the opportunity to nip at my neck. When I look up at him again, our eyes lock and the moment sobers. Nodding, I confess again. "Yes. Miles, I still love you," I tell him, leaving out that I have a feeling I always will. But if he needs to hear it a thousand more times, I'll give him each and every reassurance.

I am about to ask if he still loves me, when the very next moment, the restaurant's playlist changes from "Bye Bye Blackbird" to Donny Hathaway's "A Song for You," and the descending arpeggio of the piano transports us to a place far from all clear and present danger. As Donny sings about acting out his life in stages with ten thousand people watching, I think back on all the crowds Miles and I have appeared in front of and yet never shown our full selves to. How we've borne the heartache of private betrayal and public scrutiny, all while preserving the most honest and true parts of ourselves. And through all of that we found each other— hiding in the melodies.

I take his hand in mine to interlace our fingers and kiss each of his knuckles. And then I repeat myself. "I am in love with you,

Miles Westbrook. So in love that I was afraid I could get lost in the depth of it. But now I know that's not possible. You wanna know why?"

"Why?" he asks. But he's not smiling anymore. He watches me soberly, eyes searching for something real and true.

"Because you see me," I tell him as the dam finally breaks and my tears fall. "And you actively *love* what you see. I can feel it in your touch, hear it in your voice, see it on your face. And I see you too."

He bites his lip and swallows as a single tear slips from his eye. "You . . . s-see me?" he asks.

I nod, smiling—cradling his face in my hands.

"This mean you'll come to my games?" he asks, with his mouth drawn down to a pout.

"Yes!" I laugh and kiss him once. Then, looking at him, I sober for a second. Smoothing one hand down from his face until it's placed at the center of his chest, I tell him, "This is not just an escape for me, Miles Westbrook. This is my destination."

Snaking his hand up my back to cup the nape of my neck, he gently brings my face up to his before whispering, "You are going to be the love of my life, Elladee Robinson."

Then we kiss, with trembling hands on beating hearts. With our bodies wholly entwined. And like this love, our kiss has no end in sight. All at once, it is letting go and holding on, a secret and a confession, a fight and a surrender. But most of all, it is a promise that neither one of us will have to be alone, not so long as a love like ours exists in the world.

Epilogue

E LLADEE ASHLEY ROBINSON, GET up off the floor. It's time for shots!" Rodney yells through the bedroom door.

My best friend has always had a knack for the dramatics, and now is no exception. The only reason I'm on the floor to begin with is that I just tripped over the air mattress that *he* crowded our hotel room with.

We're in Dallas for the final of the World Series and Murphy's Law has exploded all over our plans, because everything that could possibly go wrong has in the past two days. We left the last leg of my European tour to make it here in time to watch Miles and the team vie for the championship. After our flights got delayed, turns out, the four-bed suite we reserved got double-booked and we got bumped. So the Glam Squad is packed into what could very well be a slightly upscale college dorm—and fittingly it's taken us no time to revert to our old antics as well.

Peeling myself off the floor, I make my way to the kitchenette, where Angelo has just emerged from the bathroom. "Oh. My. God," I exclaim. "What bet did you lose to end up in that?" I ask him, gesturing toward his very novel attire.

Jamie whistles from her perch at the bar. "Looking like you walked off the set of *90 Day Fiancé*."

"Ha. Ha. Very funny," Angelo replies. "Having our luggage swapped at customs isn't something to joke about. There could have been contraband in those bags. We could have been . . . arrested." He whispers the last word, and we all split at the seams with laughter. Everyone except for Angelo, who is sporting an oversized polo and wrinkled cargo pants. He had the option to pair the ensemble with a trucker's ball cap that read *Bass Pro*, but he decided against it.

"It's okay, sweetie," says Rodney, who lucked out with a pair of overalls and a flannel. "The airline will have our things back to us by tomorrow. Till then, let's just call it role-play." He makes a little growl sound with a claw hand.

Angelo aims a wilting look at his now fiancé. "That's it. Go without me. Nothing is worth being seen in public like this."

"Oh, don't be ridiculous," I tell him. "Miles would be crushed if you missed the big game on account of a wardrobe malfunction. You of all people should know we don't let those get in our way." I offer him a wink, and it draws just the tiniest smile.

Then, suddenly, a flash goes off. We all turn in the direction it came from and to our collective surprise, Sheryl struts in with her camera raised. "What? Y'all didn't plan on documenting a special occasion?"

Jamie leaps off her stool to give her a tight squeeze. "I thought you'd never show up! We were this close to hiring a replacement," she says, before dropping her voice to a whisper. "Between you and me, Ella's protective hairstyles need a little bit of guidance."

Sheryl scoffs, turning to me. "You thought you were going to find someone to replace *me*? Like my granni says back home in Jamaica, 'Her mother is dead and she ain't born yet.'"

Jamie and I eye each other with confusion until Rodney chimes in, "It means it ain't happening."

"Sheryl, we could never replace you," I tell her. "But that's not even what's important right now. How are Chris and the kids? How are *you*?"

She updates us all on Chris's remission and the kids' latest accomplishments with track and orchestra. Turns out, in her off time, she started to build a massive following on social media for content on Black hair care. She has plans now to develop her own product line and, of course, eventually return to working with the team.

Once we've had our celebratory shots, I get a ping that our transport to the stadium is downstairs. It's a moment I've been anxious about all day, since I know Gabe will be on the party bus too. In the year since their whirlwind week together in Los Angeles, Jamie hasn't told me why the two of them cut off contact. But anytime his name is mentioned, she either gets very quiet or changes the subject.

But tonight, I can't let any distractions get in the way of celebrating Miles and all he's overcome to get to this very moment. Once Elliot followed through with pressing charges against him it was the biggest mistake he could have made. Because within days of doing so, the security footage of what really went down in the alleyway was not so suspiciously leaked to TMZ—from an "unnamed" employee of Sempre, Mia restaurant. Only Miles, Gabe, and I know it was his mom who retrieved the tape, and me and Gabe who saw it through to the proper "journalistic" channels.

The video showed, without question, that a visibly impaired Elliot charged Miles and then lost his footing, which caused his own, and subsequently Miles's, injuries. Elliot was fined a pretty penny and sentenced to probation and community service for battery and filing a false police report. And given that he was already on thin ice at

Onyx Records, based on unofficial reports of maintaining quid pro quo relationships with employees *and* artists, they dropped his ass.

Last I heard he's starting his own label and, sure enough, Miss Thing is his first artist. As for that twenty-five percent royalty he claimed he *deserved* to earn off my tour, the request miraculously vanished when time came to finalize our divorce settlement. I have my suspicions that Janet and Miles might have engaged in some unofficial blackmail to get him off my case. But I'll neither make them confirm nor deny.

When all the dust settled, Miles still had a long road to recovery with his pitching arm. Ten months of rehabilitation put him out of commission for the season, but thankfully, Coach Carlin championed his return to the starting lineup once Miles was able to show he was back in top form. And though my tour kicked off last June, Mamie Houston was more than happy to accept the terms that Janet laid out for my contract, and I flew back at every opportunity to be with Miles and support his recovery. And, of course, our voice memos never stopped flowing.

So tonight, after a string of successful showings during the playoffs, he's starting again for the final game in a series that is tied so far. And it's the Rangers, go figure. As we pack up our things to head out the door, I get a ping on my personal cell phone. When I check it, I'm shocked to see it's a message from Miles. With everything riding on the game, and us being so close to first pitch, I'd expect his phone to be locked up somewhere. But when I swipe open his message, my heart beats like a rhythm section, and I can't help but smile.

MILES: Win or lose. Tonight, will you dance with me on the field?

ME: Always, baby. I thought you'd never ask.

Acknowledgments

T O SAY THAT COMPLETING this novel has been a journey would be the understatement of a lifetime. At the start, *No Ordinary Love* was supposed to be a fun, soapy, outlandish escape for me creatively. But to quote Alanis Morissette, "Life has a funny way of sneaking up on you when you think everything's okay," and I found myself in a position to identify with Elladee Robinson in more ways than I ever imagined I would. I ended up writing from a place of knowledge and empathy, rather than a place of pure imagination. And while it's my trade, I cannot find the words to capture the heights and depths of the roller coaster that has been the past year of my life. But I am grateful for this book helping me through it. And so, I will find the words to thank the people who have helped me through it too.

I'm forever grateful to my sister, Faith, my bestie and travel companion. It is only right that we'd be walking hand in hand through the ebbs and flows of life together. To my "Waiting to Exhale" girls—Caelayn, Lauren, Tawny, Allison, Chelsea—we've done life together year in and out, rain or shine. And I wouldn't have us any other way.

To my son, who gave me the greatest gift of all—motherhood. You came into my life and inspired me to write. I will be here for you always.

To the authors whose work I adore and who have become cherished friends in this business that so often can make you feel alone—Naina Kumar, Ellie Palmer, Danica Nava, Lauren Ling Brown, Riss M. Nielsen, Shirlene Obuobi, Nikki Payne, Regina Black, Alexandra Vasti, Jill Tew, Kristina Forest, Elise Bryant, Nekesa Afia, Sami Ellis, Kennedy Ryan, Etta Easton, Audrey Cleo Yap, and Laura Piper Lee—thank you from the bottom of my endlessly grateful heart.

I am also forever indebted to my incredible publishing team. Without my literary agent Kim Lionetti, my film and TV agent Rukayat Giwa, my editor Esi Sogah, assistant editor Genni Eccles, marketer Anika Bates, publicist Tina Joell, cover artist Oboh Moses, as well as the Berkley social media team, art department, sales and production teams, this storytelling dream of mine could have never taken flight.

And to my readers: Thank you for spending time with Ella and Miles. I hope you found love in the pages, right where I left it for you.

KEEP READING FOR AN EXCERPT FROM

WHEN I THINK OF *You*

1

*P*ING!

My head pops up at the sound of the elevator. Like Pavlov's dog, I'm conditioned to snap to attention at the sound of a call, a text, even a microwave. It's an occupational hazard.

Some people call me "The Face" of Wide Angle Pictures, a specialty production company on the Galaxy Films back lot. Never mind the fact that those "people" are mostly Tommy—everybody's *favorite* mail courier whose daily greeting almost always borders on harassment.

On paper, I'm the receptionist. To the execs that call the shots, I'm "the front desk girl." And to the directors, writers, and producers who churn through each day to pitch ideas and hawk scripts—I'm a greeting committee of one. And it gets old.

What felt prestigious about this job to a once bright-eyed film school grad has slowly faded over the years. Yet here I sit with a forced smile on my face. Eyes forward. Shoulders back. Soul empty.

The elevator deposits a clique of my colleagues onto the glistening marble floor of the reception area. Like gum, they always come in a pack. And because I'm of no use to them at the moment, they dodge me like a speed bump in an empty parking lot. Still, I manage to catch snippets of their conversation.

"You won't believe the clusterfuck I had to sort out last night with Allison and Keith's travel. Apparently booking flights in coach is always the wrong choice. Even when first and business class are full. Even when it's the last flight out of New York and their kid's spelling bee is the next day."

"Well, at least you didn't have to bail on a hot date after an SOS text from Louis. I had to pull out midthrust and drive the Outlaws *digital print all the way to the Palisades for a last-minute request from the Bel Air Circuit."*

Believe it or not, I envy them.

Their work/life balance might look like a lone panda on a see-saw but at least they've managed to ace *Industry Gatekeeping 101*: Get a job supporting the daily functions and navigating the erratic idiosyncrasies of a Hollywood executive for one to two years. In your nonexistent spare time, make sure to ear-hustle every call said executive takes. Never enter that executive's office without a notepad or tablet for documenting their demands. Before bed each night, speed-read every book, script, or article that's come across their desk. Write up coverage that's whip-smart and spot-on. Do it all well—and *voilà!* You're promoted and on the executive fast track.

Or at least a track fast*er* than the one I'm currently on, which seems to have taken the off-ramp toward *Admins 4 Lyfe R-Us.*

Ping!

I flinch again. This time, it's my desktop. I click out of Outlook and scan my cluttered screen for the culprit, grimacing when I find a little snarky gray bubble of a message from Nick-in-Publicity.

NickatNite: Hey Kaliya. I'm not sure if you've made your
rounds yet. But tracking says my Vitamix should have arrived in
the mail room an hour ago. Just wanted to put this on your
radar!

Unfortunately for me, at WAP, being receptionist means both
business *and* personal deliveries fall under my purview. While I'm
never one to say a task is beneath me, I won't pretend that tending
to the emotional wounds from this dead-end job hasn't taken its
toll. I'll probably never crawl out from under all the debt I've
racked up from the top film school in the country by sorting other
people's mail, either. But when duty calls, I answer. So with a huff,
I'm up and on my way to the dusty dungeon of the mail room.

Posters of the top films WAP has made over the last two decades line my path down the hall, and for a moment, my soul stirs.
Corny as it may seem, this corridor of hits is why I'm still here.
Right now, I may be on the hunt for someone else's juicer. But
some day, the name *Kaliya Wilson* will be on one of these posters
with the hallowed words *Produced by* in front of it.

But as I've come to expect from this place, any flicker of hope
is quickly doused by reality—this time in the frazzled form of
Sharon-in-Accounting as she barrels toward me looking stern
and impatient. I am briefly distracted by the lack of movement in
her blunt, red bob. And after a few failed attempts to blink myself invisible, I'm swiftly cornered with a USB thrust beneath
my chin.

"Kaliya, the Xerox is on the fritz again." Sharon's tone drips
with accusation, like the printer and I have conspired against her. I
fight the urge to roll my eyes because her version of "on the fritz"
usually means it's either unplugged or experiencing a paper jam.

Her French-tipped fingers wave the USB beneath my nose like smelling salts. "I need you to get twenty copies of these budgets printed, stapled, and collated," she demands. "And I need them on my desk in fifteen minutes."

"I'm on it!" I announce. Then begrudgingly, I accept the memory stick and pop it into my pocket. Training a false smile at her, I note that she's still blocking my path. We're essentially in a standoff until she squints at me for a beat then spins on her heel to stalk back down the hall.

Upon entering the mail room I head straight for the sorting bins, which have been filled to the brim with Amazon boxes and AmEx bills. I am elbow deep in the slush when a call comes in from the main line. My boss, Gary, whom I've un-affectionately titled the VP of Paper Clips, upgraded me to a headset with a long range—heaven forbid the reception line ring more than once because I stepped away.

I fumble to click on my earpiece without dropping a package, but it's already on the second ring, *dammit*, when I catch the call.

"Kaliya . . ." Speak of the devil. My name out of Gary's mouth might be my least favorite sound.

"Yes, Gary," I reply, biting back my irritation.

"I just got an email from Tom-in-Business-Affairs, and it appears the ants are back in the twelfth-floor conference room," he says in a clipped tone. "I thought you'd gotten to the bottom of that last week."

I grimace. "So did I," I say. "But don't you worry, Gary, I am on it."

"I certainly hope so," he shoots back coolly before clicking off the line. I take a few calming breaths, open my eyes, and spot the juicer.

LUNCH TIME ARRIVES LIKE A COLD GLASS OF WATER ON A HOT day. Even though I'm stuck downing a smoothie at my desk because there aren't any interns around to cover the phones, I seize the opportunity to dive back into my current audiobook obsession.

Normally, I wouldn't dare listen to this type of material on my work-issued computer. But in this case, WAP has optioned the novel and given the green light to go into preproduction on a feature adaptation soon. Since employees are encouraged to become familiar with the studio's newest projects, *technically*, I'm just doing my job.

I pick up where I last left the young billionaire and his impressionable new girlfriend. Moments into my listening, he's just yanked out her tampon so they can *do the deed* and I've crossed my legs in shock. I hear a gasp, realize the sound came from me, and shut my mouth so quickly I almost chip a tooth. *No way this scene gets past the MPA.*

Ping!

I'm still clutching my proverbial pearls when the sound of the elevator provides a sobering jolt. Quickly, I reach up and press the button on my earpiece to power off my headset. Then, the unthinkable happens.

"Tell me how bad you want this rock-hard cock," Caleb groaned *through gritted teeth, hands firmly gripping the globes of her ass.*

"Yes! Yes! Give it to me, Caleb. Please don't make me wait," Ashley cried in wanton ecstasy at the same time he thrust into her swollen cleft.*

I am a deer in headlights, immobilized at the sound of smut blasting from my desktop at my place of work. The voices coming from the elevator are growing louder, too. Their footsteps are drawing nearer. Panicking, I fumble with the mouse in search of the X that will put an end to the rapidly escalating scene.

"*Come for me, Ashley!*"

"*I'm close, Caleb! So close!*"

And *I'm* close to being caught red-handed—like Shaggy with the girl next door.

But not today, Satan.

I am frantically scanning my desktop in search of the elusive culprit window that's hidden somewhere among the fifty tabs cluttering my screen. With time running out, as a final Hail Mary, I grab the plug to my speakers and yank it like a lasso. In the name of all things holy, everything goes silent. Heart racing and chest heaving, I'm still gripping the speaker plug when two figures enter my periphery. Stiffly, I turn to offer my customary welcome. But the words seize up in my throat when my eyes land on him.

Danny Prescott.

I am a slab of granite. For seven years I have on equal fronts feared and anticipated our reunion—even rehearsed it in my mind. I'd run into him on a hot afternoon in the South of France at the Cannes Film Festival. I'd have a flute of champagne in one hand and Idris Elba's bicep in the other. I certainly wouldn't be attempting to hide the fact I'd been listening to erotica on my treasonous computer at a reception desk on a Friday afternoon.

I decide my best shot at salvaging the dregs of my dignity is to get through this cursed encounter without being recognized. So, against all odds, and past the lump in my throat, I force out a greeting as they both close in. "Welcome to Wide Angle Pictures. H-how can I help you?"

At the sound of my voice, Danny's sage-green eyes scan upward and lock with mine. He freezes, causing his glamorous companion to collide with his shoulder, which in turn knocks him slightly off-balance.

"Um. Hello," he says, cocking his head to the side like a confused puppy. "I'm . . . Danny—" He stops short and that voice—it's a shallow fragment of the one I remember. He falters for a moment or two, fidgeting with his collar, before abruptly burying his hands in the pockets of his jeans and carrying on. "—Prescott. Um, I'm here to meet with Jim Evans?"

To my utter dismay, it seems as though he knows who I am. Still, I desperately cling to my act, practically chirping, "Sure, I'll let Jim know you're here!"

I will my hands steady and dial up Jim's office to notify his assistant their one o'clock appointment has arrived. Hanging up, I clear my throat and gesture toward the plush sofas to my right.

"If you'd like," I say to Danny and his companion as I channel the poise of a flight attendant, "you can have a seat while you wait. But do let me know if I can bring you coffee, tea, or water."

He's saved from responding to me when the phone rings—my constant companion. With my headset now charging on its base, I pick up the handheld and avoid Danny's stare of astonishment.

"Hi, Gary, what can I do for you?" I try to project calm, as if everything is business as usual and my college ex isn't standing before me watching my every move. Gary honks into the phone at a volume loud enough for Danny to hear a few feet away. I turn slightly, cupping a hand over the receiver to create an auditory shield.

"Kaliya, Rose-in-Marketing is complaining of a foul odor coming from the love seat in her office. I'm concerned we have a rodent problem again—" Gary drones on about checking mouse traps and procuring rat poison and I'm grimacing, eyes shut tight, hoping that when I open them, by some miracle, Danny will no longer be standing here witnessing my humiliation.

Damn it all to hell, Gary.

I inhale sharply and breathe out a plan: "I'll call Peter in pest control ASAP and then I'll set Rose up in the conference room with a temporary workspace."

If nothing else can be said for this utterly desolate moment, it's that I'm damn good at my job. People throw their problems my way and I fix them. I return the phone to its receiver and stare at it in surrender—trying to ignore the sustained bafflement on Danny's face.

Then, his friend looks up from her magazine. "Umm . . . hellooo," she coos, waving to get my attention. "I'll take a green tea, no sugar, bag out."

I recognize her now as Celine Michèle, the lead actress from a nighttime soap I'm ashamed to admit I watch. She's pushing thirty but plays a high schooler at the apex of a love triangle with two vampire brothers. She's tall and willowy with pale skin and a mane of silky brown hair. She's stunning. Worst of all, she's Danny's creative partner and girlfriend—the things I once wanted to be.

Snapping out of it, I rise to go prepare the tea. But remembering my front desk etiquette, I stop and turn to Danny. "Anything for you, sir?" The *sir* rolls off my tongue like a hairball and by the look of it, he's not too fond of it, either.

Danny does a micro grimace before clearing his throat. "No thanks, Kaliya—um, I mean I'm fine." The corners of his lips turn up in a small, contrite smile and his eyes soften just slightly.

When Danny Prescott says my name, it does strange things to my executive function. No longer capable of processing it all, I bolt away on wobbly legs toward the kitchen. Once tucked away in its tight quarters, I finally feel like I can breathe again. But that just conjures all the *feelings.*

Kaliya, you will not cry on the Keurig.

No, I'll save that for later when I'm in my car, as I do often. LA traffic tends to have that effect on me.

With trembling hands, I head back to the reception area cupping a piping hot mug for Celine, only to see the backs of her and Danny as they glide down the hall toward the elevators with Jim's assistant.

I zero in on Danny's retreating form. His tight russet curls gradually disappear into a close fade that brushes the collar of a crisp white shirt that's fitted to perfection across broad shoulders and strong arms. Dark-wash jeans cling to his slim hips and taper down two very long legs. His signature, impeccably clean and uncreased Jordans finish off the look. What can I say? The man still has swag.

When he steps onto the elevator, somewhere in my chest there's a wave of relief running beneath a strange sense of loss. Defeated, I slump back into my seat and take a long sip of Celine's tea. As if on cue, the ominous theme from *Jaws* rings out from my purse. Swiping open my screen, I find a text from Gary, who must be away from his desk.

> **VP, Paper Clips**: Kaliya, Sharon has emailed to say she
> feels you have no sense of urgency. Let's have a chat on
> Monday about how you might better show up in this role.

And for the briefest moment, I envision sending a company-wide email. Two words. All caps. I QUIT.

One day. Just not today.

Photography by Dawan M. Brown

Myah Ariel's early love of movies led her from Arkansas to New York City, where she studied film at New York University's Tisch School of the Arts. She went on to earn an MA degree in specialized journalism for the arts from the University of Southern California. As a medical mom and a hopeless romantic, Myah is passionate about inclusive love stories. She lives in Los Angeles with her family, where she works in academia.

VISIT MYAH ARIEL ONLINE

MyahAriel.com

Ready to fir
your next great

Let us help

Visit prh.com/nextread

Penguin
Random
House

nd
read?

.